GOLDEN LORD

Books by Mary Jo Putney

The Dangerous Gifts series
Silver Lady

The Lost Lords series
Loving a Lost Lord
Never Less Than a Lady
Nowhere Near Respectable
No Longer a Gentleman
Sometimes a Rogue
Not Quite a Wife
Not Always a Saint

The Rogues Redeemed series
Once a Soldier
Once a Rebel
Once a Scoundrel
Once a Spy
Once Dishonored
Once a Laird

Other titles
Dearly Beloved
The Bargain
The Rake

Anthologies
Mischief and Mistletoe
The Last Chance Christmas Ball
Seduction on a Snowy Night

MARY JO PUTNEY

GOLDEN LORD

KENSINGTON
PUBLISHING CORP.

www.kensingtonbooks.com

KENSINGTON BOOKS are published by

Kensington Publishing Corp.
900 Third Avenue
New York, NY 10022

All Kensington titles, imprints, and distributed lines are available at special quantity discounts for bulk purchases for sales promotion, premiums, fund-raising, educational, or institutional use.

Special book excerpts or customized printings can also be created to fit specific needs. For details, write or phone the office of the Kensington Sales Manager: Attn.: Sales Department. Kensington Publishing Corp., 900 Third Avenue, New York, NY 10022. Phone: 1-800-221-2647.

ISBN: 978-1-4201-5504-4 (ebook)

ISBN: 978-1-4967-5125-6

First Kensington Hardcover Edition: September 2024
First Kensington Trade Edition: December 2024

10 9 8 7 6 5 4 3 2 1

Printed in the United States of America

To my wonderful agent Robin Rue, my most excellent editor Alicia Condon, and all the other terrific people at Kensington who help guide my stories to see the light of day!!

Chapter 1

Penrose Hall
Near St. Austell, Cornwall
Early May, 1803

The deed was done. It was a perfect day for a wedding, with sunshine and soft breezes and a sky full of birdsong in this warmest part of Great Britain. Cade Tremayne had performed his duties as witness as he stood up with his brother Bran, who was marrying the enchanting Merryn Penrose. The newlyweds glowed with happiness and a sense of rightness.

After the ceremony and wedding breakfast, everyone flowed from the house onto the lawn of Penrose Hall, sipping drinks and chatting with friends old and new. The house and gardens were on a bluff that commanded a striking view of the ocean. Cade found a quiet corner of the lawn where he could watch the guests and look down to the beach below the bluff.

He smiled when he saw that Bran and Merryn had slipped away from the gathering and were descending on the slanted path that led down to the sand. Both of them were very good at avoiding notice when they chose to. At the bottom of the path, both peeled off shoes and stockings before moving to the water's edge, holding hands as small waves rolled over their bare feet.

Cade felt bittersweet pleasure at the sight of them together. He was profoundly happy for Bran, who deserved the love he'd found. Cade tried to suppress the unworthy envy that he felt because he wouldn't find the same. This wedding day was a watershed for Cade as well as Bran because the marriage would change his relationship with his brother forever. Though they weren't blood kin, they'd been as close as two boys could be ever since they'd met at a baby farm where unwanted children were sent to die. Even as small children, they'd worked together well. Bran had planned their escape and was calmly certain they would find a better life, while Cade had figured out how to make it happen.

In the depths of winter, they'd spent days clinging to the backs of northbound carriages and mail coaches, sometimes for only a few miles, other times for hours until the coach stopped and guards chased them away, often with kicks and curses. The journey had been so nightmarish that even now Cade preferred not to think about it.

They'd arrived in London on a bitter cold night. Bran's intuition had brought them to Lord and Lady Tremayne, aristocrats who were gifted with the mysterious abilities that some people envied, and others feared and despised. The Tremaynes had both been fortunate to come from families that valued such talents.

But it wasn't uncommon for gifted children to be thrown out of their homes when their abilities appeared, as had happened to Cade and Bran. They would have died of neglect and abuse if they hadn't found their way to Rhys and Gwyn, who rescued gifted children in dire straits.

As a quartet of musicians began playing a bright, celebratory tune, Cade let his gaze travel over the guests, who were taking full advantage of the beautiful grounds and the sunny day. His foster father, Rhys, was ambling toward him, two glasses in hand. "I suspected that you'd prefer some good French brandy to more champagne."

"You figured correctly." Cade accepted a glass and took a sip. Merryn's father had a well-stocked cellar, though no one was mentioning that one of Cornwall's most profitable industries was smuggling and this brandy had probably never seen a customs agent.

Cade gestured at the beach below, where Bran and Merryn were laughing together as they walked along the waterline, holding hands. "Is this what a happy ending looks like?"

"Marrying the right person isn't an end, but a beginning." Rhys glanced across the lawn to Gwyn, who was chatting with several of the younger women, including bright blond Tamsyn, the eldest female of the Tribe of Tremayne and a legitimate daughter of the couple. She looked very like her beautiful mother.

Rhys's eyes lit with warmth as he watched them. "Gwyn and I knew we'd found our true loves as soon as we met, but we had no idea of how splendid the future would be. Bran is the first of the Tribe of Tremayne to marry, but there will be more marriages soon. We look forward to being grandparents."

"Don't look at me like that!" Cade ordered. "I might be the eldest male in your tribe, but I intend to be the eccentric bachelor uncle to all the nephews and nieces."

"God laughs when mortals make plans," Rhys said with amusement.

Ignoring the comment, Cade said, "Saving gifted children in desperate straits has been a vital mission for you and Gwyn, and no one knows that better than I. You placed most of your rescues with other loving, accepting families—how did you decide which of us to keep?"

His foster father grinned. "Gwyn wanted to keep Bran, and since it would have taken an ax to separate the two of you, I resigned myself to the inevitable."

Cade laughed. "Still another reason to be grateful to Bran."

"I'm glad he and Merryn will be dividing their time between London and Cornwall. We want to see them as often as possible."

Cade took another sip of the excellent brandy. "Did Cameron make it here in time for the wedding? I thought I saw him earlier, but not since."

"Cam arrived from London just in time to slip into the back of the church for the ceremony. He was glad he hadn't missed it, but he was rather travel stained so, when last seen, he was heading into the house to clean himself up properly. He said a wedding would surely include pretty young ladies, and he wanted to look presentable."

Cade smiled. Cameron was the next youngest Tremayne son after Cade and Bran, and he had wavy brown hair, an outgoing personality, and an infectious smile. Any pretty young ladies would be equally interested in meeting him. "I assume he was held up in London so he could bring an important message to you?"

"Exactly. I'm sure you can guess what that message was."

"The renewal of war we've been expecting has arrived," Cade said flatly. "And in the blink of an eye, my father has transformed into my superior in the Home Office."

Rhys nodded. "Exactly. We'll be kept busy for a long time to come." The Home Office was charged with the safety and security of Britain, and Rhys was chief of a department that recruited gifted agents for that work. Many members of the Tribe of Tremayne worked for him in a variety of ways.

"What's the latest news?"

"Britain will officially declare war within a matter of days," his father said quietly. "Ambassador Whitworth is preparing to leave Paris with the entire British delegation, which in itself is an announcement that the fighting is about to resume."

It was a relief to have the waiting over. "What do you need me to do?"

"Ensure that Lord Whitworth and his wife reach England safely," Rhys said. "You may recall that several months ago, Napoleon attacked Britain and Ambassador Whitworth in a screaming tirade in front of the entire French court."

"It was quite the scandal," Cade said. "Whitworth apparently endured it all with great British calm, which surely infuriated the First Consul even more. Is there reason to believe that Napoleon might try to have Whitworth killed before he can leave France?"

"Napoleon's rage was real, but he is too canny to murder a foreign ambassador." Rhys frowned. "My fear is that one or more of his courtiers might think that killing Whitworth would be a way of winning favor with his master."

"Rather like when Henry II raged against Archbishop Thomas Becket and several of his knights went to Canterbury and murdered him in his own cathedral," Cade observed.

"Exactly, and that's an outcome we want to avoid. Whitworth is one of Britain's finest diplomats. He is needed."

"Do you have evidence that his life is in danger?"

Rhys shook his head. "No, just intuition."

But Rhys's intuition was very, very good. "So you want me to go to Paris and very discreetly guard Lord Whitworth and the rest of the delegation until they're all safely back in England."

"Yes. Tamsyn will go with you."

No! Cade's gaze involuntarily snapped to Tamsyn. She must have sensed his look because she glanced up at him with a sweet, intimate smile. Tam, who was all warmth and light and love.

He felt a wrench in his heart. He could not possibly work

with her on a dangerous secret mission. "Why Tam? Better to send Cameron or one of your other agents."

"It needs to be a woman, and Tamsyn is the best I have."

Cade frowned. "Is it really necessary to send her into an enemy country that is collapsing into war?"

"She may look like a spun sugar angel, but she's a first-class agent, intelligent and very skilled. I feel she's the best choice to go with you."

"How can you bear to send your daughter into danger?" Cade said, his voice tight.

Rhys caught Cade's gaze, his eyes bleak. "It's hell every single time I send any one of my children or other agents into danger. I do it because I must."

"And we go because duty requires us to do so," Cade said quietly.

"That doesn't mean you can't enjoy stopping mayhem, and you do," Rhys said with a sudden smile. He glanced across the lawn. "I need to talk to Mr. Penrose. You and Tamsyn must leave for France as soon as possible, and I believe that Penrose can arrange a swift ship to take you." He laid a hand on Cade's shoulder. "Travel quickly and return home safely."

"I'll do my best." Cade watched as Rhys headed purposefully toward Merryn's father, thinking of the family Rhys and Gwyn had created, which they called the Tribe of Tremayne. It included three biological children and ten fosters. Cade privately thought it a miracle that all of the Tribe got on so well together, though it was probably not really a miracle but the love and generosity Rhys and Gwyn showed to everyone.

Even though he was looking away, he knew when Tamsyn joined him. He always knew where she was. When she reached his side, she gazed down at the beach as Bran and Merryn turned at the far end to retrace their steps. "This may be the first marriage in the family, but it certainly won't be the last. I wonder if future spouses will blend so seamlessly into the Tribe of Tremayne as Merryn has."

He considered her question. "Probably not. She's powerfully gifted, which must have helped."

"Do you think any of us will marry people who aren't gifted?"

"I expect not, since being gifted is so much a part of who we are, and our abilities are often annoying to those who aren't gifted." He gave her an amused glance. "Wondering about future brothers- and sisters-in-law seems like the sort of thing a female is more likely to ponder."

Tamsyn laughed. "I'm sure you're right. Marriages and matchmaking are important concerns for most females."

Though Cade doubted that was as true for females who were agents of the Home Office. "Rhys just told me that we need to leave for Paris as soon as possible. I wish he didn't feel he had to send you into what is about to become enemy territory."

Tam laughed. "With people like us, saying 'I have a feeling about this,' shuts down any argument. You've said that often enough yourself."

He had to chuckle. "True, but I'm usually right, aren't I?"

"Yes, and so is Rhys. And Gwyn. And Bran." She gave him a cherubic smile. "And so am I, big brother. Remember that time . . . ?"

"No need to mention that unfortunate episode," he said hastily. "I was young and made a mistake."

"And now you are old and wise and never make mistakes," Tamsyn said in a dulcet tone. Turning serious, she continued, "I feel this mission could be very simple and straightforward. Or it might not. There is the potential for complications."

"If so, we'll deal with them. Lord Whitworth has the reputation of being a reasonable man, which helps. I don't know about Lady Whitworth. Have you met her?"

"Yes, and she's a capable woman, but her first husband was

a duke and that left her with an exaggerated opinion of her consequence. She would not take kindly to a guard who was lowborn, which is why I'm needed." After a pause, Tamsyn continued, "That's one of the reasons I need to go to France with you. I'm not sure about the other reasons."

The back of his neck prickled. Yes, there were likely to be serious complications on the mission.

Luckily, he was very good at dealing with complications.

Chapter 2

✎

Paris

Traveling at the fastest possible speed, Tamsyn and Cade reached Paris and hired Moreau, a craggy and gifted French driver, to take them to the British embassy. Moreau was part of a loose network of gifted people spread across Europe. The fact that most of the gifted had experienced trouble because of their talents created bonds with others like them, and they helped each other as needed.

"Not far now to the British embassy," Moreau said, speaking around the clay pipe stem clamped between his teeth.

Tamsyn gazed at the tall houses that loomed on both sides of the street. One of her gifts was sensing emotions. Often she kept that ability tamped down because the feelings of others could be overwhelming, but today she was deliberately listening to the city around her. "Paris seems very tense," she said thoughtfully. "Most people worry about the coming war, but others find the prospect exciting. I feel a desire to fight and triumph over France's enemies."

"The First Consul has a gift for inspiration," Moreau said gruffly. "For making men, especially young ones, feel that it is France's destiny to rule all of Europe and beyond."

"Do women share the lust for conquest?" she asked.

"Some do. Most don't. Men who have seen war usually prefer peace." He pulled his pipe from his mouth and spat over the side of the carriage.

She realized that he'd lost someone close to him in the earlier wars. His brother, perhaps?

"France is a mountain of tinder waiting for the spark to set it afire," Cade said. He and Tamsyn shared a glance. That was why they were here, after all.

The carriage turned into a wider street, revealing a rather shabby mansion surrounded by a high stone wall topped with iron spikes. The British flag flying on the gatehouse identified the property as the embassy.

The gatehouse was manned by a pair of British soldiers. They swung the gates open so a heavily loaded wagon could exit the embassy compound.

"The delegation is obviously packing up and pulling out." Tamsyn surveyed the mansion. "Not very impressive for a British embassy."

"For years there was no British embassy in France," Cade explained. "After the peace treaty was signed, both countries took their time establishing diplomatic relations, so Whitworth didn't arrive in Paris until this past December. Rhys said there was a rush to find a walled estate within the city, and this was the best available at the time."

"If they've been here for less than six months, they probably hadn't even finished unpacking, and now they're leaving," Tam observed. "We live in uncertain times."

After the wagon lumbered away, Moreau drove to the gatehouse. Cade showed his Home Office credentials to the sergeant in charge, who studied the document carefully before waving them through the gates.

Another wagon was parked in front of the embassy entrance and more boxes were being carried to it and packed. Moreau pulled up behind the wagon and said laconically, "I'll wait here for a bit."

Cade nodded thanks and stepped from the carriage, then turned to help Tamsyn to the ground. After he wielded the heavy knocker, they were admitted into a large reception room that was in a state of controlled chaos. Embassy servants were carrying in boxes and trunks, and eight or ten well-dressed men were pacing about anxiously and muttering to each other.

Tamsyn's gaze went to the group of men. They were all British and desperate to get official passports signed by the ambassador and a high French official so they could leave France swiftly and without complications. She'd seen that sort of passport, and the engravings and signatures were very impressive, but she had a sense that the documents wouldn't be half as much use to the men as they hoped.

They were approached by a brisk official with an air of command. He had a military bearing and was a few years older than Cade. "I'm Mr. Holland, the ambassador's private secretary. Do you have business here? This is not a good time for courtesy calls."

"We're here *because* it isn't a good time." Cade showed their credentials. When they traveled together, they had a variety of documents, some of which made it appear they were a married couple. People who assumed that were inclined to underestimate Tamsyn. Which was often useful.

"We need to speak with Lord Whitworth as soon as possible," Cade said.

Holland handed back his credentials and beckoned a young clerk over. "Murray, take the lady and gentleman up to his lordship's office."

One of the waiting men said in a surly voice, "Why can they see the ambassador when we've been waiting for our passports for hours?"

"These visitors have other business with Lord Whitworth," Mr. Holland said sternly. "Be patient. The passports will be ready soon."

"They damned well better be!" another man growled. "I need to get my family to safety before it's too late!"

"We have been encouraging Britons to return to England for some time now," Mr. Holland said in a cool voice. "You should have listened rather than waiting this long."

There was more muttering, but no further protests. After Holland gestured for the visitors to go upstairs, Tam wondered why so many people lacked common sense. It had been clear to anyone who paid attention that the peace would be short-lived, but the giddy delights of Paris had made fools of too many Britons.

They paused outside the door of the ambassador's office, where Tam did some hasty tweaking of Cade's coat and cravat. "After making the fastest possible journey from Cornwall to Paris, we're barely presentable," she said. "We'll have to rely on our persuasive powers rather than our appearances."

"Luckily, you can persuade any male to do anything," Cade said as the clerk knocked twice, then opened the door.

"Visitors for you, my lord," the clerk announced.

A distracted voice inside the office said, "Yes?"

Taking that as permission, Cade ushered Tamsyn inside. Lord Whitworth was about fifty and as handsome as his reputation promised. He had been signing papers but laid his quill aside. "Should I know you, sir?"

"We've not met, my lord, but we were sent here by the Home Office," Cade replied. "I'm Cade Tremayne and this is Lady Tamsyn Tremayne."

The ambassador collected several documents and handed them to the young clerk. "That's enough passport signing for now, Murray. Take them downstairs and distribute them to the men waiting. I'll do the rest shortly,"

After the clerk accepted the passports and left, Whitworth said, "I know Lord Tremayne, of course, and the work his people do." He studied them both. "The reputation of the Tribe of Tremayne is excellent, but why are you here?"

"To protect you and your lady wife, my lord," Tamsyn replied.

Whitworth's brows arched. "Is that necessary?"

"We hope not," Cade said, "but you are too important to England to take any chances."

Whitworth waved them to seats. "Granted, we're on the verge of declaring war, but as diplomats, my people and I should enjoy a safe passage home. Is there reason to believe otherwise?"

Cade took one of the two guest chairs while Tamsyn sat in the other. "Not reason, precisely, but intuition inspired by the screaming tirade that Bonaparte directed against you and Britain just two months ago."

"The First Consul displayed a complete lack of propriety and decency that one would not expect from the leader of a great nation." A faint smile touched the ambassador's lips. "Not even of France. But surely Lord Tremayne doesn't think that Bonaparte will try to assassinate me because of that one intemperate scene!"

"He doesn't think that," Cade said, "but he fears that one of the First Consul's men might hope to earn favor by killing you on his master's behalf."

The ambassador frowned and leaned back in his chair as he considered. "I can't say that is impossible," he said slowly. "Some of Bonaparte's revolutionary followers are rather rough men."

"It might not happen," Tamsyn said in her soft voice. "But those of us who are gifted have learned not to ignore our intuition, and far better to be too careful than not careful enough. An attack on you would be a potential danger to all of your delegation."

Whitworth sucked in his breath. "Arabella . . ."

He stopped, then continued, "You're here to protect my wife, Lady Tamsyn? She has had much to endure these last months."

"She and I have met briefly in the past. I'll look out for her until you're all on your way home." Tam smiled. "I'm much more dangerous than I look."

"It's the truth, sir," Cade said with a hint of a smile. "We are not here to interfere with your activities, only to quietly watch for possible trouble."

"Very well. If you are to guard us, it's best you stay here in the embassy so you can travel with us when we leave. You met my private secretary, Mr. Holland, downstairs. He'll assign quarters to you. " The ambassador's gaze shifted to Tamsyn. "If you wish to meet with my wife and tell her of your mission, she should be in her rooms on the floor above this one. I think she will welcome the companionship of another woman of rank. Now if you'll excuse me, there is much to be done before we depart."

Cade and Tamsyn thanked him for his time and quietly left the room. "Thank heaven for reasonable men!" Tam said. "I think Lord Whitworth may be somewhat gifted himself."

"That might explain how well he's done in Russia and Denmark and his other posts," Cade agreed. "While you speak to Lady Whitworth, I'll get our luggage from Moreau and tell him he can leave."

Tamsyn shook her head. "Not Lady Whitworth. Since her first husband was the Duke of Dorset, she continues to use the title of duchess as it's much grander than being a mere baroness."

Cade snorted. "As a bastard, I have trouble taking such things seriously, but if anyone can handle a proud duchess, it's you."

"Let us hope." Tamsyn hesitated. "As we drove up to the embassy, I had a feeling that it might be a good idea to commandeer a couple of the soldiers on guard duty to search around the walls of the embassy. The shrubbery is overgrown and could be a good place for explosives to be concealed."

Cade caught his breath, his gaze briefly going out of focus. "You could be right. I'll take care of that now."

"Be careful." Frowning, Tamsyn headed to the floor above. The walls of the stairwell were in need of paint, and she guessed that there hadn't been enough time to renovate the private quarters as well as the public rooms.

It wasn't difficult to find the duchess's rooms—the door was open and a footman was carrying out a trunk. Tam knocked on the open door and entered the disordered sitting room of the apartment. "Your Grace?"

The Duchess of Dorset was surveying the tangle of possessions, her face strained. She was a handsome woman in her early thirties, a number of years younger than her husband. Tam remembered her as coolly collected, but today she looked on the verge of tears.

The duchess looked up and frowned when she heard Tamsyn's voice. "We've met, haven't we?"

"Yes, Your Grace. I'm Lady Tamsyn Tremayne. We've had brief encounters at one or two receptions, but never a proper conversation."

"Oh, yes, you were with your mother, Lady Tremayne." The duchess's expression eased. "She's such a lovely restful woman. Are you accompanying her?"

"She is indeed lovely, but she's home in London. I'm here with one of my brothers, Cade Tremayne."

"You've picked a poor time to make a call," the duchess said wearily. "We're packing to leave for London, and my dratted French maid abandoned me to return to her family. I don't know how I'm going to manage!"

Tamsyn's greatest gift was healing emotions, so on impulse she approached and took the duchess's right hand in both of her own. "You'll manage," she said quietly as she channeled warmth and relaxation into the other woman. "You will be as strong as you need to be."

The duchess jerked in surprise when Tamsyn first touched her, then released a sigh and began to relax. "Thank you. You're very like your mother."

"So people tell me. It is the greatest of compliments." Releasing the other woman's hand, she said briskly, "I'll help you. Where shall I start?"

"You should not be doing such menial work!" the duchess exclaimed.

"I'm rather good at packing and enjoy creating order from chaos." Tamsyn smiled. "Of which there is no shortage!"

"Your aid would be very helpful," the other woman admitted. She glanced around the room. "Perhaps . . . perhaps you could pack garments from that wardrobe into one of the trunks?"

"It will be my pleasure." Tamsyn opened the wardrobe doors and surveyed shelves full of folded chemises, unmentionables, and nightwear in the finest of fabrics. As she pulled a small trunk to the wardrobe and lifted the lid, she said in a matter-of-fact voice, "I'm happy to help in any way I can, but the primary reason I've come to France is because my brother and I both work for the Home Office. We've been sent here to ensure that you and your husband and the rest of the delegation make it home safely."

"Surely the French won't attempt to stop us from leaving!" The other woman gasped.

"Probably not, but some of Bonaparte's followers who hate Britain may not believe in diplomatic immunity." Tamsyn stacked neat piles of chemises into the trunk.

The duchess bit her lip. "The sooner we leave this benighted country, the better!"

Tamsyn tucked a dozen silk stockings into a corner of the trunk. "If you're willing to join me in packing your belongings, you'll be that much closer to leaving, and I promise I won't tell anyone that you undertook such a menial task."

The duchess gave a sudden laugh. "And it will keep me busy and less likely to fret. It's very pleasant to have the company of an English lady. Court life has been a poisonous swirl of politics. I've been afraid to talk to anyone." She set a small case on her dressing table and began packing brushes and scent bottles and small mirrors.

"In a fortnight you'll be back in London and able to breathe easily again." Tamsyn finished packing the first trunk and looked around for another.

"I look forward to that." The duchess snapped her toiletry case closed. "And I hope the government doesn't have a desperate need to send my husband to another potential battleground!"

"The time for diplomacy with France has passed. Now it's time for the generals and the admirals." Tamsyn chuckled. "And for packing so you can get away from here!"

The duchess smiled, and they spent the next several hours working and laughing and avoiding talk of anything serious. But in the back of her mind, Tamsyn sensed that Cade was dealing with more challenging issues. She wondered what tangles he'd found.

Chapter 3

The trip from Cornwall to Paris had been swift and tiring; the day spent at the embassy was demanding in a different way as Cade talked to staff and guards and investigated the surroundings. It was dark now and he'd done as much as he could for the day. Now it was time to find Tamsyn to discuss what they'd learned and perhaps raid the kitchen for a late supper. But first he needed to find his assigned quarters.

The young aide who guided him up to the top floor said apologetically, "I'm sorry there is no better room available, sir, but the embassy is full to bursting because no one wants to stay outside the compound with Paris in such a disturbed state."

"I understand. It's not for long, and I guarantee that I've stayed in worse quarters." In barns and bushes when nothing better was available. He hoped they'd found a more suitable room for Tamsyn.

"Here you are, sir." The aide indicated a door with a sliver of light underneath. "Sleep well."

Cade opened the door to a slant-ceilinged attic illuminated by a single lamp, which revealed a neat stack of baggage, a not-very-wide bed, and Tamsyn, who was perched on the edge of the bed, brushing her shining blond hair so that it spilled over her blue robe. The sight of her beauty and the intimacy of the setting blazed through him like lightning, shattering his nerves and control.

Tamsyn's gaze snapped to him. "Is something wrong? I just felt a blast of shock from you."

He clamped down on his emotions with the iron control he'd cultivated all his life. "I didn't expect to see you here. What are you doing in my room?"

"*Our* room," she said cheerfully. "Mr. Holland assumed we're married so it wouldn't be a problem for us to share."

Cade wanted to grind his teeth. "I should have made it clear that we prefer separate rooms."

"We're lucky to have this. Two servants were moved in with two other servants in order to give us this room." She began plaiting her hair into a long braid. "We'll manage. Though we aren't married, for much of our lives we've lived under the same roof. We've even shared the same bed."

"That was when you were about four years old," he pointed out. "Living under the same roof is different from sharing a room. You're not just my younger sister, but a well-born young lady. It feels very . . . improper for me to be here."

She laughed. "Cade, it isn't like you to worry about propriety! We're on a mission and we'll do whatever is necessary. And what's necessary now is eating. I'm hungry!"

"So am I," Cade said, glad to change the subject. "I haven't eaten since breakfast, which was many miles and hours ago. Shall I go down to the kitchen and see what I can beg, borrow, or steal?" "

"I already have." She stood and lifted a basket onto the small table. "One of the cooks provided us with a good selection of meats and cheeses and breads as well as a rather fine-looking bottle of red wine." She began taking food parcels out of the basket.

Relaxing, he moved to the table, knowing that sharing a meal with Tam would make the situation feel more normal. "You're the best forager I know."

"It's not a dramatic gift, but useful," she said as she opened a parcel of sliced ham. "Would you like ham and cheese on excellent French bread?"

"Please!"

She assembled a well-filled sandwich, poured wine into a tumbler, and set it on the other side of the table. He settled in the wooden chair and took a large bite of his sandwich. Delicious. After chewing and swallowing, he asked, "How did you get on with the duchess?"

"Surprisingly well. We packed her belongings into trunks together because her French maid has left her."

"The duchess was willing to do such menial labor?" Cade said, surprised. "With her reputation, I'd have thought such tasks would be beneath her."

"She's felt very isolated here, so she welcomed my company." Tamsyn sipped her wine before continuing, "I've heard that her first husband, the Duke of Dorset, married her for her beauty but was a notorious womanizer with a passion for cricket and little time for his young wife."

"No wonder she's prickly." He shook his head. "Beauty can be such a curse for women. I'm glad you won't ever be forced into a situation like that."

"So am I. Beauty is a decidedly mixed blessing. Money is more useful." Tamsyn looked reflective. "I have the feeling that the duchess's cool composure and demands for the respect due to her rank were her way of protecting herself in her difficult first marriage. But the duke's death left her a wealthy woman, so she was able to marry a man she loves. Whitworth is very different from her first husband. She wants to be a good wife to him, but this time in France has been very hard for her."

Tamsyn's assessments of people were always astute, and this analysis gave Cade a better understanding of the ambassador's wife. "It sounds as if she'll be cooperative in getting them to safety."

"She will." Tamsyn ate another bite of her sandwich. "What have you been doing all day?"

"Talking to the guards to organize protection for the journey to Calais. There are several wagons which will leave together, carrying furniture and the like, but the most important papers and embassy staff members will leave later in two carriages. There will be no flags or coats of arms to attract attention, and each wagon and carriage will have an armed guard."

Tamsyn finished her sandwich. After washing it down with a sip of wine, she asked, "Will you and I travel with the Whitworths?"

"I'll be one of two outriders, moving back and forth and watching for trouble. I thought you should ride inside with the ambassador and his wife as the last line of defense if one is needed."

"That makes sense as well as sparing me from any rain that may fall." She sipped more wine. "Did you find anything dangerous hidden in the shrubbery around the embassy?"

He grimaced. "Unfortunately, yes. I did the search with Hansen, the captain of the embassy's military guard. We found a hidden cache of gunpowder large enough to destroy most of the building if it had been set off."

Tamsyn gave a soft whistle. "A good thing you searched!"

"We took care of the immediate threat," he said seriously. "But the bad news is that I sensed the explosives had been placed there by a strongly gifted man. Ordinary searchers would almost certainly have missed them." He hesitated before continuing, "The energy that marked the explosives was very distinctive and very focused."

Frowning, Tamsyn set her wine tumbler down. "That's deeply disturbing. Would you recognize the man if you met him in person?"

"Yes, though I hope that doesn't happen. He's as cold and poisonous as a scorpion. He radiates hatred toward Britain and the British."

"He's not alone in that, but being gifted makes him particularly dangerous," she agreed. "A scorpion indeed."

"Rhys was right that our services will be needed to get everyone safely home," Cade replied. "Luckily, I think that Hansen, the captain of the guard, is more than a little gifted himself. He has good military instincts, so he takes me and my suggestions seriously. He'll be the other outrider."

She nodded in approval. "I've often thought that soldiers who have survived multiple battles have to be at least somewhat gifted."

"Hansen might agree, though he said that most soldiers would loathe being called gifted, we being such a despicable lot," Cade said dryly. "Instead, they talk about having a sixth sense for danger."

"The description doesn't matter as long as they know when to duck!" Tamsyn's expression became serious. "Do you have a sense of what the journey to Calais will be like?"

He closed his eyes and wished he could predict the future accurately. Or maybe not. Knowing what was going to happen might be more knowledge than a man could bear. But he did sometimes have a sense of the shape of the future. "I think we'll get them there safely," he said slowly. "But there will be trouble with . . . an unexpected twist at the end. Something impossible to predict."

"I do not find that comforting, but I'm sure we'll contrive. We're clever that way." Tam swallowed the last of her wine, then covered a ladylike yawn. "I'm ready to go to bed. It's been a long day, and that small glass of wine is hitting me like a draft of opium."

Both of their gazes went to the bed. "I'll sleep on the floor," Cade said. "That bed is not large enough for two."

"But you're older and you should have the bed to spare your weary old bones," she said mischievously.

"Not that much older." Cade swallowed the last of the wine. "But as your older brother, I insist that you, my delicate younger sister, must take the bed."

She laughed. "You know I'm as tough as old boots, but I'll never win an argument when you're in protective big brother mode." She stood and stretched with catlike grace. "In deference to our delicate sensibilities or perhaps our elevated status, the maids arranged a tiny washing area behind the screen in that corner. You'll have to bend your head, though." She headed to the corner, still yawning.

The maids had also left a good supply of blankets so Cade folded a couple together to make a pallet, placing it as far from Tamsyn as the room would allow. As he improvised a pillow, he did his best to ignore the sounds of her splashing in the corner.

After she'd washed up, she emerged from the screened corner and slid under the bedclothes, murmuring, "Good night, Cade. May tomorrow not bring more adventures!"

She rolled away to face the wall and pulled the covers over her head. Perhaps she was trying for invisibility, but he was still sharply aware of her.

He stripped down to his shirt and drawers, then moved behind the screen. There was a chamber pot and a very small washstand with basin, water pitcher, soap, and a pair of towels. As Tam had said, he had to duck his head.

After washing up, he checked how much oil was in the lamp,

then turned it down to the lowest possible level, just enough to provide dim illumination so no one would stumble over baggage if they had to get up. Fortunately, the one narrow window faced east so the room would receive dawn light, which would help for rising early. The next day would be at least as busy as the one ending.

Wearily, Cade lay down on the pallet. Tamsyn's soft, regular breathing indicated that she was sleeping soundly. He should fall asleep as swiftly, but he didn't. He was too aware of Tamsyn.

Her mention of the fact that they'd sometimes shared a bed had stirred up memories of when he and Bran had first been taken in by Gwyn and Rhys. The Tremaynes could not have been warmer or more welcoming, but Cade had been cold and afraid for too long to feel safe at first. He'd envied Bran's ability to embrace their amazing good fortune and relax into their new life.

Later Cade had recognized that Bran's earliest years in a prosperous household with a loving mother had given him a kind of confidence Cade had never known. Despite their differences, they'd bonded right away when they'd met at that vile baby farm.

They were both so young that it was hard to believe that they'd managed to leave Cornwall and travel all the way to London, but they'd done it. Bran had recognized that they must escape if they were to survive, and he'd come up with a bold plan. Cade was a couple of years older and stronger, and he had a powerful instinct to protect, so he'd successfully executed Bran's plan with his practicality and fierce determination.

But for the length of that nightmare journey, Cade had been terrified that he wouldn't be strong and clever enough to bring them to the unknown safety that Bran was sure they'd discover. Bran had been right, and they found their future with the two finest people either of them had ever met.

The Tremaynes knew better than to try to separate the boys, so they'd been given a room that had two beds. They had been fed and scrubbed and given new clothing; all should have been well. That first night, Bran had relaxed and settled in, sleeping as soundly as a contented kitten. But Cade had been unable to relax or sleep well because he was still desperately frightened inside. His father had been brutal, and Cade's early years had been precarious. Fear had always been part of him.

With her gift for reading emotions, Tamsyn had recognized his inner terror, so on his second night in Tremayne House, she'd quietly entered the boys' room even though she could barely reach the doorknob. Cade's gift for awareness of his surroundings had shocked him to full, heart-pounding wakefulness when he heard her soft steps.

"It's only me, Tamsyn," she'd whispered as she approached the bed. He'd exhaled with relief and reached down to help her up onto the mattress.

"Why are you here?" he said in an equally soft whisper.

"To persuade you that you're safe now." She set one small hand on his chest and pushed him down, then cuddled up against his side. After a moment of shock, he wrapped his arms around her small form and began to shudder with silent tears.

Slowly he realized that she was sending warm, healing energy into him. "All will be well," she murmured, sounding like a wise old sibyl, though he didn't have the words to describe her then. He only knew that she was a miracle of warmth and understanding despite her tender years.

Gradually his fear faded, and he fell asleep with his arms around her. When he woke fully rested the next morning, she was gone.

She came again the next night to be sure that he was well and whole. He hugged her again, murmuring his thanks. They lay peacefully together until she sat up and pressed her soft childish lips to his cheek, whispering, "I'm so glad you're my brother now."

She'd left then, taking away his fear, and along with it, his heart.

Tamsyn woke the next morning to find that Cade had already left, as quiet as a cat on the hunt. She smiled at the thought as she pushed aside her covers and crossed to the tiny washroom. That soft-footed stealth was part of what made him such an excellent agent.

But as she splashed cold water onto her face, she realized he'd been right that sharing a room was different from traveling together with separate rooms, as they'd always done in the past. It was more . . . intimate.

In the darkness, hearing his soft breathing, she'd been very aware of him as a man, not only the brother she'd known most of her life. She'd always been very close to both Cade and Bran, though in different ways because they were different men. The previous night had created a different kind of closeness with Cade. More physical awareness.

She thought back to the two nights when she'd joined Cade in his bed after he and Bran had arrived at Tremayne House. As soon as he'd entered the household, she'd sensed his courage, strength, and honor, but she'd also felt his shattering fear that he would never be strong enough or good enough to do what must be done.

She couldn't remember a time when she didn't have her gift for sensing people and emotions, and she'd learned that she could calm people who were upset by touching them, usually taking hold of a hand. Hoping she could help Cade, the next night she'd slipped from her bed and gone to find him.

He'd welcomed her presence, so she settled beside him and laid her hand over his heart. She enjoyed the warmth of being next to him, but she was shocked to feel a surge of healing power so intense that surely it must have come from the divine. Awed, she sensed his fear dissolving, leaving the strength and integrity and loyalty that were the bedrock of his spirit.

It was a night she never forgot. She'd given Cade a gift of healing, and in return he'd shown her what she was born to do.

Today there were new challenges to meet. She dressed and prepared for another busy day of helping the duchess as a combination of companion and lady's maid. The next morning, they'd be on their way home to England.

And then what? Frowning, she realized that for once she really had no sense of what the future held.

Except, she realized with a chill, that it would be different, unexpected—and dangerous.

Chapter 4

The courtyard in front of the British embassy churned in the dawn light. Carriages were being packed, horses snorted restlessly, and servants and staff members raced about making last-minute adjustments.

Cade sat quietly on his horse, watching. Next to him was Captain Hansen, the commander of the embassy's military guard. He was lean and tough, with watchful eyes. They'd become friendly, developing a degree of trust as they worked together.

Cade said, "Do you think we'll be moving before noon?"

Hansen laughed. "Yes, and the sooner the better! I can't wait to get back to England."

Cade hesitated before asking a personal question, but he sensed an unusual kind of tension in the other man. "Does trouble await you there?"

Hansen's brows arched. "This is why people resent those who are gifted."

"You're more gifted than you want to admit," Cade observed.

The other man shrugged. "I just have a soldierly sixth sense for danger. How did you know that I'm concerned?"

"There seems to be more on your mind than this escort duty."

Hansen hesitated as he considered whether to say more, then sighed. "A month ago I received word that my father had died unexpectedly. As soon as we reach London, I'll need to resign my commission and go home to take charge of the family estate. My mother is grieving and I have a young sister and brother. I need to be there for them."

"I'm sorry. I don't even want to think about what it will be like to lose my father," Cade said quietly. He meant his real father, Rhys Tremayne, not his birth father, the brutal smuggler who'd thrown Cade away when he was a child.

"We'll all miss him," Hansen said tersely. Then his voice lightened. "There was also good news arriving in the same post. My wife informed me that she's with child."

"Congratulations! That's a very good reason to want to return home."

Hansen nodded. "I wanted to return to England immediately, but it was obvious that the embassy would be closing soon and I couldn't abandon Lord Whitworth when there were no other officers with as much experience."

"Staying was the honorable thing to do."

Hansen smiled wryly. "Yes, but I now better understand the temptations of being dishonorable!"

"Sometimes being less than honorable is the best way to get the results you need," Cade said.

"Spoken like a man who works for the Home Office," Hansen said. "But you have the bearing of an officer. Were you ever in the army?"

"No, though I rather like giving orders," Cade replied. When the other man chuckled, he added, "My Home Office assignments have been varied—some were rather military in nature."

"You're quiet about it, but you're good at getting people to do what you think should be done. Is that some kind of gifted trick?"

"We're not mesmerists, if that's what you're suggesting," Cade said dryly. "It's more a matter of looking at a situation and deciding what is the best solution, then persuading the man in charge to think it's his idea."

"That's what you did with me, and it was very successful." Hansen grimaced. "We wouldn't have found that cache of gunpowder if not for you."

"My sister Tamsyn was the one who suggested that we should search the shrubbery around the embassy."

"That pretty little blonde was the one who sensed the gunpowder?" Hansen said, surprised. "She seems too ladylike for such things."

"She is not to be underestimated," Cade said with an inward smile. His gaze went to the front door of the embassy. The Whitworths were coming out together and heading down the steps, the duchess holding her husband's arm. Behind them, Tamsyn and Mr. Holland, the ambassador's private secretary, were quietly following.

The day had brightened, and it was easy to see Tam's face. She looked relaxed and calm. Her gaze went to him, and he felt a stab of sharp connection. They'd always worked well together, and he felt that connection even more intensely this time, perhaps because of the seriousness of their mission.

He nodded to her, then said, "It looks like we're ready to leave."

"I'll be glad to get out of Paris and onto the open road." Hansen set his horse forward to the ambassador's carriage. He had a brief conversation with Lord Whitworth before the ambassador, his wife, Tamsyn, and Holland climbed into the vehicle.

The gates of the embassy compound opened and the carriages rolled out. Great Britain was officially leaving France as thunderclouds of war gathered over Europe.

Tamsyn was glad when they reached the countryside. The narrow Parisian streets would be dangerous if an enemy wanted to attack, and while that didn't happen, she could feel the hostility around them.

French roads were generally good, especially major routes like the one from Paris to Calais, and the well-sprung ambassadorial carriage was as comfortable as one could be on such a journey. She shared the backward-facing seat with Mr. Holland. The opposite seat was occupied by the Whitworths, with the ambassador quietly working at a lap desk.

The duchess sat next to him, gazing out the window with her hands clasped tightly in her lap. It didn't take a gifted person to recognize her tension and her desire to be back in England.

Just three days earlier, Tamsyn and Cade had made this journey south at top speed, riding the best available horses and changing frequently at the post houses along the way. She'd been dressed as a boy because riding astride was faster. Cade had perhaps slowed his pace a little so she could keep up, but if so, she hadn't held him back much. Though she was small, she'd always had excellent stamina.

When they reached Paris, they'd stopped to change to more respectable clothing and gone to the embassy in Moreau's carriage. This journey would be slower and less exhausting physically, but they must both keep alert. She was always aware of Cade's location, and on this journey, her consciousness shadowed his as they both watched for danger.

After a long, boring day of travel, Tamsyn was glad when the ambassadorial party stopped for the night at an inn that was adequate, though no more than that. She and Holland dined with the Whitworths in a private parlor, but when they were done, she went in search of Cade. He'd eaten in the common room, then taken a sturdy tumbler of wine outside to sip while he relaxed on a bench and watched the last fading streaks of sunset.

Tamsyn smiled and sat next to him. "One day passed without disaster, but by the time we reach Calais, I'm going to be really tired of traveling!"

"I'm already tired of it, but at least this is slower than our mad journey to Paris." He wrapped a casual arm around her, and she leaned into him with a sigh. She always felt relaxed with Cade.

She borrowed his glass for a sip. "A rather nice red wine. One of the advantages of being in France." She returned the tumbler. "Have you sensed any signs of trouble?"

"Not really, but I have a sense that we're being watched." He hesitated before continuing, "The disturbing part is that it feels as if we're being stalked by the man who planted the gunpowder by the embassy wall."

Tamsyn frowned. "Your scorpion. Can you describe what he feels like?"

"Cold. Focused." He sipped more wine. "Ruthless."

"Can you share that feeling with me so I'll recognize him if he's near?"

"I'm not sure, but it's worth trying." He raised the arm around her shoulders and touched warm fingers to the middle of her forehead.

After a still moment, she felt a jolt of energy so startling that she gasped and jerked away from Cade. "I didn't know it was possible to transmit the feeling of another person so intensely!"

He caught her other hand to steady her. "What did you experience?" he asked quietly.

"Give me a moment to sort it out." She closed her eyes and stilled her mind so she could analyze the complicated mix of energies she'd received from her brother. "I felt you very strongly, as if you were protecting me from the Scorpion's energy. He's as cold and vicious as you've said."

"You're the expert in reading people. Do you think he'll attack the ambassador on the journey to Calais?"

She sent her perceptions deeper. "I don't think so, but I feel there will be trouble in Calais. Serious trouble." She thought more. "He hates Britain and passionately supports Bonaparte, but there's also a personal element in what drives him."

"He enjoys killing?" Cade suggested.

"Nothing that simple. But don't take my word for any of this." She opened her eyes and felt a different kind of startling awareness as she looked at Cade. She'd known him most of her life. She'd been instantly drawn to his desperate courage when her parents had first brought him home. He'd grown up to be tall, strong, and good-looking, but she was so used to him that she hadn't really *seen* him in years.

He really was a remarkably fine figure of a man—strong and intelligent and competent, not to mention strikingly handsome, with lurking humor in his eyes. She smiled to herself. Familiarity hadn't bred contempt, but she had certainly been taking his appearance for granted.

His brows arched. "Have I just grown a second head?"

She shook her head. "No, it's just that when I know people very well, they become so familiar to me that I don't really think about what they look like. Then I'll suddenly see them as if for the first time, and it's rather startling. Doesn't that happen to you?"

He chuckled. "No, I only see people in a regular sort of way."

She wondered for perhaps the first time in her life how he saw her. With a shiver, she pulled her shawl around herself. "It's getting chilly."

Cade wrapped his arm around her shoulders again. He was always reliably warm.

"Time to go in," he said. "Where are you sleeping tonight?"

"With the landlord's daughter. She has a room with two

beds and is used to accommodating female travelers as long as they aren't too alarming. What about you?"

"I'm sharing a room with Hansen. I hope he doesn't snore."

She stood, covering a yawn. "He probably hopes the same of you. At least none of our party must sleep on straw in the stables."

"I might head out there myself if Hansen snores loudly," Cade said darkly. "I'll be glad to get back to England. We should be there in a few more days if bad weather doesn't hold up our channel crossing."

"And if the French officials don't prove difficult." She frowned as they went inside. She had a strong feeling that they wouldn't be home in a week. If not, she hoped it was just weather that would slow them down.

No. It wouldn't be the weather.

Chapter 5

The next day's travel was long but uneventful. Tamsyn continued shadowing Cade's mind so that their joined abilities could sense possible trouble. She had the itchy sense that the Scorpion was watching them, biding his time. Waiting for Calais, perhaps?

It was early evening when they stopped at another inn much like the one they'd stayed in the night before. Lord Whitworth climbed from the carriage, turning to help out first his wife, then Tamsyn. He smiled as she took his hand and stepped to the ground. "You're having a rather boring journey, Lady Tamsyn."

"That's the way we like it!" she said with a chuckle as she stretched her tired muscles. Then she felt a sharp sense of danger and snapped her gaze toward the woodland on the other side of the road. In the trees was a flicker that looked like light reflecting on a metal barrel . . . .

She threw herself at Lord Whitworth, knocking him to the ground as the rifle blasted, shattering the peaceful evening air. The bullet slammed into the side of the carriage above Tamsyn's head.

As another shot was fired, Captain Hansen and two of his men who were still mounted kicked their horses into a gallop and headed, shouting, across the road toward the place in the trees where the shots had originated.

Cade moved equally fast, swinging his horse crossways into the line of fire between the shooter and Lord Whitworth. He vaulted from the saddle and caught Tamsyn's hand, pulling her off the ambassador. His gaze burned into hers as he asked, "Are you all right, Tam?"

"I'm fine," she assured him. Bruises didn't count.

Cade turned to Whitworth and offered him a hand up. "Sir, were you injured?"

"No," Whitworth said as he rose to his feet. "But look to my wife!"

Ignoring her bruises, Tamsyn did exactly that, guiding the shocked duchess behind the barrier of the carriage so they were out of the line of fire. "No one was hurt," Tamsyn said as they entered the inn.

Once they were inside, the duchess folded into a chair in the entryway and buried her face in her hands. "I can't wait to leave this damnable country!" she said in a shaking voice.

Tamsyn rested a comforting hand on the other woman's shoulder. "You have every reason to be upset. But no one was hurt and the extra security precautions worked. You and the ambassador have very good protectors."

"You're sure my husband is all right?" the other woman said as she uncovered her face and looked toward the door.

"I'm fine, Arabella," the ambassador said as he entered. "Lady Tamsyn, you're very good at knocking down larger men!"

"I learned that playing with my brothers," she replied as the duchess stood and went into her husband's arms.

"We'll be home soon, my dear girl," he said softly.

The caring between them was palpable. Tamsyn turned away

and motioned for Cade to follow her outside again. "Let's take a look at the carriage," she suggested.

They walked around to the stable yard where the carriage stood and the horses were being unhitched so they could be fed and groomed. She looked up at the side of the carriage. "I wasn't sure at the time, but both bullets struck very high."

Cade immediately understood. "So either the Scorpion is a bad shot or he wasn't really trying to hit anyone."

"Just as he placed the gunpowder by the embassy but seems to have made no attempt to set it off." Tamsyn considered the bullet holes thoughtfully. "Do you suppose he might just want to harass and intimidate our party but doesn't intend to kill Lord Whitworth?"

"That's possible, though I wouldn't bet anyone's life on it," Cade said. "Or perhaps because he's gifted himself, he's testing us to learn how strong we are."

"He might want to prove himself superior to gifted British people?"

"Perhaps," Cade said. "Though rather contrary given that our kind are usually very cooperative with each other even if we're of different nations."

Tamsyn grinned. "Well, French, you know. Many of them glory in being contrary."

As Cade chuckled, Captain Hansen rode into the yard, saying tersely, "The devil got away. My men are pursuing in the direction he probably went, but I'm not optimistic. He was prepared to gallop away as soon as he fired his rifle. He also timed his shots for a break in traffic on the road and just before a string of heavy wagons came along, which slowed us down."

"Did the Scorpion leave any traces behind?" Cade asked.

"The Scorpion is a good name for him," the captain said. "I didn't see anything, but perhaps a closer look might turn something up."

"Then let's go across the road to see if we can find anything. Where was he exactly, Captain Hansen?" Tamsyn asked.

"I'll show you myself." The captain handed his horse over to an ostler, then led the way from the stables to the edge of the road.

This late in the day, traffic was light, so they were able to cross quickly. Hansen guided them to a thick clump of trees directly opposite the inn. "We think he shot from this tree. His horse was tethered out of sight a little farther back and must have been saddled and ready to run."

There was crushed grass around the foot of the tree and faint prints from large boots. Cade went down on one knee to study the prints, taking a pinch of earth from the edge of one and rolling it thoughtfully between his fingers. Then he stood and surveyed the tree. "He'd have to be fairly tall to jump to the lowest branch."

Hansen eyed the height doubtfully. "It would be difficult. Maybe he had help?"

"Let's see if one man can do it alone." Cade took a couple of long steps and then leaped powerfully upward. He caught the broad branch with both hands, then pulled himself up to a sitting position. "So it's possible. Likely he's about my height if not taller."

Tamsyn sucked in her breath, experiencing another of those moments of intense awareness. She'd seen Cade grow from a skinny urchin to a powerful athlete, but hadn't consciously noticed his sheer lithe power, rather like one of the lions at the Tower of London zoo. No wonder female gazes followed him whenever they were out together.

"So your Scorpion is very tall and a good jumper as there are no signs that he had a companion to boost him up," Hansen said. "I don't think a man could jump that high holding a rifle, so he must have tied a rope to his weapon and pulled it up when he was in position."

Cade raised his arms and mimicked the action of aiming a rifle. "It's a well- chosen spot with a good clear view to the area in front of the inn."

Tamsyn had been studying the rough ground below the tree. "He was smoking a pipe, I think. There's a scattering of pipe ashes here."

She turned and moved slowly through the scruffy grass toward where the horse had been tethered. There was only one set of footprints.

She caught a glimpse of something white on her right and looked closer. Yes, there, a slender white shape was half concealed in the grass. "Here's a clay pipe with a broken stem."

Cade had moved to join her. "A pipe stem that long means the Scorpion prefers to have a smooth smoke, but they break easily."

"It surprises me that a careful criminal would leave anything behind, but perhaps he tossed it aside without thinking." Tamsyn leaned over, picked up the pipe, and received such an intense jolt of energy that she cried out and dropped it. She would have fallen if Cade hadn't caught her around the waist and pulled her against him.

"Tam, what happened?" he asked urgently.

She shook her head to clear it, grateful for his support. "Touching the pipe was rather like the jolt from one of those demonstrations of electricity you've taken me to, but . . . personal. It was charged with Scorpion energy."

"I wonder if he left the pipe as some kind of deliberate taunt," Cade said as he bent to pick it up.

"Don't!" Tamsyn grabbed his wrist, stopping him. "I think it was meant for you and might hit you harder than it did me."

"I'll pick it up," Hansen said. "Since I'm not gifted, it shouldn't affect me."

He leaned to pick up the pipe, then swore, almost dropping

it. "The bowl is still a little warm, as if tobacco was still burning when he dropped it."

"Do you feel only the heat, or something more?" Tamsyn asked.

The captain hesitated. "Something more? A feeling like the one you described of a cold, evil man. But surely that's impossible because I'm not gifted."

"You are, though," she said gently. "Not as strongly as we are, but you definitely have some talent. It's probably helped you survive as a soldier."

Hansen looked unnerved. "I don't think I wanted to know that."

"Gifts often run in families, so it's good to know because your children might inherit some abilities," she observed.

"Did your brother tell you that my wife is with child?" he asked, startled.

"No. It just seemed like something that would happen sooner or later." She smiled. "Sooner, obviously! Congratulations."

"As you see, Tamsyn and I are surviving on our gifts very well," Cade said. "A lot of people have subtle gifts that they don't recognize. They may just think they're lucky, or have good judgment, or some such."

"That doesn't sound so bad," Hansen admitted.

Cade reached for the pipe. "I want to see just what kind of vicious energy the Scorpion put into this."

"Let me see it first, Cade," Tamsyn said. "Since I'm a healer, maybe I can reduce whatever wicked energy was infused in it by the Scorpion."

"If you're sure," Cade said doubtfully.

Tamsyn carefully took the pipe from Hansen. She flinched, but it affected her less this time. She concentrated on sending calming power into the raw, jagged energy that was in the white clay.

After several minutes, she said, "I think it's safe now, but the harm was definitely aimed at you, Cade. It has the feeling of you."

Her brother took the pipe, rolling it around in his hands as he studied it. "I can feel the malice. I don't think it would be possible to make an object like this kill a person, but it might have affected my mind or my abilities if you hadn't defused it."

Tamsyn frowned as she contemplated the pipe, and hoped they would reach Calais without any more interference from the Scorpion.

Chapter 6

The ambassadorial party made it to Calais without further incident, but then stalled as they waited for permission to leave. They were fortunate to have found rooms in a pleasant hotel near the docks, but it was a mixed blessing to spend three days looking across the English Channel at the white cliffs of Dover. "So close and yet so far!" Tamsyn said as she gazed out the window in the duchess's room.

The duchess joined her at the window. "Waiting is hard, but I like knowing how close we are to home. A mere twenty miles or so."

"Does Lord Whitworth know why the French officials aren't allowing us to depart?"

The duchess smiled wryly. "Charles says they do it because they can. He's not concerned that they won't let us leave. Within the next day or so, he said."

Tamsyn hoped that would be the case. She worried that the port authorities were waiting for the official declaration of war. In theory, even that declaration shouldn't prevent a diplomatic mission from leaving, but in Bonaparte's France, traditional courtesies could not be counted on. And her sense of foreboding, of imminent disaster, was growing.

"I hope he's right," she said aloud. "Since we're all packed, we can be out of here like a group of mad March hares as soon as permission is granted and the tide is right."

The duchess laughed. "I like the image of us as a group of hares leaping!"

Tamsyn thought uneasily that hares were often caught in snares. "The port is the busiest it's been since we arrived here. There are several ships flying British colors, and passengers are boarding very efficiently."

"Like us, they want to go home! But I find it encouraging to see others leaving." The duchess sighed. "Surely our turn will come soon."

While the duchess was focused on the ships preparing to depart, Tamsyn couldn't help noticing the small clusters of blue-coated French soldiers who were scattered along the waterfront. Were they there to maintain order in the crowd, or for some more sinister reason?

Tamsyn's gaze sharpened as she saw a carriage swing onto the street in front of the hotel. Though the port area was only a few minutes' walk away, for safety's sake Whitworth had been using a carriage because walking made him more vulnerable to assault.

Cade swung out of the carriage first, followed by the ambassador and Holland, the secretary. "Look, my lord is smiling!" the duchess exclaimed. "Permission must have been granted for us to board our ship and leave!"

They both raced down the stairs to intercept the men in the lobby. The duchess asked, "Have we been granted permission?"

Whitworth smiled. "We have indeed! The heavy luggage has already been loaded onto the *Princess of Wales* and we have only our small bags of personal belongings to carry on board. The tide is right and we can be on our way within the hour!"

The duchess gave a rapturous sigh. "I'm so glad! Let's check our rooms to make sure we have everything."

The Whitworths headed for the stairs while Tamsyn turned to Cade. In a low voice, she asked, "Has there been any trouble? I have a sense of doom hanging over my head."

"So do I," Cade agreed, "but there have been no threats. Just that damnable feeling of being watched. The streets are so crowded that it will be better to walk to the ship rather than try to drive the carriage. I hope the Scorpion doesn't decide this is the time to attack."

"If so, we'll sense him before he can strike," she said reassuringly. "I'll carry your bag as well as mine so your hands will be free to deal with any trouble. Between you and Captain Hansen and the other guards, the Whitworths will be safe."

"I feel that they will be." Cade frowned. "But I think there will be trouble from an unexpected direction."

She said lightly, "We're very good at dealing with the unexpected."

He smiled a little. "True. Time to get our bags and say goodbye to Calais."

She nodded and together they climbed the stairs. His room was opposite hers. He let himself in, collected his bag, then crossed the passage to her room. They had identical canvas carry bags that could be tied shut, then slung over a shoulder and across a person's chest so there was no need to think about it.

After she arranged her bag across her chest, he gave her his bag and she hung it over her other shoulder so the straps crossed in front of her. "With two bags balancing each other, I hardly notice I'm carrying anything," she said.

Since it was a bright, chilly May day, she donned her soft brown cloak, covering the bags. As she tied her rather boring bonnet on, Cade said with a chuckle, "You look like a well-behaved spinster on her way to arrange flowers at the parish church. I assume your knife is convenient to hand?"

She arched her brows. "Of course it is. All the best spinsters of the parish know how to defend themselves."

"Here's hoping we won't need to." He held the door for her and they proceeded down the stairs together. Mr. Holland came next, then the Whitworths. As they stepped outside of the hotel, Hansen and his four soldiers gathered protectively around their small group. All of them were in civilian clothing because British uniforms might prove inflammatory under current circumstances.

Cade laid a warm hand on Tamsyn's lower back. "Stay close and be careful, Tamkin," he said softly.

"And the same to you, number one brother," she said with equal softness.

The streets had become even more crowded, but with Cade and Hansen and the other guards to clear the way, they made good time toward the port. All of them, even the duchess, were alert and watching their surroundings carefully.

Finally they emerged onto the broad street that ran along the waterfront. Hundreds of people were crowded into the area along with carts of luggage, street peddlers, sailors, and soldiers. Travelers were boarding ships. Their vessel, the *Princess of Wales,* was directly ahead of them, with a welcoming gangway in place.

Tamsyn gave a sigh of relief. They'd made it. Just a hundred yards or so more and they'd be safe. . . .

Her relief was premature.

With a clatter of horses' hooves and the steady beat of drums, a French colonel and a group of subordinates rode into the center of the dock area and pulled to a halt a little left of the route Cade and the others were taking. An aide handed the colonel a cone-shaped speaking tube, and the commander bellowed through it with a voice that echoed harshly off the waterfront buildings.

"*Attention! Attention!*" he shouted in French. "I am Colonel Gagnon, and by the authority of Napoleon Bonaparte, First Consul of France, all Englishmen from the age of eighteen to sixty who might be enrolled in the militia shall be made Prisoners of War to answer for the Citizens of the Republic who have been arrested by the vessels or subjects of his Britannic Majesty before the declaration of war!"

There was a stunned silence, then an uproar of English voices. A man with a London accent bellowed, "Are you sayin' we can't go home? Why the bloody hell not? I'm not in the militia and I don't know anyone who is!"

The clusters of French soldiers that had been waiting on street corners marched swiftly forward and began to form a line in front of the docked ships to prevent potential travelers from boarding. The ambassador and his entourage stopped. "Absurd!" Whitworth said, shocked. "The militia barely exists! It's not a trained fighting force like the regular army. There is no legal basis for arresting civilians and declaring them prisoners of war!"

"It's hard to argue the law with armed men," Cade said tersely. "Hansen, you and your soldiers are in the army and legitimate targets. We need to get you and the rest of our party onto the ship before the French troops organize themselves. Stay close!"

He and the other guards formed around the Whitworths and forced their way toward the *Princess of Wales*. The ambassador had a protective arm around his wife and Tamsyn brought up the rear, her gaze scanning the rioters and her senses on full alert.

To their right, a group of shouting Britons pushed forward against the line of soldiers. As fighting broke out, some soldiers raised their muskets and shot over the heads of the crowd. Apparently they didn't want to shoot foreign nationals, but that might change.

As more French troops moved to help control the group of Britons, a gap opened in the line in front of the ambassador's party. "Now!" Hansen snapped.

They all moved forward and closed half the distance to their ship before Colonel Gagnon and his aides galloped forward to stop them. The colonel barked, "All of you men will be arrested and detained as prisoners of war!"

Lord Whitworth said in his excellent French, "I am the British ambassador and have permission to leave. Here is my signed and sealed official passport."

He produced the document and handed it up to the colonel, who scowled at it before saying grudgingly, "You and the women may proceed, but the rest of you damned Englishmen will be detained."

Tamsyn stepped forward and caught the colonel's gaze. She'd removed her dull bonnet and the sunshine made her blond hair shine like gold. Speaking in flawless Parisian French, she said, "Monsieur le Colonel, only the ambassador and his wife are English. The rest of us are French. These men were ordered to escort the ambassador to his ship to ensure that he left the country promptly."

Cade almost laughed aloud. Tam had a powerful gift of persuasion, and when combined with her beauty, there were very few men who could resist her.

The colonel's gaze ran over the other men disbelievingly. "You're all French?"

"Of course!" Tamsyn said, her bright voice utterly convincing. She shifted her gaze to Cade. "Captain Tremayne, speak to Colonel Gagnon to prove you are French."

All the children of the Tribe of Tremayne had been raised with French tutors and spoke the language flawlessly, so Cade responded in French that was a little less aristocratic than Tamsyn's accent. "Indeed we are citizens and soldiers of France, sir. We are not in uniform because we were ordered to escort the ambassador and his wife to Calais as quietly as possible. If we were in uniform, rumors would spread that France had arrested the British ambassador." He cast a contemptuous glance at Whitworth. "The British may ignore the rules of war, but the sons of France are always honorable!"

Amazingly, the colonel believed him. "Very well, Captain. Once you've delivered the ambassador and his wife to their ship, join my soldiers in arresting these other Englishmen!" He turned his horse and rode down the waterfront, his aides following him.

Whitworth said with a laugh, "Lady Tamsyn, Mr. Tremayne, that was an amazing performance! I now understand why the Home Office supplied me with Tremaynes." Taking the duchess's arm, he strode toward the *Princess of Wales.*

They reached the gangway of their ship and several sailors bolted down to help the passengers aboard. The duchess went first, followed by Whitworth and Holland, then the guards other than Hansen.

With most of the ambassador's party safely on board, Cade scanned the area behind them and saw several Britons who had made their way through a gap in the French cordon and were now looking around in confusion and despair.

Tamsyn hadn't yet boarded. Taking in the situation, she said, "The *Princess of Wales* isn't full, so let's get some of these people aboard!"

Hansen was nearby. "The ambassador will want to help them get home," he agreed, "but we have to be quick about it!"

The three of them split up and headed toward the nearest desperate travelers. Tamsyn approached a young family with two small children. The couple moved slowly since they were carrying the children as well as a bag of the family's belongings. After a brief conversation, Tamsyn took the larger child so the father could manage the travel bag, and Tam and the family walked swiftly toward the ship,

Hansen jogged over to what looked like a father and son. The father was limping slowly with a cane. He could be heard begging his son to leave him behind, but the son flatly refused. Hansen joined them, and after exchanging a few sentences, he and the son lifted the father between them and carried him to the ship at a near run. When they reached the gangway, two crewmen carried the older man up, and the son hurried behind.

Farther away, Cade spotted an elderly man wearing a vicar's collar moving forward with his wife, both of them looking frantically for their ship. A French soldier swooped down on them and grabbed the vicar's arm. "You're under arrest!"

The vicar cried out, "No! I'm sixty-three, too old!"

Refusing to release her husband's arm, his wife said furiously, "Let him go! Clergymen and doctors are never taken prisoners of war!"

The French soldier gave a nasty laugh. "You can take it up with the First Consul once I have you safe in a cell!"

Cade sprinted over and jerked the French soldier away from the vicar, then knocked him to the ground with a hard punch to the jaw. He pointed at the *Princess of Wales.* "Sir, you and your wife can board this ship right here! You can sort things out when you get to Dover."

The vicar looked at the chaos around them. Some Britons were trying to force their way through the cordon while others fled back to the town, hoping to escape and hide. Occasional gunshots were heard, and shouts of fear and anger mingled in a fearsome chorus accompanying the actions of the relentless soldiers. They'd rounded up an ever-growing group of detainees, mostly men, but also some women refusing to leave their husbands.

"God bless you, sir!" the vicar gasped. "Quickly, Elizabeth!"

Cade kept an eye on the elderly couple until they were safely aboard while he scanned for others in need, but by now the British travelers had already boarded ships, fled, or been captured. Only Hansen, Tamsyn, and Cade remained free in this area.

Gagnon or one of his aides must have noticed that most of the ambassador's group were staying on the ship, not leaving, and realized they were likely English. At a shouted order, several French cavalrymen turned their horses and began to gallop toward the spot where the *Princess of Wales* was docked, closely followed by a small carriage.

Cade swore to himself as he realized that he'd waited too long. He bolted toward the *Princess of Wales,* but the cavalrymen blocked the route between Cade and the ship. He was searching for a way to weave between the horsemen when the carriage thundered to a halt right behind him. Cade was trapped.

The door of the carriage opened and Cade prepared to attack the occupant, hoping to fight his way free. But the tall, dark man who emerged from the carriage had vicious eyes and a pistol in one hand. "Now I have you, my British spy!"

Swearing to himself, Cade recognized that this was the Scorpion, so he immediately hurled himself at his attacker. After Cade wrenched the pistol away, there was a brief, violent skirmish between the two men. Cade almost managed to break free. . . .

"You'll not escape me!" the Scorpion snarled as he clamped a large hand across Cade's forehead. An uncanny energy surged between them, unlike anything Cade had ever experienced. There was pain and searing light. Then the world disappeared.

The last thing he heard was Tamsyn's scream.

Chapter 7

Tamsyn and Hansen watched in horror as Cade was attacked. Several gunshots sounded along the waterfront and Cade collapsed, his body obscured by the French cavalrymen. Tamsyn screamed but she couldn't go to him because French foot soldiers were closing in on her and Hansen.

Hansen made an instinctive movement toward Cade, but Tamsyn grabbed his arm and said fiercely, "Board the ship and tell the captain to set sail!"

Her companion hesitated, looking agonized. "But I must help your brother!"

"I'll take care of him, but you have to board the ship *now!*" she ordered. "You have a family in England that needs you."

Hansen took her arm. "Come with me! You have a family also, and they won't want to lose you both."

Tamsyn broke free of his grip. "I'll be fine, I promise you! Now *go!*" She shoved him toward the gangway. "I will find Cade and *I will bring him home!*"

"Then go with God, Lady Tamsyn!" Hansen pivoted and raced up the gangway. The ship was in the process of casting off and a watery gap was opening between the dock and the ship even as the gangway was hauled aboard.

Certain the ship would get away successfully, Tamsyn swung around in time to see Cade's body being loaded into the carriage. He wasn't dead, *he couldn't be dead!*

Tamsyn forced herself to calm down and looked around for a place to hide. An empty cart had been abandoned to her right, so she ran toward it and dived underneath. Some French soldiers had gathered at the dock and were shouting at the departing *Princess of Wales.* A few muskets were fired, but Tamsyn guessed that was out of sheer outrage rather than a serious attempt to shoot the passengers. She huddled into a ball under the cart, trying not to sneeze at the acrid black powder smoke.

One of Tamsyn's gifts was to be easily overlooked. She wasn't invisible, but when she didn't want to be seen, she usually wasn't. Huddled under the cart in a plain brown cloak, she was safe enough. Even if she were discovered, no one would take her for a man eligible for arrest, and with her flawless French, she could pass as a Frenchwoman who had been caught in the turmoil and had hidden for safety.

She drew in a deep breath, releasing it slowly to help calm her mind before she reached out to Cade. Even when she was a child, she was always aware of him when they were apart, and he'd told her that the awareness was mutual.

He wasn't there. *He wasn't there!*

Her heart began pounding frantically as she tried to analyze his absence. She would surely know if he was dead, but this felt different, as if he was out of reach because he was blocked by some kind of barrier.

She had a sudden memory of Merryn, her new sister-in-law, whose mind had been paralyzed by a gifted woman who could take away a victim's memory and awareness. She'd done so to Merryn, who was powerfully gifted but had been untrained at that time. Could something similar have happened to Cade? He was both powerfully gifted and very experienced.

The Scorpion!

She and Cade had both sensed that the man was a powerful and a dangerous enemy. If he had the ability to block another person's mind, he could have done that to Cade before taking him away in the carriage.

She needed to search mentally for Cade not as the mature, powerful man he was now, but as someone whose mind had been dampened. She sought for calm, then reached out again, this time looking for the faintest shadow of Cade's essence.

As she opened her mind, she sensed the members of her family whom she was closest to. Her mother, Gwyn; her father, Rhys; Bran and Merryn, other members of the Tribe of Tremayne. Each had an emotional signature like a clear pure note of music, and they made up a choir of love in the back of her mind. Cade's note had always been deep and rich and resonant, but he was no longer there.

Suppressing her fear, she summoned memories of things they had done together, of the times when they had been closest. When he'd first come to Tremayne House and she'd healed him. Riding together across the green acres of the Tremayne family estate; Cade teaching her how to swim, and how to fight in ways suited to her small size; cooking together in a country kitchen on their recent mission to help Bran and Merryn.

Those memories flowed through her mind until . . . there! She sensed a shadow trace that was unmistakably Cade. His mind was suppressed much more thoroughly than if he were sleeping or unconscious, but it was him. Cade was alive and she thought he wasn't seriously injured physically.

His mind must have been blocked as Merryn's had been. Well, she'd cleared the block from Merryn, and she could do it for Cade once she located him.

Soon she would inventory her resources and start thinking

about how to find him, but for now, she concentrated on maintaining and strengthening her connection to her brother. She doubted that she could remove the block unless they were within touching distance, but maybe she could reduce it a little through their nearly lifelong connection.

She stroked that connection as gently as if it was one of the Tremayne family cats. *"I'm here, Cade, and I'll find you no matter how long it takes. I will find you—I swear it!"*

As she sent him her energy, she felt the connection grow a little stronger. She kept up the flow until she felt tired and depleted. *"Good night for now, Cade. I shall return. Stay strong!"*

As she was gathering her physical strength, a voice barked, "Come out from under there, Englishman, or we'll drag you out!"

Jerked back to her present circumstances, she said in a shaking voice, "I'm no Englishman, sir, but a French girl! I'll come out. Please don't shoot me!"

Donning her meekest expression, she crawled out from under the cart, clutching her cloak around her. The man who had spoken was a French soldier, a sergeant.

Looking surprised, he offered a hand to help her up and said not unkindly, "Were you here with an Englishman? If so, he's been arrested."

She shook her head and said in the soft accent of a French girl who might work in a rather superior shop, "No, sir, I live in the town. On fine days I like to come down to the harbor to look at the ships. I didn't expect the madness today! The soldiers, the shooting! That's why I hid." She shuddered. "What was the rioting about?"

"War has been declared and our job was to stop all Britons of militia age from going home and taking up arms against us," the sergeant explained.

She looked at the nearly empty harbor. "Did they all escape?"

The sergeant shook his head. "A few did, but we arrested most of them."

She widened her eyes. "What will become of them? There were women and children as well as men."

The sergeant shrugged. "The women and children could leave or stay with their menfolk. The men will be detained till the war is over, I expect. France has the best army in Europe, so that won't take long."

"I hope you are right and this ends soon." She tugged her cloak around her more closely. "You be careful in the fighting, *monsieur le sergeant!*"

"I always am," he said with a smile. "Do you need an escort home?"

She shook her head. "It isn't far. Thank you for your kindness." She turned and walked briskly away. She must now find a place to stay and decide what to do next.

And do some praying as well.

Chapter 8

Consciousness was slow in returning. Cade was bruised all over and his mind was so clouded that he had no idea where he was, or even who he was. He managed to open his eyes a slit and found that he was lying on a bed in a drab room. When he tried to roll over so he could sit up, he heard a metallic rattle and realized that a long chain was manacled around his right wrist. It was fastened to a heavy metal ring embedded in the wall. He was a captive.

He had only the barest spark of awareness and no curiosity about who or what he was or why he was imprisoned here. He closed his eyes numbly. After a long blur of time, his body insistently woke him. He opened his eyes and saw a china pot in the corner of the room. He dimly recalled what it was used for. Luckily, the chain was long enough for him to reach the chamber pot and use it before he stumbled back to the bed.

Then, in the formlessness of his spirit, he felt a touch of warmth. Of life, of recognition. That touch strengthened the faint spark of his being. He was called Cade, and that spark of warmth was from a friend.

Tamsyn. The name formed in his mind. A female. She was his best friend, and she was looking for him.

That knowledge was a warm comfort as he drifted into darkness again.

Chapter 9

Tamsyn walked briskly into the town as if she knew where she was going. She couldn't return to the hotel where the ambassador's party had stayed. Where might she find refuge?

During the days of waiting for permission to leave France, she had explored the town with Cade, partly from curiosity but also from a general habit of learning the territory they were in.

They had stopped at a bakery to buy coffee and exquisite French pastries, and discovered that the woman who ran the shop liked to talk. She had mentioned that the building on the corner of the street was Madame Bernard's boardinghouse for young ladies, most of them country girls who had come to Calais for work. The baker had emphasized that it was a *respectable* house, not for the naughty sorts of girls. Tamsyn had nodded gravely and done her best to look very respectable.

The memory made her bite her lip. That day had been so pleasant and normal. She and Cade had been enjoying each other's company and preparing to escort the ambassador and his wife home. Though they'd both expected some kind of trouble in Calais, they'd not imagined the catastrophe that had just occurred.

Disaster had struck, however, and now it was necessary to keep moving forward. The boardinghouse should be a a good place to go to ground. She had money and could afford to rent a room, but she would need a reason to explain why she was in a strange city on her own.

By the time she reached her destination, she had her story ready. The house was well kept, and a neatly dressed maid admitted her when she knocked. Tamsyn said shyly, "I'm Therese Martin and I was told that this is a respectable place for a single woman to stay. Do you have a room available?"

"You'll have to speak with Madame Bernard." The maid gave her a conspiratorial smile. "But I believe there is one. Wait in the parlor while I summon the mistress."

Tamsyn sat in the comfortable room, her hands folded in her lap and her eyes downcast. She was the portrait of unhappy respectability.

She stood when Madame Bernard entered. She was a short, well-rounded woman with a firm chin and kind eyes. "Good day, Mademoiselle Martin. I'm told you need lodging. Why are you here in Calais?"

"I'm a lady's maid, *madame*. I speak good English, so I was offered a position with a wellborn English lady and was given the money for a ticket to Dover." She bit her lip. "But when I went to the port to board the packet, all was madness! I was told that war had been declared, all Englishmen in France were being detained, and it was unlikely that there would be any more ships sailing to England."

"You were at the docks today?" the landlady said with interest. "What did you observe?"

Tamsyn gave a succinct description of what had happened, concluding with, "I was afraid, so I hid under a cart and prayed to the Blessed Mother."

"She seems to have looked out for you." Madame Bernard cocked her head to one side. "Could you have taken passage on one of the departing ships?"

"Perhaps, but I could not leave my country in wartime," Tamsyn said emphatically. "I might never see my family again if I left!"

The landlady nodded. "It was wise of you to understand that. What are your plans now?"

Tamsyn spread her hands. "I have no idea! I need time to rest and think. Your house was pointed out to me, so I thought this would be a good place to decide what to do next. I might not be here for long, but I hope very much that you can accommodate me for a few days."

Madame pursed her lips, then nodded. "The only room I have available is in the attic, and it's the smallest in the house. But it's clean and comfortable. I also offer three meals a day but that's extra. Do you want to see the room before you agree?"

"I have no other choice so I'm sure I'll find it very suitable," Tamsyn said ruefully. "I would like the meals as well."

"Very well. Do you have any belongings?"

Tamsyn unfastened her cloak to reveal the crossed straps of her carry bags. "I thought this was the safest way to carry my things."

"Very wise. Come along and I'll show you the room."

There were four increasingly narrow flights of steps up to the room. Madame unlocked the door to reveal a very small attic space with a slanting ceiling. But it was indeed clean, a window let in sunlight, and the narrow bed looked adequate. There was a washstand and a wooden chair and a small piece of carpet to warm the feet. There was even a rather nice water-color picture of ships in the harbor hanging over the bed.

"This is perfect," Tamsyn said.

"It's fortunate that you're short or you'd be bumping your head against the ceiling all the time!" Madame said. "I'll send the maid up with water for your washstand. Dinner will be served at six o'clock. A gong will be sounded ten minutes before."

Tamsyn pulled out her small purse and carefully counted out enough francs to cover a week of room and board. "You have my most sincere thanks, *madame*."

The landlady accepted the money and handed over the key to the room. "I hope you will find the peace you need here, my dear. I'll see you at dinner."

As soon as the landlady left, Tamsyn peeled off her cloak and lifted the carry bags from her shoulders, hanging the bags and cloak on pegs behind the door. A wave of fatigue swamped her. She hadn't realized how tired and bruised and drained she was.

Not even taking off her half boots, she sprawled onto the bed and let exhaustion take her.

The hollow sound of a distant gong wakened Tamsyn. She wanted to stay in bed for the next week, but she needed to eat. Wearily she pushed herself to a sitting position and hoped that the dinner would be good enough to justify the four flights of stairs down and back up again later.

She stood and peered into the small mirror above the washbasin. She looked as bad as she felt. Remembering that Madame Bernard had said she'd send up water, she unlocked the door and found that a full pitcher was set against the wall.

After splashing cold water on her face and combing her hair, she felt ready to find her meal. The dining room was in the back of the house, next to the kitchen, and Madame appeared to introduce her new guest to the seven other residents.

They were friendly and interested in hearing her account of what had happened at the port. There were gasps of shock from some of the young women who sympathized with the poor Englishmen who were prevented from going home, but others said they should have stayed in England in the first place. Tamsyn supposed that was a fair reflection of what most of the French thought.

Dinner was a great pot of hearty stew that contained sausage and beans and barley and other vegetables accompanied by slices of fresh warm bread and a mild, pleasant white table wine. There was enough stew for seconds. Tamsyn finished her second bowl with a happy sigh, feeling much better than she had earlier.

"I needed that!" she said. "Is the food always this good?"

The other young women nodded. "Madame's cook is very good. No one goes hungry," a cheerful girl named Lucille said. "I'm glad you liked the stew. If you stay very long, you'll be seeing it regularly!"

Tamsyn laughed. "French cooking is still another reason for staying on this side of the channel. They say the English are dreadful cooks."

"Which is why wellborn English folk are always hiring French chefs." Lucille frowned. "With the war resumed, there won't be many people crossing the channel to work. Have you decided what you'll do now, Therese?"

"I haven't had much time to think about it," Tamsyn said. "I'll probably return to Paris, where I know people who can help me find work." She sighed. "But I'm sure I won't be paid as well as the English milady promised me."

"The English need French style as well as French food," another girl said.

A third said, "This war is good for no one. Soon all the young men will be sent away to fight and then what will we do?"

Silence fell over the table. Tamsyn rose and said quietly, "Then we must pray for peace. Good night, my friends, and thank you all for your welcome."

Climbing four flights of steps several times a day would certainly keep Tamsyn fit. She'd been given a short piece of candle to light her way, and when she reached her attic, she used it to light the lantern on the small table. It was time to evaluate her resources.

Both of the carry bags had been made by a younger sister,

Naomi Tremayne, who loved to sew. The bags were sturdily constructed and had small pockets inside to hold special items. Each also had the beautifully embroidered initial of the owner. Tamsyn's initial *T* was done in a soft rose color.

Cade's bag had an elegant *C* and was sewn in a very dark blue, the same shade as his eyes. When they'd first met, Tamsyn thought his eyes were brown, almost black, but the color turned out to be an intense blue. Compelling eyes that could light with laughter or warmth or icy determination.

Tamsyn knew that her own bag carried several items of clothing, including a boy's outfit for when she needed a disguise or more freedom of movement or both. Money and a few pieces of jewelry were tucked into pockets that were secured with buttons.

There was also a folded list of gifted people in France who might be able to help if Tamsyn or Cade needed assistance. The names and addresses were coded so a searcher wouldn't be able to decipher them and perhaps threaten their allies.

She opened Cade's bag and froze. The contents carried his scent, subtle and masculine and as distinctive as if he was sitting next to her. The effect was shattering. She closed her eyes and mentally reached out, needing to feel him even though he was not his full self now. In return, she sent her own caring energy and thought it strengthened him a little.

When she felt steady again, she examined the contents of his bag, assuming that they would be similar to her own. There were fewer items of clothing because he was so much larger than she, so his garments took more space. Their additional belongings had been packed into a small trunk and carried to Calais on an ambassadorial wagon and loaded onto the ship. Those things would reach London long before they did, but no matter if they didn't. Clothing was easy to replace.

Cade had been carrying even more money than she had, which could prove useful. He also had a copy of the list of gifted people they might call on. In the same pocket she found the sleek folding knife she'd given him several years earlier. It was a very nice specimen, compact and potentially lethal.

She held it a moment, wondering if Cade had ever used this blade to kill someone. He'd probably had to kill on occasion and if so, she was sure the killing was justified, but she was grateful that she'd never had to kill anyone herself. If the necessity ever arose, she hoped that she'd be strong enough to do the right thing.

There was one more pocket to search. Something hard and rectangular was inside. She unbuttoned the pocket and found a golden case about two inches square. It looked like a watch, though she couldn't remember ever seeing Cade use it.

She clicked the case open, then gasped. Inside was a miniature of her, a small version of the laughing portrait her parents had commissioned. Each child of the Tribe of Tremayne had a similar portrait, and the paintings covered a whole wall of her parents' private sitting room. Opposite the miniature was a small lock of blond hair under glass. Her hair.

She closed the golden case, unnerved. It pulsed with Cade's distinct energy as if he held it often. She was probably closer to him than any of the younger sisters, but even so, this seemed . . . extreme.

For an instant she wondered if his feelings for her went beyond brotherly affection. She buried the thought immediately. They were brother and sister and that was more than enough.

She prepared for bed, weary to the bone. When she put out the lantern, moonlight poured through the window, keeping the small room from complete darkness.

She laid down, forcing herself to relax, muscle by muscle. Then she reached out mentally to her parents. When she felt their presence, she sent a wordless message that she and Cade had been delayed in France, but not to worry. They'd be home soon.

She sensed that they understood and were sending her warmth and reassurance. She wanted to crawl into Gwyn's arms and be told everything would be all right, but held back her longing. If she communicated how serious the situation was, her parents would be upset and want to do something, but war had been declared and no Englishman was safe in France.

Telling Bran would be even worse because he'd want to come to France immediately. That would be too dangerous for him. Her intuition told her if Cade was to be rescued, it must be done by her.

Though God only knew how she would be able to free the brother she loved.

Chapter 10

Cade was pulled from his dark fog when the door of the room opened and a man entered with a tray of food. The newcomer was tall and dark, and he radiated malevolence. "You must be hungry by now, Englishman."

A primitive instinct of self-protection stirred Cade to sit up and lean against the headboard—lying on the bed felt very vulnerable. Plus he was hungry. Though he was stiff from bruising and lack of movement, his mind was a little clearer than earlier.

The newcomer handed him the tray. Bread and cheese and a tumbler of white wine. The man asked, "Do you know who I am?"

Cade and Tamsyn had talked about this dangerous fellow. "Scorpion."

He took a bite of cheese and bread and washed it down with the wine. It was a low-grade table variety, but the combination was good because he was famished.

The other man laughed. "Scorpion? I rather like that, but I'm known as Claude Bastien. I am sometimes called Frossard."

A fragment of knowledge floated into Cade's mind. "Frossard. To break. Shatter."

The other man's brows arched. "Your French is very good for an Englishman. You are correct. I am called that because I am very good at breaking people, and I intend to break you."

Cade's gaze met Bastien's. "No." He took another bite of bread and cheese.

"So confident," Bastien said with a sneer. "Do you know who you are?"

Cade hesitated, feeling uncertain. What had his friend called him? "Cade."

"What else do you know about yourself?"

He would not mention his friend Tamsyn to this man. "Not much."

Voice hard edged, Bastien said, "You go by the name Caden Tremayne, but you're the bastard son of a Cornish smuggler named Jago Evans."

Cade hesitated again as the image of a small dark-haired girl with large speaking eyes appeared in his mind. Ellen? No, Es-elde. His daughter? No, not that, but the child was important to him. With a brief flash of knowledge, he remembered that she was the young daughter of Jago Evans, his half-sister. He couldn't remember anything more about her except that now she was safe from Jago.

He shrugged and resumed eating. Bastien's information might be accurate, but it didn't seem relevant at the moment.

"I'm going to have to wake you up a bit to learn anything worthwhile," the other man muttered. He approached Cade and laid a hand on his forehead.

Cade jerked back from a jolt that felt like electricity. His mind was immediately clearer, though he knew he was still far less acute than he should be. His eyes narrowed as he looked at Bastien. "Why am I here?"

He must have looked dangerous because Bastien stepped back out of Cade's reach. "You are said to be strongly gifted, one of the Home Office's most effective agents." He frowned.

"A pity you weren't accompanied by Bran Tremayne, who is said to be equally effective but more intelligent."

Bran! Cade's brother of the heart if not of the blood. Several images appeared in his mind. Bran as a small but preternaturally wise child. The two of them standing together against the world. Laughter and kindness and soul-deep trust.

From Bastien's expression, he expected Cade to be insulted at being told his brother was more intelligent. Amused, Cade said, "Bran is indeed more intelligent than I am. Too intelligent to be here in France."

Bastien scowled. "He might have been here if you hadn't insisted on bringing your bit of fluff instead!"

It was Cade's turn to frown. "Bit of fluff?"

"The little blonde. Very pretty, but I doubt she's useful outside of a bed. Your wife, I assume."

So Tamsyn was more than a friend. She was his *wife*! No wonder they were so close. No wonder he'd been haunted by dreams of holding her. "Did she escape the riot at the port?"

"I believe so. She reached your ship when it was boarding." Bastien shrugged. "I didn't pay much attention because you were the one I was after."

Cade finished his wine. "Again, I wonder why."

"You know things about Britain's intelligence activities that I wish to learn," Bastien said. "You can answer my questions when I ask politely, or I can torture you to get the answers. Answering my questions would be quicker, but torture would be more interesting. The choice is yours."

"I doubt I know much of interest." Cade bared his teeth. "And if I did, I wouldn't tell you, so bring on the red-hot knives."

"I have a gift for persuading people to do what I want." Bastien moved forward, raising his hand again.

Cade grabbed the length of chain in both hands and whipped it into his captor's ribs with vicious force, wishing the chain was long enough to do more damage. Bastien howled and staggered backward, clutching his left side. "You bastard!"

Bastien recovered enough to make a wild swing at Cade and managed to land an open-palmed slap on Cade's face, striking his left eye and part of his forehead. Excruciating pain ripped through Cade's face and head. Red-hot knives would have hurt less, he thought dizzily as he fell back onto the bed and slid into darkness.

Chapter 11

⟞⟝

Tamsyn jerked awake as pain slashed through her. Cade's pain, she realized. As a healer, she automatically neutralized it, but the aftermath left her shaken. Dimly she realized that the Scorpion must have a gift for inflicting pain. She'd heard of such an ability but had never known anyone who had it. Tamsyn couldn't think of any use for such a gift other than torture.

She swore under her breath as she reached out to Cade. He was sleeping, she thought, recovering. She must find the best way to mitigate Cade's pain, because surely there would be more such assaults on him.

"*Tamsyn!*" She was jolted by a mental call from Bran, who must have felt his brother's pain as keenly as she had. They couldn't speak in words, so she sent an image of Cade, alive but imprisoned.

She sensed that Bran wanted to come to France to rescue his brother. She sent a powerful *No!* Since they couldn't speak with actual words, she created a mental image of France as a hellish red fire burning a British flag.

He seemed taken aback, so he must have understood some of

what she was trying to express. Then his wife, Merryn, joined her mind to Bran's and Tamsyn's. She was powerfully gifted but never knew it until she'd met Bran, and she was still learning what she could do. She brought calm and clarity to their exchange, and her presence steadied Tamsyn. "*Tomorrow morning,*" Merryn seemed to be whispering. "*Tomorrow . . .*"

Tamsyn sent thanks and agreement, then forced herself to relax. The last fortnight had been exhausting and today had been an endless nightmare. She rolled onto her side and clutched the pillow to her chest. Tonight she would sleep, and order her deepest mind to come up with a plan for tomorrow.

The window in Tamsyn's attic room faced east, and the sunrise wakened her. She lay motionless in the bed and went over the events of the day before. Seeing Cade attacked and kidnapped had been shatteringly painful, but she forced herself to go through that scene again and again, this time looking for any clues that might help her learn more about the Scorpion so she could track him.

The fierce, destructive energy displayed in his earlier threats against the ambassadorial party made him easy to identify. Might that help her locate him?

She would explore that idea later, but now she needed to connect with Cade. Though he might be sleeping at this hour, she reached out gently and touched his mind. "*Cade?*"

He responded to her warmly. "*Tamsyn?*"

"Yes." He was still mind blocked. Could she reduce the blocking even though they were separated?

It was worth a try. She visualized him as a ball of light that was trapped in an iron cage, then imagined the cage dissolving as she poured healing energy into it. She sensed him becoming more focused. She poured her power into him, trying to form words so he'd be more likely to understand her.

"*Tam . . . safe?*" he asked, his thoughts labored.

"Yes, and looking for you. Do you know where you are?"

She felt his confusion. He did not reply.

"I will find you," she promised. *"Stay strong!"*

She sensed gratitude and apology from him before he faded from her mind, leaving her drained. A casual mind touch just to check that a family member was well wasn't difficult, but this level of communication required much more focus and strength. It was difficult for her, and surely much harder for Cade in his current state.

When he was restored to himself, he would loathe knowing how weakened he'd been. He'd always had limitless strength. He was the protector who looked out for her and everyone else he cared about. More than once she'd seen him go to the aid of complete strangers who were in need. She ached at the knowledge that at the moment he couldn't even defend himself.

After several minutes of gathering her mental strength, she swung her feet to the floor, then stood and walked the two steps to the washstand to splash water on her face and prepare for the day. It was her job to rescue Cade, and she damned well *would*!

She guessed that he was still in the vicinity of Calais because there was no indication that he was being moved when she'd contacted him the day before. That could change today, which would complicate the situation enormously. But without knowing where he was, it was impossible to make plans.

The meal gong sounded through the tall, narrow house, so she dressed and headed down the stairs. After a good French breakfast of warm bread, berry preserves, and strong hot mint tea with honey, she returned to her room and considered possible ways to locate where Cade was being held captive. She didn't have a strong finder gift, but maybe desperation would help her.

She pulled a piece of paper and a pencil from her carry bag

and drew a simple map of Calais and the surrounding area. She relaxed her mind and scanned the drawing, hoping an area would attract her attention.

Nothing stood out for Cade's location. Nothing for the Scorpion.

She was wondering what to do next when she felt a deep, powerful mind touch from Bran, Merryn—and Gwyn and Rhys? The combined Tremayne power was a flood of warmth and support. Tamsyn could feel each of them as distinct presences.

And startlingly, she could understand the messages clearly, not with the vagueness that was usual with mind touch. Bran's thoughts were as distinct as if they were in the same room together. *"Tam, we needed Gwyn and Rhys in this mind touch to increase the power and clarity."*

Tamsyn replied, *"I wanted to spare them worry, but it's so good to feel you all here!"* Her mother's presence was like a warm hug.

Merryn's mental message was equally distinct. *"I found a way to bring us together with great clarity. But much power is needed and I can't hold the connection for long."*

Tamsyn could feel the bonds Merryn had generated to bring their minds together and was awed at the other woman's strength, but it was clear why this conversation would be brief. Bran's thought was the most urgent. *"Bring Cade into this mind touch! I need to feel him!"*

Tamsyn warned, *"He's not fully himself and he's tired now, but surely your energy will help him."*

Together she and Merryn reached out and drew Cade together with the rest of the family. He reacted to the love and assurances like a thirsty flower welcoming water. He wasn't fully aware, but she sensed that their caring was gradually strengthening him.

"*He feels the way Merryn did when mind blocked,*" Bran said. "*You healed her. You will be able to heal him as well once you locate him. I'll come help find him.*"

Once again, she said emphatically, "*No! France is detaining all Englishmen from eighteen to sixty. Not safe for you to come here, Bran!*"

Reluctantly he said, "*I agree for now, Tam. You're best placed to rescue him, but if you need help, I'll be there!*"

She had expected no less. He and Cade had been as close as any two brothers could be. But her intuition told her it would be very dangerous for Bran to cross the channel. Possibly fatal—and she couldn't bear to lose both of them.

Rhys spoke, his mental voice as deep and powerful as his physical voice. "*Gwyn, you found Cade when he was a shivering child. Find him again.*"

Tamsyn felt her mother gather her finding power and her love for her missing son. After a long moment of stillness, Gwyn said, "*Tamsyn, do you have a map of northern France?*"

"*Just drew a crude one.*"

"*Gaze at it and I'll see what I can learn.*"

Again, Tamsyn relaxed her mind as she looked at the map. Her mother's focus was very strong, and she was supported by the power of the other Tremaynes.

At length, Gwyn whispered, "*Southwest. Along the coast a little beyond Frethun. Only a few miles from Calais.*"

Tamsyn caught her breath with desperate hope. "*Can you see the building?*"

After another long pause, Gwyn thought, "*Gray stone. An old fortified farmhouse? Right on shore.*"

"*This may be enough. Thank you!*"

Sounding strained, Merryn said, "*Can't hold much longer. Anything else?*"

What did Tamsyn need to know most? "*His captor. We called him Scorpion. Can anyone add more?*"

Rhys's thoughts came slowly. *"A fanatic supporter of Bonaparte. Hates Cade for . . . complicated reasons."*

A surge of pain swept through the gathering. Cade's pain. The Scorpion was tormenting him again. Tamsyn instinctively worked to neutralize his pain, and she was supported by her family's love and strength, which helped her and Cade alike. But their joining was strained to the breaking point.

Merryn gasped, *"Can't hold longer, sorry!"*

Tamsyn felt the shattering of the bonds that held them together and a flash of images flooded her mind. Cade vanishing as his mind was blocked again. Merryn collapsing with exhaustion into Bran's arms. Bran cradling his wife while sending a last despairing thought. *"Find him, Tamsyn, and heal him!"*

Gwyn and Rhys were holding each other as Gwyn sent her blessing. *"Go with God, my darling girl!"*

Rhys thought urgently, *"Look at list of allies in Calais! Bar . . ."*

The last of her family's thoughts faded away. Tamsyn collapsed on her narrow bed, almost too tired to breathe. None of them would want to undertake such a joining again anytime soon! The clarity achieved had given her vital information about Cade's location, but the price had been high for everyone.

She envied her parents and Bran and Merryn, who had mates to offer strength and comfort, for she felt very much alone. But all of them believed that she had the ability to rescue Cade, which bolstered her confidence and determination.

Once she discovered where he was imprisoned, she'd surely be able to find a way to free him. She should have thought of seeking aid from her list of gifted allies herself, but now that Rhys had reminded her, intuition told her that she'd find vital help there.

Despite her exhaustion, she reached out to Cade again. He was barely there, deeply unconscious as he recovered from the

Scorpion's assault, but there was a stir of awareness when she touched his mind. Recognition and pleasure at her presence.

Holding that touch as if they were holding hands, she slid into unconsciousness herself.

Tamsyn slept until the dinner gong sounded. She awoke groggy and ravenous but managed to rise and lurch to the washbasin. There were tearstains on her cheeks and dark circles under her eyes. She did not look like the bright golden Tamsyn depicted in Cade's miniature of her.

She splashed cold water on her face and neatened her hair, then descended to the dining room on the ground floor. Her appearance drew glances from the other residents, and the friendliest, Lucille, said sympathetically, "When great changes are forced on us, it takes time to find the next step."

Tamsyn managed a smile. "So true! I spent much of the day feeling sorry for myself and thinking of what I've lost." She sighed. "Not only was the English milady most pleasant and generous, but she had a footman who was very handsome. We exchanged interested glances, but now he is in England. I will not see him again."

There were sympathetic murmurs from the other residents. Lucille said, "That's unfortunate, but surely a Frenchman would be a better choice."

"Yes, and with the coming of war, it is better to stay in my own country rather than being stranded among the enemy," Tamsyn agreed. "From now on, I will be looking to the future. And good food will certainly improve my mood!"

"You're in luck," one of the other girls said with a smile. "Tonight's meal is one of my favorites."

The cook and her assistant entered the dining room, each of them carrying a steaming casserole of sliced potatoes, onions, bits of ham, and a creamy bubbling hot cheese sauce. It smelled delicious and Tamsyn learned that it tasted even better. Madame

Bernard's kitchen was skilled at producing satisfying meals with ingredients that were simple and not expensive.

After two servings of the potato dish, a piece of apple tart, and more fragrant mint tea, Tamsyn was ready to face her search again. She bid polite good-nights to the rest of the residents and headed up the stairs again. The first thing she would do was to consult the list of gifted allies to find someone who might help her find the mysterious stone building. And there she would find Cade.

Chapter 12

Cade had begun the day when a burly guard brought him a simple breakfast. Vaguely he thought that once he would have been able to best that guard in a fight, but now he was chained and had no strength. He could barely remember being that other man.

After eating, he lay in a twilight haze until a wave of love surrounded him. Dimly he recognized that these were the people he cared about the most. Tamsyn, of course, first and foremost. His wife and the guide who'd brought the others to his damaged mind.

At first he wasn't sure who the others were. Ah, it was his brother Bran! His closest friend, connected by a bond that was too deep for words. Were his parents there? Yes, they were. He couldn't remember their names, but the caring and protection he felt was familiar and warmed his heart. He almost wept with the knowledge that he had people who loved him.

He felt his mind becoming clearer and realized that he had reasons to live. He must work his way out of this poisonous weakness.

The door to his cell opened and Bastien entered. He stopped and frowned, his eyes narrowing. "You're connected to your friends by mind touch. Can't have that."

Bastien grabbed Cade's wrist and sent a blast of pain into his prisoner. Cade gasped as the assault tore him away from his family and destroyed the sense of well-being he'd been given.

Then he felt Tamsyn's power moving through him, cooling the pain and saving his sanity. He could see her very clearly. Petite and blond and achingly beautiful. She held his soul as he slid again into sleep . . .

It was still daylight when he woke again. Realizing that lying here like a lump of coal was doing him no good, he gathered his strength and sat up, then stood, the chain rattling. He couldn't move far, but he began to improvise exercises within the range of what he could do. Stretching his limbs. Standing by the stone wall and doing push-ups against it to build his strength. He had a sense that exercising was a basic part of his nature. He had always been strong and fit, and even these simple exercises gave him more a sense of himself.

Bastien had said he was Caden Tremayne. Tamsyn called him Cade.

He must find his way back to her.

Chapter 13

When Tamsyn returned to her room, she dug into her carry bag for the coded list of potential gifted allies. The list was divided into geographical regions with half a dozen listings for the Calais area. Frowning, she decoded the names. It had sounded as if Rhys was saying, "Bar . . ." when he reminded her to check this list.

There were two surnames that began with "Bar . . .": Jacques Bardin and Marie Barriere. She gazed at the two names and Barriere's drew her attention. She had a vague recollection that the name meant something like gatekeeper, which was appropriate for a gifted ally. Madame Marie Barriere.

She then decoded the address. Her brows arched when she saw that it was listed as Madame Barriere's Tearoom, and it was on a nearby street.

Since Tamsyn was going to be moving about in public, she needed to make herself easy to overlook. Her carry bag contained a temporary color rinse that would make her hair an unremarkable brown. Her boring tan bonnet and brown mantle were good, but she also needed to get more boy's clothing because she would be unable to ride around the country as a lone female without drawing attention.

The one male outfit she had needed to be augmented with more rugged clothing, suitable for riding, climbing, and possibly breaking into houses. There should be used-clothing shops in the town; she'd visit them with the explanation that she was buying for her young brother.

She also was going to need a horse to ride around the countryside. Madame Barriere might be able to point her toward a reliable dealer. At the same time, she would keep an eye out for a mount that would suit Cade.

But the first step was to call on Madame Barriere. She would dye her hair on another day. The most important part of going unnoticed was to think herself plain. It was a trick she'd developed to avoid the attention of annoying men. Cade had said once that when she wanted to be overlooked, it was as if she'd doused her candle.

Cade. She squeezed her eyes shut, fighting off a wave of painful memories. They had done so many things together for so many years. The thought of losing him put a hole in her heart.

She reminded herself sharply that he wasn't lost, just in trouble. She would find him and heal him, and they'd go back to London, where life would return to normal.

Wouldn't it?

She made her plans and a list of things she'd need to buy, then went to bed. She had much to do the next day.

After breakfast the following morning, Tamsyn went out in her plainest mode and did more exploring. She found a used-clothing shop and bought a sturdy outfit for her younger brother, who was about her size.

At the edge of town, she found a large livery stable that also sold horses. She told the owner that she was interested in buying a mount for her younger brother. He smiled indulgently. "Take a look around the stable, mademoiselle. The stalls of the horses that are for sale are marked, but be careful not to open any doors. A restless horse can be dangerous. If you need advice about which of the mounts are best, feel free to ask me."

"I'll be careful," she said. "Horses are so large and frightening!"

She headed into the stables without mentioning that the male members of her family usually took her along when they were considering buying new mounts because she had very good instincts about horses. The dealer had a dozen or so full-sized riding horses for sale. She intended to look for a smaller equine since she was small herself, but she was drawn to a sizable white gelding called Zeus. He had a good temperament and a look of stamina, and he would be up to carrying Cade's weight if necessary. There was a smaller chestnut that might do well for her later, but first the white gelding.

When she left the livery, she told the owner that the white gelding might do well for her brother, and she would send him over to look at it for himself in the next few days.

The owner's brows arched. "You have good judgment. Zeus is the best mount I have for sale. Sound limbs and good conformation and very well trained."

"I've always fancied white horses. So pretty," she said artlessly, thereby persuading the owner that she didn't know much about horses.

After dropping her clothing purchases back in her room, she headed to Madame Barriere's Tearoom. It was a pretty, feminine space with colorful calico curtains, the scents of good baking, and small vases of spring flowers on each of the mismatched tables. It was well into the afternoon and there were only two other customers, elderly women who were chatting like old friends.

The tearoom was presided over by a competent-looking young woman who watched Tamsyn's entrance with mild interest. Tamsyn approached her, asking, "Are you Madame Marie Barriere?"

"No, I'm her daughter Julie," she said. "Marie is my mother. Are you interested in having a tea reading with her?"

Tamsyn blinked. "I didn't know she did readings! I came by to say hello because a friend said I should call on Madame Barriere if I came to Calais, but I'd love a reading as well if it's convenient."

"I'll ask her to join you. If you'll step back through these curtains, I'll start your tea. Would you like some cakes to go with it?"

Realizing how long it had been since breakfast, Tamsyn said, "Indeed I would." She stepped through the curtains and found herself in a cozy chamber with a round table that had several chairs set around it. She took a seat where she could look into the tearoom through the crack in the curtains.

A few minutes later Marie Barriere joined her. She was a pleasantly rounded woman with shrewd eyes and only a few silver strands in her dark hair. After they exchanged greetings, the older woman said, "What is the name of the friend who referred you to me?"

Tamsyn hesitated a moment before replying. "Tremayne."

"Ah, one of the Tribe of Tremayne," Madame Barriere said thoughtfully as she sat down on the opposite side of the table. "You're surely Gwyn Tremayne's daughter. You look very like her."

Tamsyn smiled. "I've been told that often, and it always pleases me to hear it. I'm Tamsyn."

"The Tremayne heiress. You're a long way from London." The other woman offered her hand and Tamsyn took it. Among gifted people, this form of greeting helped strangers assess the other person's power and decide if they were trustworthy. This woman was both powerful and trustworthy, traits for which Tamsyn was very grateful.

As they released hands, the other woman said, "Call me Marie. You're powerfully gifted and you're surely here because you need information and aid."

"I see you don't actually need tea leaves for readings," Tamsyn said wryly.

Their conversation was interrupted when Julie brought in a tea tray with a steaming teapot, two white china cups, and a plate of sweet and savory cakes. As Julie left, Marie poured tea for them both. "Your parents once did a great service for me so I am happy to help you in any way I can. As you drink your tea, tell me how you come to be here in Calais when the war has just resumed."

Tamsyn took a swallow of tea. "The Home Office was concerned about the safety of the British ambassador, so my brother Caden and I came to Paris to provide extra protection for him and his wife on their return to England."

Marie nodded. "I heard that the British ambassador left Calais just as the order was issued to detain all British men of military age. Quite outrageous!"

"As you must have guessed, that's why I'm here. In the turmoil at the port, my brother was detained. I stayed in Calais to find a way to free him." Tamsyn paused, unsure how much more to say.

"And there's something unusual about his detainment," Marie said. "Finish your tea and we'll take a closer look."

Tamsyn took another swallow, leaving just a bit of liquid in the cup. "Is there really wisdom in tea leaves?"

"They help me focus my intuition," Marie said. "Tea leaf reading is a tradition in my family. I had a Romani grandmother so the gift is in the blood. Julie has the gift also."

Glancing at the tea leaves left in the cup, Tamsyn asked, "What now?"

"Swirl the cup clockwise three times while thinking of your question. Do it vigorously enough for the leaves to spread around the cup."

Tamsyn obeyed, then set the white cup down between them. Dark brown tea leaves were spattered across the bottom and sides.

Marie studied the leaves, frowning. "Though traditionally tea leaf readings are positive, telling of the good things in life, there is a serpent in the middle of this cup." She pointed at a twisting group of leaves.

"But also much more," she added, indicating a vaguely heart-shaped clump of leaves. "Love."

"Most assuredly. Cade and I have been best friends since we were small children." She loved every member of the Tribe of Tremayne, but none of them more than she loved Cade.

Marie's eyes narrowed. "Danger, and in more than one form. But you already know that."

"That's why I'm here," Tamsyn agreed.

"Change, profound change," Marie said slowly, "and in ways you never expected. Not necessarily disastrous, but a disorienting surprise."

"Isn't there always change around us?" Tamsyn said wistfully as she thought how Bran's marriage had created change. His wife, Merryn, was wonderful and had become a true sister, but the close little triad of Tamsyn, Bran, and Cade would never be the same.

Marie indicated a sweep of tea leaves high on the side of the cup. "A guardian angel. I think that is you."

"I hope I'm a good one, because that is what Cade needs," Tamsyn said softly.

Marie raised her gaze to Tamsyn's. "Do you want to tell me more about your situation? That might help with the interpretation. You can trust me. No one outside this room will know what is said here. My calling is to help, not harm."

Grateful for that, Tamsyn said, "Between Paris and Calais, we were stalked by a gifted man we called the Scorpion. He's the one who arrested Cade, and he has the terrible gifts of mind blocking as well as the ability to inflict hideous pain by touch."

Marie looked appalled. "Claude Bastien! He is notorious in gifted circles. He works for the French government, but also for himself. You must get your brother away from him as soon as possible!"

"My thoughts exactly. I can feel Cade through mind touch, but he is almost paralyzed mentally. I'm a healer and I'm sure I can lift the paralysis, but first I must free him. Do you know where Bastien lives? And how well guarded the place is? It was suggested to me that the Bastien property is a bit beyond Frethun and right on the sea."

"Your information is good," Marie said. "I've only seen Château Bastien once from a distance. It is formidable, a very old fortress."

"Do you know of anyone who works for him, or has worked for him in the past? It would be very helpful to know what to expect."

"The few servants he has managed to keep never speak of the fortress. They all fear their master."

"With reason," Tamsyn muttered.

"The château is built on a rocky rise above the sea, and it's said there are caves below that were used by smugglers in the past." Marie shrugged. "Perhaps they are still used that way."

Tamsyn was hit by a powerful certainty that those caves might be her way into the château. "I think I'll do some exploring."

"Be very, very careful. Bastien is the worst kind of gifted man, one who uses his powers for gain and cruelty."

"He destroys. I heal," Tamsyn said fiercely. "Whose power is greater?"

"You have great power," Marie agreed. "But even more you need luck and guile."

"I can manage guile. Luck I'll have to pray for." Tamsyn frowned. "After I rescue Cade, do you know any smugglers who could take us back to England?"

Marie bit her lip. "When the time comes, transport over the

channel can be arranged. I do know a gifted woman in Frethun, a widow, who could help you enter Château Bastien if she's willing. Her aid would come at a price, however."

"Whatever her price, I will pay it," Tamsyn said flatly.

"The price wouldn't be in money," Marie said. "I'll send her a note to say that you will call on her tomorrow. She can decide how much she wants to say."

"Thank you," Tamsyn said, praying that the gifted widow would be in a cooperative mood.

Chapter 14

Cade's mind and memory were still clouded, but he found that physical exercise helped him feel not only stronger, but more himself—whoever that was. Besides push-ups against the wall, he found he could jog in place next to the bed.

The only window in the room was high and narrow, but it was within the range of his chain. He found that he could jump up and catch the sill, then raise himself to look outside. The sea was there, and the sight of the broad sweep of water lifted his spirits.

Though it took practice because his balance was off, he found after cautious experimentation that he could do hand-stands as his strength and balance increased. None of his exercises offered much help to his mind, but they helped combat the deadly boredom.

His only regular visitor was the burly servant who brought food and drink in pewter vessels, then removed the empties left from the previous meal. He looked strong and brutal and never spoke or responded to questions. Unfortunately, he took care to stay out of Cade's reach. Though even if Cade could bring the man down, he wouldn't be able to escape the chain or the room.

Damn, he wanted his full mind back!

On what might have been the third or maybe the fourth day, Bastien entered Cade's cell, his expression predatory. "I'm going to lift the mind block enough that you can answer questions, but not enough to restore you fully. Answer my questions and I will restore your mind to its full power. I might even release you." He briefly laid his open palm on Cade's forehead.

After a shock of dizziness, Cade felt a sharpening of his thoughts, though there was much he still couldn't remember. He studied the other man, who was tall, dark, and somehow familiar, but if they'd ever met in the past, Cade couldn't remember when or where. "You're a bad liar, Bastien. You'll see me dead before you'll free me."

Bastien looked amused. "Perhaps, perhaps not. I haven't decided. If you give me the names and locations of other British Home Office agents, things will go much better for you."

"I won't, so you might as well go directly to the torture," Cade said. "You know that you want to."

Bastien's eyes narrowed. "Indeed I do, but I don't want to do so much damage that you'll be useless to me."

"I will always be useless to you," Cade said in a flat tone. "I will not betray my friends and family and country."

Bastien caught his prisoner's wrist, his gaze ferocious. Pain blazed through Cade's body, every nerve screaming with agony as Bastien said in a ruthless voice, "Where are the London headquarters of the gifted branch of the Home Office?"

Cade gasped, feeling as if his body was on fire. In his mind he could see the headquarters, but damned if he'd tell this monster where to look. "No!" He followed his refusal with a string of French curses.

"Your knowledge of French profanity is impressive," Bastien snarled. "But it won't stop the pain." His grip on Cade's wrist tightened like the talons of a falcon, and the pain magnified, exploded beyond endurance. Cade knew down to the marrow of his bones that he was incapable of betraying his oaths and friends and family, but death would be welcome. . . .

Then he felt the touch of Tamsyn's mind, countering the agony, surrounding him with calm and caring. He hoped to God that she wasn't taking on the pain herself because he truly would prefer death to subjecting her to such torment. Tamsyn, his wife and salvation. His beloved, delicate and blond and stronger than steel.

But he didn't have any sense that she was taking on his pain. She was using her gift for healing to dissolve it, and now she was sending him to sleep. As **he slid** into blessed peace, Bastien barked, "Stay awake, you bastard! I'm not done with you!"

But Cade was done with Bastien for now, and good riddance. His last thought was a desperate wish that he could be free and holding Tamsyn in his arms in some safe place.

Chapter 15

When Cade suffered another excruciatingly painful assault, Tamsyn collapsed onto her bed, giving thanks that she'd been in her room. All her concentration and most of her strength were needed to counter the effects of what Bastien was doing. If Cade wasn't so strong, he might have been driven mad by what he was suffering.

Tamsyn remembered Merryn's theory that strongly gifted people might be able to develop new abilities in times of crisis. Even though she was a healer, she'd always worked through physical touch. While healing usually included reducing pain, she'd never done anything like this, neutralizing pain at a distance through mind touch.

Perhaps this was possible because it wasn't normal physical pain but an assault by a viciously talented man that was inflicted directly to the nerves and mind? Or maybe she was able to mitigate Cade's pain because he was so dear to her, one of the handful of people she always carried in her heart.

When this was all over, she'd do some research and find out if any other gifted healers had dealt with this sort of situation. But mostly she just wanted it to be *over!*

She closed her eyes and calmed herself so she could make a mental list of the things she must do the next day. First on the list was buying that promising white riding horse, which meant acting as her imaginary younger brother. She would call herself Thomas since it was similar to her own name.

In the morning she would leave the house wearing her boy's clothing and boots under a skirt and cloak. She'd find a quiet alley and strip the outer items off, then go to the livery stable to buy Zeus and a saddle and the other gear required. Then she'd ride the few miles to Frethun to call on Madame Agnes LeBlanc, the woman Marie Barriere thought might be able to help her find the caves below Château Bastien. Marie had not mentioned the other woman's name until Madame LeBlanc had agreed to help

Tansyn also needed to find a quiet, isolated cottage where she and Cade could stay safely for a few days while he recovered. Perhaps Madame LeBlanc would help with that?

She smiled humorlessly. Then all she had to do was find where Cade was being held, break into his cell, free him, and lead him to safety, all without being seen by Claude Bastien.

She drew a shaky breath, knowing she mustn't let the task overwhelm her. One step at a time. If all went miraculously well, she'd be able to rescue Cade within the next two or three days, preferably before Bastien assaulted his mind and body again.

She shuddered at the memory. Her gift was healing, not torture, but she'd be willing to use a more old-fashioned form of punishment on Bastien, the sort inflicted by a very sharp blade.

She sighed. No, she was incapable of deliberately hurting any living being. But if Cade wanted to give Bastien a beating, she wouldn't try to stop him.

Her bloodthirsty thoughts were interrupted by the deep gong of the dinner bell. Time for a good meal in the company of normal, good people.

* * *

The next day started smoothly. The owner of the livery stable remarked on "Thomas's" resemblance to his sister, but she'd lowered her voice, and he didn't notice that his customer was a female. After a test ride on the white gelding, they bargained over the cost. Tamsyn wouldn't have minded paying the asking price, but doing so would be suspicious.

In fact, she paid a very reasonable sum for her new mount and his tack, which included a spacious set of saddlebags. She filled the bags with their least essential belongings, hoping there would be a safe place to leave them if today's mission went well.

The three-mile ride along the coast road to Frethun was pleasant and relaxing. Zeus was a strong mount with smooth gaits and it felt good to be doing something.

Marie Barriere's directions on how to find Madame LeBlanc's home on the far edge of Frethun were clear and easy to follow. The house was sizable and clearly prosperous. Tamsyn paused on the road before turning into the drive and gazed south along the coastline. She could *feel* that Cade wasn't far away. If Madame LeBlanc wasn't helpful, Tamsyn would start searching on her own and take her chances.

Marie had told Tamsyn to take her mount to the stables in back. When she entered the open doors, she saw a pair of carriage horses and two good riding hacks. A stable hand greeted her, speaking with a strong Cornish accent. "You're the guest Madame LeBlanc is expecting?"

"Yes, I'm Tam Tremayne," she said, using a lowered voice and a neutral name.

"Milady is expecting you," he said, taking Zeus's reins. "I'll look after your mount."

Used to caring for her own horses, she hesitated, but the stable hand looked capable, and Tamsyn was impatient to speak with the woman who might be able to help her find Cade. She thanked him and left the stables to walk around the house.

The polished brass knocker on the front door was in the shape of a sailing ship. She rapped smartly and the door was opened by an elderly butler who escorted her to a well-furnished drawing room with a view of the sea. A small-boned woman with silver streaked hair and shrewd eyes was writing at the desk, but she looked up at her guest's entrance.

Tamsyn bowed. "Thank you for seeing me, Madame LeBlanc. Madame Barriere said you might be willing to discuss a certain matter."

The older woman studied her narrowly. "She did say I'd be receiving an interesting visitor today. No need to bow, young lady, and a curtsy would require a skirt. Have a seat. Would you like a cup of tea?"

So much for passing as male. "Yes, please. Is it the fortune-telling sort of tea?" Tamsyn asked as she settled into one of the brocade-covered chairs.

"No, this is tea that tells no tales. I haven't Marie's gift for such things." The older woman poured two cups of tea and handed one to Tamsyn, gesturing for her to help herself to sugar. "She said that you are a member of the Tribe of Tremayne and are desperate to rescue your brother from Claude Bastien."

Clearly the two older women were good friends and Marie trusted Madame LeBlanc's discretion. "Yes, we were caught in Calais as war was declared and the order was issued to detain all British men. My brother and I were helping some English stragglers board the British ambassador's ship when Cade was attacked and taken away. Of course I had to stay here to free him."

"Of course." A faint smile touched Madame LeBlanc's lips. "So you're brave, loyal, and reckless. A true Tremayne."

Curious, Tamsyn asked, "Do you know my parents?"

"Yes, they visited France in better times." The older woman

made a face and stirred a heaping spoonful of sugar into her tea. "Outrageous for the First Consul to detain so many British civilians, but he enjoys being outrageous."

"Can you help me free my brother from Château Bastien, Madame? Cade and I are not here to cause trouble. We just want to go home."

Madame LeBlanc stared into her teacup, stirring the sugar more than necessary. "You've been told how . . . difficult Claude Bastien is?"

Tamsyn's mouth tightened. "He's been torturing my brother. He has the most appalling gift for pain."

"He does." There was a long moment before Madame LeBlanc met Tamsyn's gaze and said quietly, "To my regret. He's my nephew."

Startled, Tamsyn said, "You're a Bastien by birth?"

"Yes. I grew up in the château and know it well. My older brother Edmond was the previous master of the estate."

"So Claude is his son."

"Officially, though I have my doubts about his actual parentage," the other woman said dryly.

"That's an . . . intriguing statement," Tamsyn said cautiously.

"I don't air my family's hidden scandals lightly." Madame LeBlanc sighed. "But it might be useful in this case. My brother was a scholar, more interested in his books than people. He married Melisande for her dowry, I believe. She was beautiful and . . . profligate. She would go down through the caves to meet lovers. She liked rough, common men—smugglers, highwaymen, and the like. She only had the one child, Claude, and she died in childbirth. He is tall and dark and craggy looking, his appearance nothing like anyone else in the family. I've always presumed Claude's father was one of her lovers."

Startled, Tamsyn said, "Did your brother realize that?"

"I assume so, but he was interested only in his studies of an-

cient Greek and Roman texts. He had his heir and that suf-
ficed." She poured more tea into her cup. "He died in a fall
down the château stairs when Claude was twenty-one."

Tamsyn caught her breath. "Did you think it wasn't an accident?"

The older woman shrugged. "I really don't know. My
brother could be very absent-minded. Perhaps he missed a step
while thinking about an inscription."

Perhaps. But Tamsyn sensed that the older woman didn't
believe that. "Madame Barriere said that your nephew works
for the government."

Her hostess nodded. "Yes, the secret police. He likes hunt-
ing the enemies of France."

No wonder he'd been so intent on capturing Cade. "Is it still
possible to enter the château from the caves below?"

"Yes, though I haven't traveled that way for many years.
There are several caves but only one leads up to the château. I
can show you that one, and you can decide if it will work for
you and your brother." Madame LeBlanc's eyes narrowed.
"But before I explain how to enter the château, I will tell you
what I need in return for helping you."

"I will pay any price as long as I am alive to do so," Tamsyn
said.

"I'm glad you're not underestimating the risks. If you're
dead, of course that absolves you of the debt," the other woman
said with grim humor.

"Tell me your price."

"I want you to take my grandson Andre to England and do
what is necessary to establish him there," Madame LeBlanc said
in a steely voice.

Chapter 16

"That's not what I expected," Tamsyn said, surprised, "but it's a reasonable request, assuming I'm alive to perform it. Tell me more about your grandson."

"Andre is twenty. My daughter Giselle was his mother. She married a Scotsman, Robert Jameson, and they went together to India, where he worked for one of the rajahs designing some kind of mechanical things. After Robert died, Giselle brought Andre home to France, but the lad is more British than French and he would surely be detained with other Britons if he is discovered." Madame LeBlanc's eyes turned icy. "Claude would dearly love to make that happen."

Tamsyn caught her breath. No wonder Madame LeBlanc was willing to work against her nephew. "I will be pleased to help your grandson to safety and give him the protection of my family. Where is he now?"

"Working in a menial job where he is unlikely to be noticed. If you succeed in freeing your brother, I will bring him to you." Madame LeBlanc stood and moved around the desk, and Tamsyn realized that she was wearing a riding habit. "Now it's time for a ride south along the seaside."

They walked out to the stables where a sleek white gelding with a sidesaddle awaited his mistress. The stable hand helped her mount. Since Tamsyn was theoretically male, she mounted Zeus on her own.

"That's a beautiful horse," Tamsyn said admiringly. "He looks like he might be kin to my Zeus."

"That's quite possible. There's a breeder on the other side of Calais who specializes in breeding white horses, so there are many in this area." Madame LeBlanc patted the sleek neck. "Clovis belonged to my late husband. He's rather large for me, but he's very well mannered and I enjoy riding him."

They set off for the coast road and followed it for a mile or two before descending a lane that slanted down to the beach and continuing south. The white sand was wide enough for the horses to ride abreast. As waves lapped over Clovis's hooves, Madame LeBlanc said, "Having been raised here by the sea, I've always loved riding along the beach."

"There is something very free and primal about it. Since I haven't lived by the sea, I've had few opportunities." Tamsyn slanted a glance at the other woman. "Once I free Cade, I'll need a safe place to go to ground with him until he's ready to travel."

"That can be arranged. I assume that his French is as good as yours so he won't be identified as English?"

"Yes, our parents hired French nurses and tutors as we grew up," Tamsyn replied. "Since our countries have been fighting for centuries, it seemed a useful skill."

Her companion smiled. "Indeed. A pity women don't run our countries. The world might be a more peaceful place."

After they'd ridden another half mile or so, Tamsyn saw a massive stone building set on a rocky bluff above the sea. It looked like a small medieval fortress complete with battlements. She felt a clench of her heart. Cade was up there, so close, she could feel him. "I presume that's Château Bastien."

"Yes, it's Norman and very old. Though it's not large enough to be considered a castle, it's very solid and makes a good prison." Her gaze rested on her childhood home. "Not very comfortable. I haven't been inside since my brother's death, but I do ride along this beach regularly."

"When I've done mind touch with Cade, I had the sense that he's in a small, rather plain room," Tamsyn said. "There's a narrow vertical window. He was able to pull himself up to the sill and look out at the sea. Do you have an idea where that might be?"

Madame LeBlanc considered. "It would have to be on this side of the fortress, of course. Likely on the top floor below the battlements. You can see several vertical windows up there and he's probably in one of those rooms."

When Tamsyn was close enough, intuition would surely take her to where Cade was imprisoned. But breaking into the fortress and escaping safely was going to be near to impossible even with Madame LeBlanc's help.

As they drew closer to the château, she saw that the bluff had been undercut by the relentless sea and the area below the overhang was a ragged wall of crevices and dark holes.

They continued riding until they were in the middle of the undercut area. Surprisingly, a sea-worn stone bench was set against the irregular wall. "Time for a break," Madame LeBlanc said. "I like to stop here under the bluff because it's protected from the wind. Over there I had iron rings installed for tethering horses. There's a little natural basin that collects fresh drinking water from a small spring in the cliff."

"It's a lovely place to sit and watch the waves," Tamsyn said as she dismounted. "There's even a stone over there that can be used as a mounting block."

The older woman chuckled as she dismounted and tethered her horse. "I had that stone placed there for exactly that reason. The Bastiens have owned this stretch of coastline for centuries.

Though I prefer living in the town, I own the estate next to the château domain. I visit my property regularly to talk to my steward about what's going on, and because it gives me an excuse to ride along the sea."

"Your nephew doesn't mind?"

Madame LeBlanc shrugged. "We politely ignore each other. He hasn't invited me into the château since his father died, but this stretch of coast belongs to both of us."

As Tamsyn dismounted, she asked, "Can people in the fortress see down here to the bottom of the cliff?"

"No, the overhang prevents anyone above from seeing us. One would have to be farther out in the shallows to be seen."

"Convenient." She tethered Zeus to an iron ring next to the little drinking basin. He started slurping enthusiastically.

She glanced around the rocky wall. "There seem to be several caves. Which one leads up to the château?"

"Most of the caves are shallow. A few are large enough that smugglers used them for storage and perhaps still do." After pulling something from her saddlebag, Madame LeBlanc raised the skirts of her riding habit above the wet sand and led the way to a particularly ragged section of rock. She ducked behind an outcropping and pointed to a narrow crevice that looked too small to be the entrance to a cave, "This is the way up to the château. It's easy to miss unless one knows exactly where to look."

Tamsyn regarded it doubtfully. "It's very narrow. Can a grown man get through here?"

"Yes, though with some difficulty." Madame LeBlanc lifted the stiff brimmed hat that she'd brought from her saddlebag. A short candle was attached to the brim. She handed the hat and a tinderbox to Tamsyn. "This will help light your way. The path inside is very rough, so step carefully. In several of the steeper sections railings were installed, but I don't know if they're still sound after all these years."

Tamsyn used the tinderbox to light the candle, glad that this little niche was protected from the wind. "Time to explore the passage. What's at the top?"

"A solid door that leads into the lowest level of the fortress. I imagine it's locked." Madame LeBlanc studied Tamsyn's face. "It is up to you to see if this passage can be used to rescue your brother. Good luck with your exploring. I'm going to sit down and have a bit of cognac while I watch the waves."

Tamsyn lit the candle, then donned the hat. "Thank you. I should be back soon." She turned and ducked to enter the narrow entrance.

The footing was indeed rough and the passageway that led upward was steep. The original natural crevice had been modified to allow people to move up and down, and crude steps had been shaped in several places, but the flaring shadows caused by the candle made every step treacherous. She'd get a lantern for her next visit. Two—one for her and one for Cade.

When she found railings, she tested them cautiously. One had deteriorated to the point of being dangerous, but the others could be used with care.

The passage would be very tight for Cade in several places. Because she was small, she moved through without a problem, but she had to scramble up several of the higher steps. The air in the passage was cool and damp and the rocks could be slippery.

Panting, she reached the top, a small level area in front of the door into the fortress. She took off the hat and held the candle close to the keyhole. The door might be stuck from lack of use, but the lock was old and simple. She should be able to open it with the right tools.

Cade was the one who had taught her how to pick locks. She swallowed hard at the memory. He was such a very helpful brother, with no foolish beliefs about what females should be allowed to learn.

She stared at the door, wanting desperately to break through and find Cade, wanting to get him away from this vile place *right now*. But she knew that acting on impulse would lead them both to disaster. She needed to be prepared for all eventualities, and she must find a place where they could safely go to ground for a few days after they escaped.

She closed her eyes and pressed her hands to the door, using her talent to estimate how many people were in the fortress. There didn't seem to be many. Several servants like kitchen staff and maids. There were two or three rougher energies that likely belonged to guards.

Bastien didn't seem to be at home now. Based on the times when he'd tortured Cade, she guessed that he might usually be away during the day so that was probably the best time to stage her rescue. Servants would be more active in daytime, but they'd be easier to deal with than Bastien.

She turned and started down again, forcing herself to move cautiously. Her impatience to get out into the fresh air caused her to slip when she was close to the bottom. She swore when she banged her knee, but it was a good reminder to be careful. She prayed that Cade's mind would be clear enough that he could maneuver through the passage. If he fell and injured himself, it would be almost impossible for her to get him out. But Cade was so strong and agile that he should be able to get down safely even if he was half dazed.

She gave a sigh of relief when she reached the sand at the bottom of the passage. After blowing out the candle, she returned the hat to Madame LeBlanc's saddlebag, then joined the other woman on the stone bench, where she was sipping her cognac from a small, elegant glass. "Cade should be able to manage, but I am not looking forward to storming the castle!"

Madame LeBlanc smiled and pulled a silver flask and another small glass from a jacket pocket. After pouring a little of the amber fluid in the glass, she handed it to Tamsyn. "You've survived one vital step without a major accident or having a screaming fit at the closeness of the passage."

"Thank you." Tamsyn took a sip of brandy, then said slowly, "I had a thought. Lengths of rope securely tied would help us both keep our balance as we descend. I saw several places where I believe a line could be safely tied. Does that make sense to you?"

Madame considered. "Do you tie knots well?"

"Yes, Cade taught me."

"Then it's worth trying. The downward passage is particularly treacherous." She sipped at her cognac. "When will you attempt your rescue?"

Tamsyn took a deeper swallow of the excellent cognac. "The sooner I free Cade the better. Tomorrow by preference, but it might take until the next day to make all the arrangements. As I said earlier, I need to find a safe place for us to hide while Cade recovers and you bring Andre to us. Then we need to find a co-operative smuggler."

"I can help you with both of those things."

"I can't thank you enough for all you're doing to aid us," Tamsyn said quietly. "I don't know what I'd have done without you."

"I have no doubt that you would have figured something out, but I'm glad I can make it easier." The older woman finished her cognac. "It's very important to me to send Andre to safety in England among people who will understand and support his gifts. But I have another request."

"Anything within my power," Tamsyn said gravely.

"Please don't kill Claude unless it's absolutely necessary. He has become an angry and dangerous man, and he may not even be my blood kin. But when he was a child"—she swallowed hard—"he was a lively, likable boy. For years we were very close because he didn't have a mother. I do not love who he is now, but . . . I loved him once."

Hearing the underlying sadness, Tamsyn said, "I can't predict what will happen. I know that danger lies ahead. But I swear I will do my best to see that your nephew survives."

Her promise was sincere, but she had no idea if it would be possible to honor it.

Chapter 17

Every day Cade felt a little stronger, a little clearer, though there was still much he didn't understand or remember. It helped that Bastien hadn't visited him in a couple of days. Probably away tormenting other poor souls.

It helped enormously that Tamsyn was a constant presence in his mind, like a bright star on the darkest of nights. He wished that she could be more fully present but sensed that maintaining that contact took power and she couldn't use all her energy in that way while she was trying to arrange his rescue. He had no idea how she would manage it, but he felt her increasing confidence.

Once, his mental powers had been the equal of hers and he prayed that would be true again, but for now, rebuilding his physical strength was the only thing he could do. When Tamsyn came, he'd be ready.

He occasionally felt mental brushes from other members of his family, but they were never as strong as those from his Tam. When his mind had been clear, he'd been able to feel the others much better.

He was quietly jogging in place when he felt the distinct touch of his brother Bran's mind. Behind Bran he felt more power from Bran's wife, Merryn. Even working together, their mind touch wasn't as strong as Tamsyn's, but it was true and real.

Bran felt his welcome and the bond between them strengthened. Might his brother be able to help him in practical ways? Cade visualized the chain that locked him to the wall, charging the image with loathing.

Bran understood and after a long moment, he sent an image of boots. Cade's boots?

Yes! It was real communication and pleased them both. Bran's image sharpened, focusing on the heel of the left boot Cade had been wearing when he was captured. Something concealed inside?

Cade looked around the stark room. When he'd been dumped here, unconscious, his coat and boots has been stripped off and piled onto the plain wooden chair that was set in a corner.

Could he reach the chair? He stretched as far as he could, but the chain wasn't long enough for him to reach that far. Frustrated, he tried to puzzle out a solution. It seemed that there ought to be a way . . .

Ah, his legs were longer than his arms! He sprawled across the bed on his stomach and stretched his legs out. His extended right foot touched the chair. He stretched himself even more and was able to hook his foot around one of the legs. Slowly he pulled it toward the end of the bed, careful not to dislodge the boots and coat that had been left on the chair seat.

Bran had focused on the left boot heel. Cade lifted the boot and tried to twist it off. Nothing. He tried pulling and twisting in various ways and found success when he pulled the heel away from the sole and twisted it counterclockwise. Yes, that worked!

The heel pivoted to the left, attached to the boot by a thin nail. The inside of the heel was hollowed out with something inside and a fluff of wool to keep it from rattling.

Removing the wool revealed a pair of slim metal bars. Picks, he realized, designed to open a lock. He stared at them, knowing he'd once been good at picking locks, but he couldn't remember how to do it. The picks felt awkward in his fingers. Swearing, he returned them to the hollow heel. He packed the wool in again and twisted the heel into place so that the boot looked normal.

He didn't want his captors to know what he was doing so he started to return boots and coat to the chair and then shove it back into the corner. But the chair was sturdy, and he realized he could use it to look out the window for longer than the brief glimpses he'd caught by jumping and grabbing the sill.

He climbed on the chair and peered out the window. Yes, he could see more than the sliver of the sea he'd viewed before. There was a sandy beach and the tide seemed to be coming in. He drank in the sight.

A low bluff edged the beach with wind-shaped grasses and shrubs at the top. In the distance he saw a few cottages belonging to farm workers or fishermen. The real world with normal people living their lives.

His sluggish mind realized that this stretch of the sea must be the English Channel, and on the far side was home. He squinted into the distance, hoping for a glimpse of England, but there was too much mist over the water to see land.

At the bottom of his field of view, two riders emerged along the sand, both riding fine white horses. One was a boy, the other an older woman. They seemed to be chatting amiably as they ambled along the beach.

The boy turned in his saddle and looked up at the stony building that was Cade's prison. With shocking suddenness, he knew it was Tamsyn, disguised as a boy and surely scouting this area. Did she know he was here? He tried to send his thoughts to her, to catch her attention, but he wasn't strong enough to reach her.

He remembered the spark of her essence that was always in his mind, and imagined it growing brighter and stronger so that she could feel him. Though she glanced up in his direction again, he didn't think she was aware of him.

But Tam was here looking for him. She hadn't given up. Knowing her, she never would.

With a sigh of resignation, he stepped down from the chair and set his boots and coat on it. Then he pushed the chair back toward the corner as close as he could get to the original position. He didn't want his captors to think that he had any will or understanding.

Then he grimly set himself to the strengthening exercises which were all he could do that might help him escape.

Chapter 18

Madame LeBlanc turned her horse into a lane that led up the low bluff to a fenced field containing sheep. "This is the beginning of my property. Château la Mer."

The great house by the sea. It was a good name for the well-proportioned manor house visible in the distance. A band of woodland grew along the bluff, protecting the fields and pastures from the sea winds. Tamsyn saw the weathered roof of a small building in the clump of trees and was unsurprised when the older woman led the way along a narrow path to the cottage. It was well-kept but had an air of disuse.

"This should suit you for a temporary refuge," Madame LeBlanc said as she dismounted.

Tamsyn also dismounted, surveying the cottage. "It appears to be in good shape."

"There are several unused cottages around the estate. I make sure they're cleaned and maintained regularly. Château la Mer is short of laborers now. The wars, you know. But that will change in time and when more people return to the land, they will need places to live."

"Plus it's convenient as a sanctuary for people in trouble," Tamsyn murmured.

"Exactly," the older woman said with a smile as they entered the cottage.

Surveying the place didn't take long. The main room was a combination kitchen, sitting, eating, and dining room. The kitchen area was surprisingly up-to-date, with a hand pump for water and a kitchen fireplace well equipped with cooking tools. There was a wooden table with several Windsor chairs and an oak settle large enough for two or three people to sit.

Behind the front room was a small bedroom with a wide, sagging bed and a neat stack of ragged blankets set on a small cabinet. Tamsyn guessed that discards from the manor house had ended up here, but the cottage was serviceable and reasonably clean. A narrow stairway against one wall led upward. She climbed the steps and found a slant-roofed sleeping loft.

Returning to the main floor, she said, "This will suit Cade and me and Andre very well. As we rode up, I saw a shed behind the cottage. For the horses?"

Madame LeBlanc nodded. "You should be undisturbed here as long as you create little light or smoke. I'll have some provisions brought in."

"Perfect." With Madame LeBlanc's permission, Tamsyn transferred all the nonessential items from her saddlebags into the bedroom cabinet. The most important possessions she'd keep with her and bring to the cottage along with Cade.

After closing the cabinet door, she said, "Now all we need is a smuggler who has a seaworthy boat and a willingness to carry passengers illegally to England."

"I know such a man." The other woman smiled a little. "This has always been a smuggler's coast. We politely overlook the trade."

Tamsyn's gaze traveled around the cottage. "Once Cade is free and we take refuge here, how long before Andre can reach us? Then how long to make arrangements with a smuggler?"

"Only a few days. Andre is working nearby, and I will speak with the smugglers tomorrow so they can be ready." She gave a faint, humorless smile. "So many things might go wrong."

"And if they do, plans will be revised. We *will* find our way to safety," Tamsyn said fiercely.

"I believe you will." Madame LeBlanc studied her. "But be ready to face the unexpected."

"Hard to prepare for the unexpected, but I'm good at improvising."

"That's one of the greatest gifts." Madame LeBlanc glanced around the cottage again. "It's time to return home."

The ride back was a quiet one. Tamsyn concentrated on making mental lists of all that must be done. She wished she could go after Cade the next day, but there were far too many things to do. It would have to be the day after.

When she reached Calais, she left Zeus at a livery stable not far from her boardinghouse. Before returning to her room, she bought a coil of thin, strong rope from a ship chandler and found a sharp knife and sheath in a pawn shop that she could give to Cade since Bastien would surely have taken away his prisoner's weapons. She also bought a pair of small sturdy lanterns.

Before that night's dinner, she talked to her landlady, Madame Bernard, and the house cook. She explained that in two days she'd be returning to Paris to seek employment, but as a thank-you for the kindness of everyone in the house, she'd like to pay for a special dinner the next night. She offered an amount of money sufficient to buy more costly ingredients than were usual at the house, but not so much as to make her look too prosperous. The two women were happy to oblige, and they were discussing menus even before she left the kitchen.

After that night's dinner, she returned to her room to organize the last of their possessions and double-check her plans. In the middle of her packing, she was flattened by a wave of pain from Cade. Bastien had returned and was once more trying to extract information from his prisoner.

She reduced the pain to a bearable level and then sent Cade to sleep again. As his consciousness faded, she whispered, "*Very soon.*"

He returned the word *soon* with relief, gratitude, and love.

As she fell into an exhausted sleep, she prayed that within the next two days they'd be together, safe, and preparing to leave France, perhaps forever.

The next morning, she collected Zeus and rode along the beach to their refuge cottage. Madame LeBlanc had supplied more bedding and basic foodstuffs as well as several bottles of wine. Tamsyn smiled at the sight. Leave it to a French woman to make sure they would drink like civilized people.

She checked the provisions to see if anything vital was missing, but all seemed to be in order. She wondered what Andre Jameson would be like. With luck, he'd have his grandmother's good practical sense.

On her way back to Calais, she stopped under Château Bastien and entered the cave with her coil of rope over her shoulder. She made her way up to the door that entered the lowest level of the château. As she had the day before, she pressed her palm on the door and scanned for inhabitants. A small number of servants; Bastien wasn't at home.

Next, she laid her hand over the lock and called on Bran to help her with his lock power. He touched her mind instantly, glad to help with Cade's escape. Joining his gift to her own talent, she pressed her hand over the door lock and quietly focused on it.

It was impossible to describe how Bran shared his gift for locks with Tamsyn. Was it the closeness between her and Bran? Was it knowledge? Magic?

Whatever the process was, she felt a click under her hand and caught her breath with relief. Cautiously she turned the knob, and it moved, though sluggishly. She fought down the desire to break in *now*, but it was too soon. She needed to make sure that she would leave no traces of this temporary life behind.

She sent Bran the knowledge of success, then added "*tomorrow.*" In return she felt him pledging to support her with his power, and Merryn would as well.

She used her new gift to lock the door again, and it worked without effort. Then she cautiously made her way down the cave passage, tying lengths of rope at different secure points. Most were iron brackets that had been used to attach railings. The wooden railings had deteriorated, but the iron brackets held when she pulled the rope as hard as she could. She wasn't sure if they'd hold Cade's weight, but it was the best she could do.

When she reached the bottom of the passage, she gave a sigh of relief, then mounted Zeus and returned to Calais. The thank-you dinner was lovely, with generous portions of beef braised in red wine until it was falling-apart tender. There was fresh bread and sliced potatoes baked with cheese and cream as well as other vegetables, along with good wine and sumptuous desserts.

It was a grand occasion that ended with hugs and best wishes for her future, along with hopes that she would find a fine man who would appreciate her. She smiled and accepted their good wishes, thinking that her father and brothers appreciated her, and that was all she needed.

The weather in Calais had been generally pleasant and sunny since Tamsyn had arrived in the town, but the day of her planned rescue was cool and misty with spatters of rain and rare moments of sunshine. The weather was well suited for her purposes. She breakfasted at the boardinghouse and said her goodbyes, thanking Madame Bernard and the other residents.

Then she called on Marie Barriere and thanked her for her

help and also changed into her boy's clothing before she collected Zeus at the livery stable. As she rode along the beach, the mist thickened into fog. Mentally she considered all she'd done to improve the chance of success and couldn't think of anything she'd missed. The trouble with plans, though, were the problems she *hadn't* thought of.

She reached the overhang under Château Bastien and tethered Zeus. The critical moment had arrived. The climb up the cave passage seemed familiar now. When she reached the door into the fortress, she took several deep breaths to steady herself. She would leave one small lantern here, unlit, and take the other inside with the flame reduced as much as possible.

She rested her hand on the door and scanned to determine how many people were in the fortress. As before, she sensed perhaps half a dozen residents, all of them in higher levels of the structure. She guessed that half of that number were in the kitchen, busy preparing food. They were unlikely to cause trouble.

She moved her hand over the door lock and used the mental trick she'd learned from Bran to unlock it. It was easier this time, and she felt the shift inside the mechanism. Carefully she turned the knob and opened the door, wincing as it squealed. She caught her breath as she looked into the dark, cluttered cellar. A tiny golden thread ran through the darkness. She blinked and looked again but the golden thread was still there.

Now *that* was interesting! Her brother Bran had a gift for seeing silver threads that would lead him in directions that were important. A silver thread had led Bran and Cade to London when they were desperate children. A silver path in his mind had led him to Cornwall, and when he met Merryn, she had blazed with silver.

Nothing like that had ever happened to Tamsyn, but perhaps the intense work she had done with Bran, learning how to open locks, had triggered this new ability to see golden threads to guide her way. So if Merryn was silver, did that mean Cade was gold? She almost laughed at the thought. He'd be appalled by the idea when she told him that!

But first she had to free him from his prison. By the faint light of her lantern, she picked her way around old furniture and battered boxes. Madame LeBlanc had drawn floor plans of the building so Tamsyn knew where to find the stairs to the higher levels. The golden thread led unerringly to the door at the foot of the stairs.

This one wasn't locked. It moved stiffly so people probably seldom came down here. Because it was daytime, there was enough light to see, so she left her dim lantern in the cellar and climbed to the next level. The kitchen was to the left and she smelled roasting meat and bread and heard the clink of utensils as well as a murmur of voices. But she saw none of the servants.

She turned right along the corridor. At the end she found the stairwell that ran all the way up to the top level. Soft footed, she followed the golden thread and prayed that her luck would hold.

Her steps quickened as she climbed and the golden thread grew brighter, leading her to a locked door. She was panting and breathless from the climb and her heart accelerated at the knowledge that Cade was on the other side of the door. She rested her hand on the lock and *pushed*. The lock clicked and the door opened under her hand.

Cade had been doing energetic push-ups against the wall, but he swung around as she entered. The misty weather outside cleared and a shaft of golden sunshine came through the window and touched him with golden light. He was less than fully himself, but he was *enough*. "Cade!"

Their gazes struck and held, and then she hurled herself into his arms. He was warm and strong and utterly familiar. Her best friend.

His heart was hammering under her ear as he hugged her

with rib-bruising force. "Tam," he whispered hoarsely. "Tamkin, I've missed you so!"

"As I've missed you," she said in a shaky voice. She wanted to hold him forever, but reluctantly she broke free of his embrace. "We must get out of here as quickly as possible."

She lifted his chained hand and rested her fingers on the manacle. It snapped open as she poured power into it. His wrist was rubbed raw underneath.

His brow furrowed as he looked at his freed wrist. "How . . . ?"

"Bran taught me the trick of it." She looked up into his beloved face and touched his unshaven jaw. He was well on his way to a beard and obviously hadn't been able to bathe, but the connection between them was as strong as ever. Stronger, perhaps, because of the way their minds had been touching since he was captured. "Is your mind clear enough to escape? I can fully remove the mental block, but we can't afford the time to do it now."

"Not . . . myself," he said with effort, "but can follow orders and run."

She smiled a little. "That will do. Now it's time to leave. We'll go down to the cellar. A cave passage leads from there to the beach. It's awkward and it will be tight for you, but I think you'll be able to manage."

"I will," he said harshly. A chair in the corner held his boots and coat, which he rapidly donned. As they turned toward the door, it swung violently open and Claude Bastien stepped into the chamber, his face twisted with ferocious satisfaction. "Now I have you both!"

Chapter 19

Everything happened at once. Horrified, Cade tried to move Tamsyn aside, away from Bastien's hungry stare.

"First I'll block her mind, Tremayne," Bastien said viciously. "Then you'll tell me everything you know about the Home Office to spare her from being tortured. A little thing like her won't be able to endure as much pain as you did." He was already swinging his palm toward Tamsyn's forehead for the mind block.

"No!" she spat out as she jerked away from him. "Neither of us will tell you a single damned thing!"

Bastien lunged toward her, and she kicked furiously upward. He twisted away so that her boot struck his thigh rather than smashing into his genitals. Swearing, he staggered a moment, then lunged at her again.

The bastard was attacking Tamsyn! Incandescent with rage, Cade hurled himself at Bastien. His mind might not be clear, but he was no longer chained, he was stronger than Bastien realized, and he was trained to fight. He stepped between Tamsyn and Bastien and slammed a punishing fist into the Frenchman's jaw, knocking the other man into the door.

As Tamsyn scrambled out of their way, Bastien swore, then collected himself and struck back. Cade dodged the blow and slammed one fist into the other man's throat and the other into his belly.

Gasping, Bastien folded down to the floor. Cade followed him down and locked his powerful hands around Bastien's neck.

Bastien struggled for breath and tried to throw off Cade's weight but failed. As his furious face slackened and he slid into unconsciousness, Tamsyn said sharply, "Don't kill him, Cade!"

It took long moments for her words to penetrate his fury. "Why not?" he ground out. "The devil deserves it!"

"There are several reasons." She rested a hand on Bastien's forehead and closed her eyes as she concentrated. Looking startled, she continued, "One of which is that I think he might be your half brother."

Shocked, Cade studied the man he held pinned to the floor. He was tall, dark-haired, powerfully built, with strong, harsh features. There was an undeniable resemblance to the face Cade remembered seeing in his mirror. "How is that possible?"

"I'll tell you more later," Tamsyn said, her voice uneven. "Your father was a smuggler and may have visited these shores. When I touch Bastien, I can feel a blood connection."

Cade was revolted by the thought, but Tamsyn wouldn't have spoken lightly. He sat back on his heels. Maybe he shouldn't kill Bastien, but he needed to secure the man so they could escape.

He dragged off Bastien's cravat and tore it lengthwise into two long strips. One strip he used as a gag and the other to tie Bastien's wrists behind him. Lastly, he snapped the manacle around the other man's wrist. He would be trapped here until one of his servants came looking for him.

Cade stood. "Time to go."

"Wait. I'm trying to make him . . . less dangerous." Tamsyn's hand still rested on Bastien's forehead and her expression was abstracted. Cade could sense the amount of power she was expending. It seemed a waste, but he had to trust that she knew what she was doing since she was in full possession of her wits and Cade wasn't.

It seemed a long time before she said, "That's enough, I think." She staggered as she got to her feet and Cade caught her arm to steady her. Her face was pale and it took visible effort for her to steady herself. He wanted to embrace her again, but they needed to get out of this fortress as soon as possible.

Tamsyn opened her eyes and cracked open the door. Silence. It seemed none of the servants had heard the fight. She opened the door wider and slipped out, beckoning Cade to follow.

Quietly he closed the door behind them and followed her down the dark stairwell. The only sounds of life were on the kitchen floor, but no one noticed them.

Down and down and *down*. The steps ended at a plain wooden door. Tam tugged it open and waved him through. A dim lantern sat on the floor, illuminating a crowded cellar.

After Tamsyn closed the door behind them, she lifted the lantern and turned it up to increase the light. "Not far to the cave," she said lightly. "Then we hope that you lost enough weight in captivity to fit through the passage!"

He smiled a little. "If need be, I'll chip the tunnel wider to get out of here. Lead on, my lady!"

She picked her way through the boxes and old furniture to a heavier door. He winced as it squealed open, but again, no one in the fortress seemed to notice. Thank God Château Bastien had thick walls and few servants!

The small landing at the top of the cave passage was barely large enough for both of them. Tamsyn was tantalizingly close but all business as she lifted a second lantern and lit it from the first.

Handing it to him, she said, "Be careful of the footing. I noticed earlier that because of the rain, water has seeped into the cave and made the rocks slippery. I tied lengths of rope in different places to help steady us, but I'm not sure they can support your weight."

"I'll take care." He studied the irregular passage that led downward. Tam hadn't been joking about the tightness, but he would cheerfully scrape off skin to make his way to freedom.

Grimly he followed Tamsyn down the passage, which was weirdly illuminated by the flaring lanterns. Had he always hated tight spaces? He couldn't remember if he had, but his breathing was strained and he certainly hated this enclosure. Because Tam was small, she didn't risk getting stuck, but there were long, irregular steps where he could hear her use the ropes to help her descend.

The worst part was when he slipped on a wet rock and grabbed a rope that broke under his weight. With ironic good luck, he slid down and landed bruisingly in a tighter area of the passage, which kept him from falling farther.

Tam called anxiously, "Cade, are you all right?"

He drew a deep breath as he tallied his bruises. "No serious damage done." It took care, strength, and ripped clothing to work himself free of that tight spot, but he managed and continued to work his way down through the dank, suffocating passage, knowing he'd remember this in his nightmares.

As they descended, the sound of waves grew stronger. When dim outside light began to be visible below, he knew the end was in sight and he had to force himself to keep moving carefully rather than recklessly going as fast as he could and risking broken bones.

The light below brightened and Tam called softly, "I'm down and out of the cave! You've only a few feet more to go."

Carefully, carefully . . .

He exhaled with relief when his feet touched sand, but the opening at the bottom that led onto the beach was so tight, he wasn't sure if he could make it through. He ended lying on his left side and crawling through the narrow opening to reach the wet open sand. When he was finally free, he paused to gulp cool, fresh air into his eager lungs.

He saw that they were under a protective cliff overhang and fog obscured the beach and the sand. All the better for escaping. He levered his tired body up using the wall. "Next time, bring a hammer and chisel I can use on the passage!"

Laughing, Tamsyn threw her arms around him. "But we made it!"

He enfolded her, never wanting to let her go. Her warm, sweet body was promise and memory and sanctuary. When she tilted her face up, he kissed her with desperate yearning. He wanted her so much, so intoxicatingly much.

For a moment she responded with all the warmth of her nature and the passion he remembered that had helped him endure his captivity and torture. Then she shoved herself away from him and stared at him with wide, shocked eyes. "Cade, what are you *doing*?"

She was wet and muddy and dressed like a boy, and she looked enchanting. He cupped her cheek with one hand and said tenderly, "I can understand if you'd rather wait for a proper bed, but I'd be happy to make love to you right here on this wet sand."

She jerked back from his hand. "How can you say such things?"

Confused, he said, "Is it strange that I want to make love to my wife?"

After a long, suffocating silence, she said tightly, "Cade, I'm not your wife. I'm your *sister!*"

Chapter 20

Shocked and deeply disturbed by Cade's words, Tamsyn continued unsteadily, "Where did you get the idea that we're married?"

Looking as disoriented as Tamsyn felt, Cade faltered. "Bastien said you were my wife and . . . it felt so right that I believed him."

She frowned, trying to make sense of his statement. "He doesn't seem like the sort of man who pays much attention to women. Since we were traveling together and we look nothing alike, it probably didn't occur to him that we were brother and sister."

"We are, Tamsyn?" He shook his head. "I don't understand."

He was glowing golden in her mind and she couldn't *think!* She inhaled deeply and said, "This is not the time or place to sort this out. A mile or so south along this shore, there's an empty cottage where we can stay until everything is organized for us to go home."

In the chaos of her mind and emotions, the clearest thought was that she had to get them away to safety. "My horse is tethered around the corner. After what you've been through, you should ride him."

Cade shook his head, and dammit, he was still glowing gold.

"You used much power on Bastien. You ride and I'll walk since you say it's not far."

This was the protective big brother she knew, and he wasn't wrong. "Very well. Let's hope this fog holds for the rest of the day."

He glanced upward. "I think it will. Your horse?"

Cade had always been good at predicting weather. Silently she led the way around the corner to the cave where Zeus was tethered.

"Nice," Cade said as he introduced himself to the gelding. "You have a fine eye for horses." He untethered Zeus, then turned and lifted Tamsyn into the saddle.

She felt she should complain about being treated like a child, but she realized that she was exhausted. And Cade's hands around her waist felt warm and protective.

The walk along the water to Château la Mer was silent, with waves occasionally washing over Cade's feet and horse's hooves. Cade gave a soft whistle when they reached the snug cottage nestled in the grove of trees. "How did you find this?"

"The network of gifted people." She slid from the gelding's back, holding the saddle for a moment until she felt strong enough to walk. "There's a stable around the back. I'll go into the cottage and start a fire."

He nodded and led Zeus around the cottage. They'd always worked well as a team. Cade was her favorite brother, not that she would ever tell Bran that.

She'd laid a fire on her last visit so it didn't take long to strike a spark and get it going, warming the cool cottage.

What next? Fighting her fatigue, she stepped into the bedroom area and sat on the edge of the bed as she pulled off her boots. She should get up and set out food, but Cade had been right about how tired she was. She'd lie down for just a moment. . . .

Cade gave Zeus a very thorough grooming, not surprised that Tamsyn had provided all the feed and tools necessary to make a horse happy. Though there was much he couldn't remember, his muscles knew what to do. He found the process as soothing as Zeus evidently did.

After the horse was fed and bedded down, Cade headed out into the mists and around to the front door of the cottage. He and Tam needed to talk, but not until after she'd cleared the mental block Bastien had forced on him.

The fire had taken the chill off the cottage, but it was so quiet that he wondered if Tam was there. One of the lanterns shed gentle illumination from its place on the single table. It didn't take long to find Tamsyn sprawled on one side of the bed, dead asleep.

She was so petite, but with the heart and strength of a lioness. Ever since he was captured, she'd been working nonstop toward freeing him and maintaining steady mind contact with him. She'd also used a vast amount of energy not just on rescuing him, but doing whatever she'd done to make Bastien "less dangerous." No wonder she was so tired.

He wasn't much better, he realized. His captivity, the mind block, the torture, the sheer physical demands of the escape, had left him reeling.

The bed had been made up, but Tam had fallen sleep on top. Several blankets were folded on the small cabinet, so he shook one out, folded it in half for more warmth, and laid it over Tamsyn, brushing her hair with light tenderness.

He needed something to eat, he realized. Surely if horse food had been provided, there was also food for people. He moved to the simple kitchen area and found cheese and ham and bread, along with good French wine to wash it down.

The food steadied him, but maybe he should have skipped the wine because after he drank a glass, he was ready to lie down on the flagstone floor and go to sleep. He couldn't remember when he'd been so tired.

Of course there was much he couldn't remember.

His gaze went to the bed where Tamsyn still slept. It was the only bed and wide enough for two. Though his mind produced intoxicating images of sharing a bed with her, he wasn't sure if they were memories or imagination.

Was he Tamsyn's husband or her brother? She said she was his sister, and surely she knew best since her mind was operating normally.

She was almost invisible under the folded blanket. Would she mind if he joined her on the bed? Perhaps, but he needed rather desperately to be close to her. Not in a romantic way, as much as he wanted that. He just needed to be near her healing presence.

He stripped off his boots and coat and shirt and realized that he must smell like a goat. And a horse. Tam would have brought his carry bag and he recalled that it included fresh clothing. The cottage was small so it didn't take long to locate the bag. He stripped off the garments he'd been wearing for days, then took advantage of the kitchen water pump to give himself a quick wash. He refused to let himself think how good a hot bath would feel. He really needed a shave, but he'd leave that for tomorrow.

Cleaner and even more ready to drop in his tracks, he dragged on a pair of drawers and his one clean shirt. Both were loose, which his body appreciated after wearing the same clothing for days on end.

He eyed the bed again. He desperately needed a good night's sleep, and the bed would be far more comfortable than the cold stone floor.

Decision made, he banked the fire for the night, then pulled a blanket from the pile and folded it in half, then spread a third blanket over both of them.

He lay down as far from Tamsyn as the bed allowed. Tomorrow would be a complicated day as Tam healed his mind, he found out what had been happening, and they laid plans for escaping home to England.

But for now, he slept in peace.

Chapter 21

Tamsyn moved gradually toward wakefulness, mostly still asleep and wanting to stay that way. She couldn't remember ever being so relaxed and happy. It was because Cade was free. In a matter of days, they'd be home. She felt so warm and safe.

Surprisingly warm, in fact. Uneasily, she opened her eyes a sliver and saw Cade at very close range. His arm was draped over her waist, holding her close.

She stiffened, wondering what to do. She didn't want to wake him when he needed sleep to help recover. Plus, blast it, his embrace felt so warm and *good*.

But this was *wrong*! They'd always been casually affectionate in a brotherly and sisterly way. Now the fact that Bastien had convinced Cade they were married changed everything. Wondering if they would ever be easy together again, she slowly disentangled herself so she could get up.

His deep blue eyes opened and they stared at each other, both frozen. She was sharply aware of his physicality. His strength, his maleness, and the dangerous look created by his flourishing whiskers.

He broke the moment with a sharp inhalation and jerked away from her. "I'm sorry! I meant to stay on the other side of the bed."

She gave him a crooked smile. "On a cool night, a warm body feels good."

He swung off the bed, muttering a curse under his breath. "How long will it take you to clear the mind block? I hate being lost in my own head!"

She could only imagine how dreadful that must feel. "The process takes time and a lot of energy. We need to have breakfast first."

"I want to know how you managed all this." His gesture included the cottage.

"Do you remember that Rhys gave each of us a coded list of gifted people in Northern France?"

His brow furrowed unhappily. "I don't remember that."

"You will soon," she said confidently, hoping that would be true. Minds were complicated and unique. "While I fix breakfast, could you take care of Zeus and bring in more fuel for the fire?"

Her request steadied him. "Of course." When she moved into the kitchen, her gaze firmly away from him, she heard him dressing. She swung a kettle of water over the fire to heat for tea, then did a simple washup and undid her braid so she could finger comb her hair loose over her shoulders. A nice pot of tea would make everything feel more normal.

She sighed. *Normal* would mean arriving safely home in London with most of her family nearby, not being solely responsible for the safety and mental health of her dearest friend.

Zeus was a very soothing horse. Cade relaxed as he concentrated on feeding and grooming. He didn't want to think how Tamsyn would soon be rummaging around in his mind. He admitted to himself that though he desperately wanted to be restored to his usual clarity and competence, he was afraid of what Tam might find. He was sure there would be emotions and crude male thoughts that would embarrass them both, and perhaps damage their relationship. But to stay in his present state was impossible.

Chopped wood was stored in a corner of the shed so he gathered a heaping armful and headed inside. When he reentered the cottage, he stacked the wood by the fireplace, then accepted the steaming hot cup of tea Tamsyn offered. He sipped it with pleasure. "Something smells good."

"Just eggs and toast, but warm food always tastes particularly good on cool spring mornings." Tamsyn scooped the eggs onto a pair of plain pottery plates, then added toasted and buttered bread. His portions were double hers, only reasonable since he was twice her size.

He set the plates on the table. "I can't remember when I last had a hot meal."

"What were you fed?"

He shrugged as he sat down. "Stale bread and cheese, mostly. The cheese was usually decent."

Tam sat opposite him and they both dug into their eggs. When Cade's plate was empty, he said tentatively, "I have a feeling that you've made many breakfasts for me."

She nodded. "You're quite a decent plain cook yourself."

He drew a slow breath. "So many holes in my memory!"

"Not for much longer," Tam said quietly. "Are you ready to have your mind restored?"

"Yes." After a long pause, he said, "But . . . I'm worried about what you'll find."

"No need to be." She smiled as she collected the dishes and moved them to the kitchen area. "We've known each other for most of our lives, Cade, so I doubt I'll find too many surprises. Besides, mind healers are hard to shock."

Maybe she wasn't shocked by what she found in the minds

of strangers, but the mind of someone she knew might be more disturbing. He couldn't bear it if she ended up hating him, but she was his only hope of regaining himself.

Tamping down his fear, he said, "I think I've seen you clear someone else's mind, but I don't remember how it's done."

"The process is different for each person. You have seen me do this before and the results have always been good. At least, so far," she said reassuringly. "Let's move to the settle, where it's wide enough for both of us to sit."

"I'll pad it with some blankets," he suggested.

"A good idea," she agreed. "This will take a while."

He spread two blankets over the settle to soften the bare wood, then sat at one end. "Now what?"

"I'll take one of your hands and place my other palm on your forehead."

He flinched, remembering his captor's torturing hands. "Like Bastien?"

She looked apologetic. "Sorry, but yes, that's what works best. The difference is that I'm clearing your mind, not blocking it. I don't think it will hurt physically, but it will probably be disturbing. Confusing. Like being trapped in a dream or a nightmare. Trust me. Soon you'll be yourself again, but it will take time to clear away everything that isn't you."

He did trust her. "Then let us begin," he said grimly.

She clasped his right hand in her left, then leaned forward and rested her warm right palm on his forehead. She must feel that he was rigid with anxiety, but she said only, "Relax, my dear. You'll feel me inside your mind. Not much different from the way we kept in touch with each other when you were a prisoner."

He liked the idea of that closeness because she'd been his link to sanity as well, mitigating the worst of the pain. He closed his eyes and welcomed the increased closeness between them as she gently began exploring his mind.

But this was more than the warm contact they'd maintained since he was captured. Her power brought welcome clarity, but the blazing light illuminating his mind was also intense and disturbing and shockingly intimate. His instinct was to fight this mental invasion, and it took all of his willpower not to jerk away from her hand.

Surely reading his mind, she whispered, "I know you're not liking this, but you're doing a fine job of allowing me in to do my work. Are you beginning to feel some lightening of the bonds?"

He realized that he could, so he gave a rough nod. "How much longer?"

"I'm not sure," she said honestly. "The blocks are very complex and strong. But I am stronger. Keep trusting me."

"I will." Though the mind blocks were fading, he wasn't sure how much more of this invasion he could take. Or how much more Tam could do; despite her calm, he sensed that her power was waning.

Dear God, how much longer?

With a final scouring blaze of light, he realized with awe that she'd done it! The blocks were *gone!* He felt that his mind had been restored, exhausted but as good as ever.

With a shuddering gasp, he bent over and buried his face in his hands, breaking the physical connection between them. "That was . . . interesting," he said in a voice that was ragged but fully his own. "You're a miracle worker, Tamsyn, and thank God for you!"

She lurched away from him, her eyes wide and her expression shattered. "Cade?" she gasped. "I didn't know. *I didn't know!*"

Chapter 22

Cade was fully himself again. She saw intelligence and aware-ness in his face, the focused power of his body. But his gaze was as stricken as hers must be. "You saw," he whispered. "I buried it in the deepest part of my soul, but you *saw!*"

"I saw that you love me the wrong way." She swallowed, feeling ill. "The images I saw in your mind . . . !"

He closed his eyes, his face pale. "Under Bastien's mind block, I couldn't tell if those images were true memories or my imagination."

"They were your imagination. I've loved you ever since you came to Tremayne House, but as your *sister*. Not as . . ." She stopped, her face flushed by the vague images of passionate in-timacy she'd sensed.

"That's why I never spoke," he said quietly. "I've loved you from the moment we met, Tam. As I grew to manhood, I began loving you as a man loves a woman, but I never spoke because I knew you didn't see me that way, or want to."

"I'm your *sister!*" she whispered again.

He shook his head. "Gwyn and Rhys created the Tribe of

Tremayne, showing us how to love each other as brothers and sisters, and we do. But there is no blood connection between you and me. You are the oldest of the three true-born children of Gwyn and Rhys. Because the Tremayne patent of nobility was written so that the oldest child inherits the title even if female, you are the Tremayne heiress and will someday become the Countess of Tremayne in your own right. I'm only your bastard foster brother."

She gave a sharp shake of her head. "Don't demean yourself like that! You are brave and capable and intelligent, and despite your start in life, you're now a wise, compassionate man who is one of Rhys's best Home Office agents. You and Bran have also become wealthy through your investments, and you've helped everyone else in the Tribe of Tremayne do well. If you want a wife, any number of women would say yes in a heart-beat."

"I doubt it," he said dryly. "Most females seem to view me with wariness or alarm. But even if it's true, the only woman I've ever wanted is you, and you've always thought of me as a brother. " His gaze shifted away from her and he said in an almost inaudible voice, "I'm afraid that now you've found out my desire, you will despise me."

She rose and began pacing restlessly around the room. "Never that, Cade! But it will take me time to . . . to accept how differently we see each other."

"I found it difficult to share that room with you in the British embassy," he said bluntly. "But you know I would never, ever do something you don't want me to do."

"I do know that." She paused in her pacing and turned to face him. He sat unmoving in the settle where she'd healed his mind, as if he feared that any movement would send her fleeing.

She was still shocked to her core, but she remembered un-easily the way he'd kissed her when they had escaped from the fortress. She'd been startled then, but for that first moment when he'd embraced her, she'd felt delight and rightness. Then shock had flooded her and she'd jerked away, baffled and upset.

She tried to study Cade as if they were strangers. He drew the eye because he had an appealing air of mastery. He was also a very attractive man, and when she looked closely, he had an irresistible golden shimmer that she saw with her mind, not her eyes. If they hadn't been raised as brother and sister, she'd had found him appealing. Very.

She had never been a girl who dreamed about whom she would marry when she grew up. Her life was too full of people she loved and interesting things to do and learn. As the heiress of the Tremayne earldom, she'd attracted her share of fortune hunters, but had been able to dismiss them instantly because of her ability to sense the emotions of others.

In her social seasons, she'd met some pleasant men and several had become friends. But she'd never met anyone she considered marrying. She'd thought very little about marriage, assuming that if she ever met a man she could imagine as her husband, she'd give the idea serious thought.

But that had never happened. It had occurred to her that her closeness to her Tremayne brothers, particularly Bran and Cade, filled any need she had for male company. Plus, they treated her as an equal rather than a delicate and possibly dim-witted female, which was how many men regarded her.

But if she'd met Cade as a stranger, would she have considered him husband material? The immediate "yes!" in her mind was profoundly disturbing.

She couldn't think any more about this now, especially since there were more important things to discuss. Shutting down any further analysis of their relationship, she said, "Let's have a glass of wine so I can answer all your questions about how we got here and what comes next."

"An excellent idea." Cade rose and poured two tumblers of

white wine, then returned to the settle. "But first I want to let Bran and Rhys and Gwyn know that I'm safe and free."

She nodded. "Are you feeling strong enough to reach them? You've just had a rather tiring session of me poking around your mind. I can help if you like."

He frowned, then gave a nod. "If I sound too weak, they'll worry."

She moved a chair close enough to the settle that she and Cade could hold hands, then hesitated at the thought of touching him. But she must if she was to augment his energy.

From his satiric gaze, she realized that he had the same thought and was waiting to see what she would do. Jaw set, she took hold of his hand. The clasp was warm, strong, reassuring. Familiar.

But was there an additional flicker of energy, something new? She refused to consider that. Firmly she said, "You're the one they want to hear from, so you take the lead."

He closed his eyes and she felt him center his energy, then reach out. He touched Bran first because they'd always been close; then his essence reached the minds of Rhys and Gwyn. It was nothing as clear as the communication they'd had days before that had exhausted everyone, but Cade was able to convey that he was free and safe and that Tamsyn was with him, and that was enough.

Tamsyn felt an invisible brush of delight and relief from the other Tremaynes; then they faded from her awareness. They'd probably sensed Cade's exhaustion and didn't want to add to it.

After the connection ended, Cade released Tamsyn's hand and leaned back on the settle again. "Now I want to hear all about how you performed your miracle rescue."

"It seems like months since we were scrambling to get the ambassador and his people aboard the ship and then you were captured by Bastien, but it's only been days." She made a face. "Do you want the short version or the long version?"

He gave her his familiar smile, the one that said they were a team that worked together seamlessly. "I probably should hear the long version as parts of it might prove useful in the future." He swallowed the last of his wine and stood to move over to the kitchen area. "But serious discussions require tea. I'll make us a pot."

She stiffened as he walked across the room. The friendship and ease were as familiar as her own heartbeat, but never before had she watched him so intently as he walked away. He moved beautifully.

And he had a splendidly fit, thoroughly masculine body. Watching him, she remembered with acute detail the times they'd held each other with casual hugs or Cade lending her a hand when they were scrambling up a tree.

And she was damned well *not* going to think about any such things!

Chapter 23

Cade added a spoonful of honey to Tamsyn's tea, then handed her the cup before sitting in one of the Windsor chairs. He was trying to create a sense of normalcy, but he recognized that the energy between them had changed. Tam wasn't meeting his gaze. Her disposition was usually steady and positive, but now she was experiencing emotional turmoil, and it was his fault.

He hated that he was the cause of her pain. Under other circumstances, he could have wrapped an arm around her shoulders to offer comfort, but not now. For years he'd buried his desire for her, and he'd never planned to reveal his feelings. But now that she'd discovered his passionate dreams about her, change was inevitable.

Perhaps change was good. The thought of losing Tam's friendship was terrifying, but he wanted more. The fact that she hadn't run screaming gave him some hope. Tamsyn had a flexible mind, and perhaps in time she could come to think of him as a lover, not a brother. He hoped to God that could happen.

For now, he must be casual and matter of fact, as if nothing had changed. "How did you manage to break me free of Château Bastien? I think you said you were helped by the network of gifted people."

"Yes, Rhys's list led me to Madame LeBlanc, who made everything possible. She's the sister of the former master of Château Bastien, and she grew up there. She showed me the entrance to the cave path that leads up to the fortress. She also owns the estate next door, which includes this cottage." Tam's expression turned fierce. "Though I would have found a way no matter what."

"Even at my most confused, I felt you and your determination in my mind." He frowned. "After my fight with Claude Bastien, I think you said he might be my half brother? It's a horrible thought. What made you think that?"

"Madame LeBlanc again. Officially she's Claude's aunt, and she has fond memories of him as a child even though she's certain he isn't blood kin. That's why she asked that he not be killed if possible."

"I thought you spoke from a general desire to avoid unnecessary violence, which I agree with, though I might have made an exception in Bastien's case." Cade thought back to their escape. "Why does Madame LeBlanc believe he isn't actually her nephew?"

"Apparently, Claude Bastien's mother was young and beautiful and wild. She would leave the fortress by the cave path to meet lovers more to her taste than her husband. She liked rough common men like sailors and smugglers."

Cade exhaled roughly. "Men like my father, the smuggler Jago Evans?"

Tam nodded. "Exactly. You and Claude Bastien resemble each other physically, and when I touched him, I sensed a blood kinship."

"What an appalling thought!" Tea wasn't strong enough to deal with such a revelation. Cade set his cup down and began to pace around the living space. "What did you do to Bastien before we left? You said you were making him less dangerous."

"He was filled with anger and a desire to destroy," she said slowly. " He hates gifted people even though he's one himself. He wants to use his gifts to annihilate the enemy."

"Meaning Englishmen?"

"Yes, but you in particular." Tamsyn frowned as she thought. "Searching someone's mind is a very imprecise process, but I think that when Claude was a boy, a servant told him who his father was. Later he had Jago investigated and learned about you and Bran. He resented you for finding a family that accepted and loved you."

"If he thinks my early years were more pleasant than his, he didn't learn enough," Cade said dryly. "Strange to have a mortal enemy you didn't know existed. What did you do to his mind?"

"I tried to remove the anger," Tam said. "I don't know how well I succeeded because I didn't have much time, but I think I reduced at least some of his rage. Better for him and for us."

"A pity you didn't have enough time to persuade him to beat his sword into a plowshare so he would become a peaceful farmer with no desire to destroy Britain."

Tam shook her head. "I don't know if that would be possible, but I wouldn't have changed him that much even if I could. He has a right to serve his country just as we do."

Cade paused in his pacing and gazed out a window. There was a glimpse of the sea through the trees that surrounded the cottage. On the other side of that water was England. Home. "Given how much aid Madame LeBlanc gave you, it was right to honor her request not to kill Bastien. Why did she do so much for us? Was it a desire to help others who are gifted?"

Tamsyn shook her head. "That's part of the reason, but more important is that she wants us to take her young grandson to England and to help him become established."

Cade turned back to Tamsyn, who was no longer avoiding his eyes. "Is he a child?"

"No, he's twenty and his name is Andre Jameson," she replied. "His father was a Scottish engineer who worked for an Indian rajah. After his father died, his mother brought him back to France. Madame LeBlanc says he's more British than French and he's in danger of being arrested as a Briton. Claude Bastien wants that to happen because his cousin is another of the people he hates."

Cade's brows arched. "No wonder Madame was willing to help you thwart Claude! So we escort young Andre to Britain and take him into the Tribe of Tremayne? I'm glad we can help her that way. Does she know Rhys and Gwyn?"

"Yes." Tam gave a swift smile. "I suspect that Rhys and Gwyn know every gifted person in Britain and France!"

He decided to voice something he'd long wondered about. "Why do we all call Lord and Lady Tremayne by their first names? Even you and your birth brother and sister, who are legitimate children, call them Gwyn and Rhys rather than Mother or Father. It's shockingly informal."

Tam looked thoughtful. "I asked Gwyn about that once. She said it was a way to remove the differences between members of the Tribe. Birth children or foster, legitimate or not, we all call the parents of our Tribe by their first names. As the oldest birth child and the heiress to the earldom of Tremayne, I'm entitled to the courtesy title of Lady Tamsyn, but I almost never use it because that would draw a line between me and my siblings. I want to be one of the Tribe—an equal, in no way superior. Does that make sense to you?"

He blinked. It was so very Tamsyn. "Perfect sense, and I don't know why I hadn't thought of that myself. As the bastard child of a smuggler, I'm at the bottom of the usual social hierarchy, but I don't feel that way when I'm among Tremaynes." He sighed. "At least, not usually. But I've very aware that someday you'll be the Countess Tremayne in your own right, and I'll still be the bastard son of a Cornish smuggler."

She scowled at him. "You are the oldest son, a vital part of the Tribe. We all look up to you not just because of what you do for the Home Office, but because of who you are. We are equals and don't you forget it!"

"I never forget who we are, Lady Tamsyn," he said quietly. "That's why I never intended to let you know how I feel about you."

She swallowed hard, then sipped her cooling tea. "Well, that cat is well and truly out of the bag and racing about the cottage, ricocheting around the furniture and knocking things over,"

He laughed. "Like every kitten a Tremayne ever rescued from the street and brought home!"

Her face lit up. "Remember Smokey the Destroyer? He was the champion at knocking things over."

He gave an answering smile. "Who could forget Smokey?"

"Or Basil the Bear, always formally dressed in black and white, who marched in the front door and laid claim to Rhys."

Cade laughed. "As the lead tomcat in Mayfair, he immediately recognized that Rhys was the lead male in the Tribe of Tremayne."

"And he's been leaving black and white cat hairs all over Rhys ever since," Tamsyn said fondly.

Remembering their shared history was good, Cade thought. He could see her becoming more relaxed.

Her smile faded. "I'll be so glad to be home again. We haven't actually been in France all that long, but it feels like months."

"So much has happened." He began moving restlessly around the room again. "I wonder how long we'll have to wait before we can leave."

"Not long, I think."

There was a crisp knock on the door. "You might want to conceal yourself," Tam said quietly as she rose to respond.

He nodded and stepped into the bedroom area, out of sight of the front door. He heard Tamsyn's footsteps as she crossed the room, a faint squeal as the door opened. "Madame LeBlanc! I'm so glad to see you. Come in. Your cottage has been most welcoming."

"I heard that your assault on Château Bastien was successful," a warm French voice said. "Is your brother concealed somewhere about here?"

Taking that as his cue, Cade stepped out of the bedroom and saw the elegant older woman who had entered the cottage. She wore a riding habit and had an air of command. He gave her a low bow. "Tamsyn has told me how much you did to help free me. I am eternally in your debt."

"I'm glad I was in a position to help. I assume Lady Tamsyn has told you how you will be repaying that debt." The Frenchwoman studied his face. "There is a definite resemblance between you and Claude."

"I find that alarming, and I gather he does also," Cade said dryly.

"You are both very forceful young men," she said thoughtfully. "But you work in more positive ways than Claude. Perhaps that comes from growing up Tremayne."

"I think you're right. I've been very fortunate," he agreed.

Madame LeBlanc's gaze shifted to Tamsyn. "You are said to be an expert in emotional healing. Did you do something to Claude before you left the château?"

"I tried to make him less angry," Tam said. "I don't know how successful I was."

"Even though we are at a distance, I sense a change in him," the older woman said softly. "I hope that lasts." Her gaze returned to Cade. "I'm glad you didn't kill Claude. You must have wanted to after the way he treated you."

"Yes," Cade said honestly. "But Tamsyn said not to, and I always do what she tells me to do."

Tamsyn chuckled. "Only if it's what you want to do anyhow."

They exchanged a smile. They always listened to each other, then did whatever they thought best.

Turning serious, Tam said, "We wish to return to England as soon as possible. Is your grandson ready to leave? Going to a new country takes courage."

"Andre feels the danger around him and he is tired of living in hiding," Madame LeBlanc said. "I will bring him to you tomorrow as darkness is falling. I'll also bring another horse so we can ride to meet the smugglers. They'll take the three of you across the channel tomorrow night."

"A quarter moon. Just enough light to guide us safely," Cade said.

Madame LeBlanc nodded. "Exactly."

"We'll take good care of Andre," Tamsyn promised.

"If I didn't believe that, I wouldn't be able to let him go," the older woman said starkly. "I'll see you tomorrow evening. It will be best if you stay inside the cottage until it's time to leave. If you need some amusement, there are books in French and English in the bottom of the cabinet in the kitchen area."

"I like the idea of doing very little for a while!" Tamsyn said fervently.

"Rest while you can," Madame LeBlanc said as she opened the door. "There is a long war ahead of us all."

"She's right," Cade said soberly after the older woman was gone. "I also like the idea of resting." He covered a yawn, then turned to the ladder that led upward. "Time to see how comfortable the sleeping loft is."

Yawning was contagious. As soon as Cade disappeared into the loft, Tamsyn headed to the bedroom. She and Cade had been on the move ever since leaving Bran and Merryn's wedding to head straight to France. She had a lot of lost sleep to catch up on.

Tamsyn was used to being busy, but spending a quiet day in the cottage turned out to be surprisingly pleasant. She awoke refreshed in midafternoon and considered what they might have for supper. After studying their supplies, she decided on a pot of hearty potato-leek soup. Chopping the vegetables was very soothing.

She kept thinking of Cade's shocking revelation about his feelings for her, but his behavior hadn't changed so she was starting to relax. Perhaps his declaration of love had been a result of his captivity and his gratitude at being rescued. He was probably regretting what he'd said.

Her reaction when he'd kissed her, thinking she was his wife, had just been surprise. No need to keep thinking about how it had felt. . . .

She was slicing the stale bread for toasting when Cade swung down the ladder from the loft. His smooth, controlled action caught her attention. He moved beautifully, all elegant male strength, and once again, he seemed to shine with a golden light.

She blinked and the golden light disappeared. Had it been only a brief splash of late-afternoon sunlight that had shafted through the window at the front of the cottage? Now the light was gone, and he was his normal self again, handsome, rumpled, and in need of a shave.

"Something smells very good," he said. "I'll go tend to your horse. Then what can I do?"

"We're having humble but delicious potato-leek soup," she said. "You can open another bottle of white wine and pour it, then toast the bread with cheese."

He went out to take care of the horse, then returned and started toasting the bread and cheese. They'd often shared a kitchen, and they fell easily into the routines of cooking and eating.

Tamsyn poured the soup into two bowls and they both sat down to their simple meal. "I'm enjoying a day of doing nothing. How about you?"

He chuckled. "So am I, though by tomorrow afternoon I'll probably start pacing around restlessly."

"So will I," she admitted. "But now—soup!"

They had a leisurely meal with seconds and, for Cade, thirds on the soup. As they sipped wine, they talked casually about the past and what the future might hold. They both agreed that the renewed war was likely to be long.

The pleasant evening was like any number they'd shared in the past. But she knew in her bones that her future back in England would be different from her life in the past.

Chapter 24

The pallet in the loft was reasonably comfortable, and Cade was still tired enough to fall asleep easily, serenaded by the soft rolling sounds of the nearby sea. In two nights, they'd be stealthily sailing home across the channel. . . .

He came sharply awake at the sound of a muffled cry from the floor below. *Tamsyn!*

He swung from the pallet and jumped straight through the hatch that opened to the main floor of the cottage, not bothering to use the ladder.

Another sound came from the bedroom, an anguished cry that was close to weeping. The cottage was dark except for the faintest glow of light from the banked coals on the hearth. He didn't sense anyone but Tam in the cottage, but he still moved carefully as he entered the open door to the small bedroom.

She was sobbing as she thrashed under the bedcovers as if fighting an unseen enemy. "Tamsyn!" he said urgently. "Wake up!"

He dropped onto the edge of the bed and gathered her into his arms. One of her flailing fists rammed into his chest with more force than one would expect from a petite woman. He caught her hand and said soothingly, "You're safe, Tam! I'm here and you're safe. You were having a bad dream."

For a moment she continued to struggle against him. Then her body softened. "Cade?" she said uncertainly.

"Yes, my dear girl," he murmured as he pulled her closer. She wore only a warm flannel nightgown, and he could feel her shaking underneath the single layer of fabric. "I think you were having a nightmare. I didn't know you were prone to them."

She pressed her face against his shoulder and struggled for breath. "I'm not! I don't have nightmares! I can't remember ever having one before!"

Her delicate features looked haunted, and tears glinted in the faint light. He wanted to kiss the tears away, but no. This was not the time for that. "Do you remember the nightmare or was it one of those chaotic dreams that make no sense?"

"I . . . I was losing you," she said in a choked voice. "I saw you going down as you were being abducted by Claude Bastien. I was sure you were dead. And then there was pain. So agonizing, it was destroying you. You were gone and . . . and I knew I'd never see you again."

"But that didn't happen," he said reassuringly. "You reduced the pain he caused until it was endurable, and you stormed the castle to rescue me. I'm right here and I have no plans to get myself killed."

"But I'm still losing you," she said starkly. "I spent the day trying to convince myself that you didn't really mean it when you said that you loved me in a . . . a passionate way. I wanted to believe you were just grateful to be free."

She tilted her head and he could feel her gaze even in the near-total darkness. "But you did mean it, didn't you?"

He drew a deep breath, wondering if it would be best to say he hadn't really meant what he'd said—he'd just been exuberant at attaining his freedom. Perhaps then they could go back to normal, being close friends who were easy with each other, the way they'd always been.

No. Honesty was essential. "I meant it, Tamsyn," he said quietly. "I would never have spoken if not for the confusion and scrambling of my wits, but words spoken can't be unsaid. I've always loved you as a man loves a woman. I always will."

"And that changes everything," she whispered. "The nightmare meant that if I don't change also, I will lose you. You'll pull away and perhaps get yourself killed on one of those dangerous missions you don't talk about."

"I survived such missions in the past and I plan on continuing to survive them, though of course there are no guarantees," he said matter-of-factly. "I certainly don't plan on pulling away from you."

"You've managed to survive so far, but there are other ways to lose you," she said softly. "If you want a home and family of your own, it won't be hard to find a lovely willing wife who isn't part of the Tribe of Tremayne. Marriage would certainly take you away from me."

He had to laugh at her words. "That won't happen! I'm not the sort to attract women unless they're desperate. I've always assumed that I was meant to be a bachelor uncle."

She gave a small snort. "You haven't noticed how women watch you?"

"Never!" he scoffed. "They tend to edge away because I make them nervous."

"That is not what is happening," she said with a touch of humor. "You look like a delicious combination of exciting and reliable. Like the Tremayne cats feel about catmint."

He was glad for the darkness because he suspected that he was blushing. "Your excellent imagination has run away with you."

"It's not imagination but observation, Cade," she replied. "If you look carefully when we return to England, you'll see interested females all around you."

"Even if what you say is true, it doesn't matter," he said

intently. "I've never met another woman who moves me as you do."

"I think that's because you never looked." She took a deep breath. "But now that you've admitted to desire, it might be more difficult for you to be around me."

He shifted uncomfortably, knowing that might be true. Passion had been a closed door, one that he felt he could never open. But it was closed no longer. His dreams of Tamsyn were explicit and passionate.

Wanting to change the subject, he said, "I've sometimes wondered if you simply aren't interested in men. Some women are made that way. You've done your share of fashionable society events and never shown much interest in the various young men who fluttered around you. You always treated them like brothers."

"It's not that I don't like men," she said simply. "It's that none of them were you."

Taken aback, he said, "Could you . . .explain that?"

"I'm just now realizing that I shut down the part of myself that might feel a normal interest in men," she said haltingly. "Because you were the only man I was interested in and you're my brother. So there was no point in encouraging any of those pleasant but not terribly interesting young men."

"Ever since Rhys and Gwyn brought Bran and me to Tremayne House, you've been a wonderful sister," Cade said. "You took responsibility for the whole tribe of foster children even when we were older than you. I didn't question that then, but I've come to realize how remarkable you were."

He felt her shrug. "That was because my gift for healing minds was so useful helping new brothers and sisters recover from the harsh treatment they'd received. Gwyn and Rhys encouraged me to help anyone who needed it."

"I remember when Cameron first arrived, he was so terrified that he vanished somewhere into the house for two days." Cade smiled reminiscently. "Bran and I wondered if he'd escaped back to the streets until you found him and healed him so well that he dared to come out and join the rest of the family."

"I always knew where Cam was, but I thought it best that no one hunted him down before he was ready," she explained. "When I sensed that he was beginning to relax, I went to his hiding place with cream cakes."

Cade laughed. "Very like coaxing a frightened kitten to come out from under the furniture!"

"Exactly. Cream cakes are the perfect bait for pets and children." There was a smile in Tam's voice. "Of course I ate my share, too."

Turning serious, Cade said, "What you did for me changed my life. Is that why you felt so much my sister that you could never imagine me as anything but a brother?"

There was a long silence in which he was very aware of her heart beating where he held her against his chest. That great loving heart had given him the warmth and acceptance that guided him to sanity, but he recognized now what a vast responsibility it had been for a very young girl. Then he'd half believed that she was an angel.

"You may be right," she said at last. "Being the eldest sister of the Tribe of Tremayne was my role and I've always been proud of that. But I'm beginning to understand that seeing myself that way was . . . limiting."

"Earlier you said that our situation has changed, and how you must change, too," he said, choosing his words with care. "Are you saying that perhaps you might no longer see me only as a brother and therefore forbidden?"

After another long silence, she said, "Shall we find out?"

He felt her head tilting back and he opened his mouth to speak, though he wasn't sure what he would say. Then her lips touched his in a questioning butterfly kiss.

He froze as lightning sparked through his veins. The passion he'd controlled for so long simmered and burned, but he knew it would be disastrous to let it run wild. As he savored the delicate pressure of their lips, his hands stroked down her back, delighting in the feel of smooth muscle over strong bones, of intoxicating feminine strength.

She gave a soft sigh and her mouth opened under his. Gently the kiss deepened and his caresses lengthened. His Tamsyn, the wise, kind girl who had held his heart since they were children.

He sensed that she was responding to him in a wholly female way, but cautiously because she was moving into what was unknown territory. His right hand moved to cup her breast, irresistibly soft and tempting under the flannel fabric.

She caught her breath and became very still. He grew equally still and moved his hand away from her breast, wondering if even this slow pace was too quick for her.

Breaking the lingering kiss, she said breathlessly, "I do want to change but I fear it will be very slowly. Can you bear that?"

He gave a husky laugh. "I can bear anything as long as we're moving in the same direction. All the choices are yours, my dear girl. Just tell me what you want."

Shyly she said, "Will you share the bed with me tonight? Just holding each other?"

"That would be my pleasure and delight, Tam," he whispered into her hair, knowing it would also be a great challenge to his self-control, but no matter. Whatever it might cost him, the self-denial would be worth it.

Chapter 25

Tamsyn moved to the far side of the bed so Cade could slide in beside her. By unspoken agreement, they rolled toward each other into a warm mutual embrace. She felt her muscles slowly relax so she molded herself bonelessly against him, her head on his shoulder. His familiar scent and breathing soothed her. She gave a slow sigh of relief and pleasure. "I always feel so safe with you," she murmured.

He gave a soft chuckle. "But you're the one who rescued me, not the other way around."

"It's the merest accident that you needed rescuing this time." She cupped his cheek with one hand, enjoying the prickle of his dark whiskers. "You've always been a protector, even when you were a small child and guided Bran safely to London."

"We worked together," he pointed out. "Bran supplied the idea and the confidence while I figured out how to steal rides on coaches and find food and shelter. Low-quality food and shelter, but they kept us alive."

"As I said, you're a protector. As the oldest male member of the Tribe of Tremayne, you always protected us from those who dislike anyone who is gifted."

He shifted uncomfortably. "It has been my responsibility to look after my younger brothers and sisters."

"Not just your responsibility, but your calling," she said. "It's why you're such a good agent for the Home Office. That work gives you a chance to protect the whole of Britain."

He chuckled. "That's too vast an undertaking for one man!"

"True, but you've always done your best."

"It's all any of us can do, my golden girl," he said tenderly as he brushed out her blond hair, which had fallen from her loose braid.

She sighed. "Sometimes our best isn't good enough."

He didn't reply, just ran a warm, wide hand down her back. She closed her eyes, understanding why cats like being petted. As they both lapsed into silence, she became increasingly aware of how this closeness stirred her senses. She wanted him to touch more of her and found that she wanted to touch more of him. Sweet intimacy.

Her hand brushed down his chest and lower until she reached a firm, unexpected barrier. He caught his breath. "Best you avoid too much exploration, Tamkin!"

She pulled her hand back, a little embarrassed but also intrigued. Though she was primarily a healer of the mind, she understood how male and female bodies came together and her curiosity had been aroused. "Perhaps some mutual exploration?" she said hesitantly. "Now that the female part of me has woken up, I've become actively curious."

"That's dangerous territory," he said ruefully. "But if you're sure you'd like to learn a little more . . ." His voice trailed off as his hand slid around her to rest gently on her right breast.

She caught her breath, thinking that felt wonderful, and pressed a little closer into his hand. Understanding her unspoken signal, he began stroking her nipple with his thumb, sending tingles in all directions.

Her breathing quickened and his hand moved gently lower.

Even with the layer of flannel between them, his touch was intoxicating. What would it be like if he was stroking bare skin?

She tugged up the hem of her nightgown till it crumpled below her waist. He hesitated before stroking lower, over the subtle curve of her stomach. Lower still until his skillful fingers reached the incredibly sensitive area between her legs.

She gave a choking sigh as her lower body began pulsing involuntarily against his hand. She'd never felt anything so enthrallingly wonderful, and she wanted more. She could feel sexual tension burning through him, but his touch remained delicate, suggesting rather than demanding. Stimulating a yearning so intense that the world faded into a golden haze of delight.

Then shockingly, a series of fierce convulsions rocked her as she lost all control, thrashing against his warm, firm touch in a surge of desperate need and fulfillment. "Cade!" she gasped. "Dear God, *Cade!*"

He drew her against him until her body stilled, his breath soft against her forehead. Shaken but trying to sound calm, she murmured, "That was . . . educational."

"You're an apt student," he said, his voice strained. "That's probably enough exploration for tonight."

He started to move away from her, but her curiosity hadn't abated. "Surely there's more." She slipped her hand under his shirt so that it rested on taut skin over powerful muscle. His deliciously male body invited further touch.

She slid her hand down his belly under the waistband of his drawers and found the interesting barrier she'd brushed against earlier. She wrapped her hand around the heated length and squeezed gently. "I know the theory. Can you show me the application?"

He jerked within her clasp and gasped. "Stop, Tam!"

She squeezed him again. "Why? I'm interested in further lessons."

He caught her hand and stilled it within his own. "It's too

soon, Tamsyn! You're only just discovering a side of your nature that you buried, and you've only just learned how I feel about you. Becoming lovers would be an irrevocable change, one we might both regret. You need to come to terms with what just happened, and what you'd like to happen in the future."

She wanted to exclaim that she knew what she wanted and he was right here in her bed, but her rational mind intervened. "You're probably right," she sighed.

"You know I am," he said gently as he started to pull away. "We need to put some space between us. I'll go up to the sleeping loft."

Becoming lovers might be unwise, but recklessness still danced through her veins. "Not yet! Though it's too soon for anything irrevocable, there is a matter of equity to be settled. What you did for me was . . . stunning. It's only fair for me to attempt to return the favor."

Before he could reply, she freed her hand from his and again clasped that heated, pulsing essence of masculinity. She stroked rhythmically, sensing his desire as it intensified to a golden inferno. Suddenly he gasped and turned rigid as he climaxed swiftly with a deep, shuddering groan that engulfed his whole body.

As he slowly relaxed, she exhaled with pleasure and cuddled against him. "I think I'm going to sleep very, very well."

"You'll have to share the bed with me since I no longer have the strength to climb the ladder to the loft," he murmured as he rolled to his side and tucked her back against his front.

She relaxed into his warm embrace, her body satisfied and happy but her mind whirling. Her instinctive feeling that they could not be physically attracted because they'd been raised as brother and sister had faded as she accepted that they weren't blood kin, but the issue was still complicated.

She'd think more about the complications tomorrow. Tonight she reveled at being cradled in Cade's arms.

Chapter 26

Tamsyn woke up from a deliciously restful sleep, every fiber of her body tingling with well-being. She'd learned wonderful new things the night before, and God willing, she'd learn more soon.

Sadly, she was alone in the bed, but the mattress next to her retained a trace of warmth. Cade was in the kitchen area. He'd quietly built up the fire and was setting a kettle of water on to heat. His glance at her was grave. "I'm going to miss this cottage."

She smiled as she slid from the bed. "So will I, but it will be wonderful to get home."

She padded across the room toward Cade. Her flannel nightgown kept her reasonably warm down to her ankles, but the flagstone floor was *cold*. "We'll have to come up with something to amuse ourselves until it's time to leave."

"Cleaning the cottage and making it look as if we were never here will take some time." He turned to their simple larder to pull out bread and cheese. After he'd set them down, Tamsyn stepped behind him and wrapped her arms around his waist. He still wore only his shirt and drawers so she slid her hand down over the fabric to rest on that fascinating ridge of male flesh. He hardened instantly under her touch.

After a frozen moment, he jerked around to face her. "No, Tam!"

She blinked at him, surprised. "Why not? We have a long dull day ahead of us."

"Because *no* means *no*, Lady Tamsyn!" he said sharply. "Whichever of us says it and whatever the reason."

She bit her lip. "I'm sorry. After last night, I assumed that . . . that things had changed between us."

"They have, unfortunately." He frowned as he sorted his thoughts. "Love and lust are not the same thing, and passion can scramble the wits of even someone as intelligent as you, Tam. We must go forward as if last night never happened."

"You seemed to enjoy sharing the bed last night. Was passion scrambling your legendary self-control?" she retorted.

"Indeed it was." He sighed. "I'm sorry for snapping at you, Tam. Passion most certainly overcame my judgment."

"If there's guilt about last night, I think it should be equally shared." She gave him a tentative smile. "But I don't feel at all guilty."

"Guilt is irrelevant. What we need is restraint," he said bluntly. "For years I buried my feelings for you so we could be friends as well as brother and sister. I should have kept them buried. I'll never forget last night and the joy of the . . . the closeness we shared."

"I'll never forget it, either," she said softly.

He caught her gaze with his. "My deepest dream has always been that someday you might be my wife. But now reality has made me realize how impossible that is. If we were to marry, we would risk damaging the Tribe of Tremayne, perhaps shattering our family into pieces."

Marriage? The idea was surprising but not unpleasant. Not unpleasant at all. She felt herself blushing. "Do you think we'd be disowned if we married? Surely not!"

He shook his head. "You wouldn't be. You're the golden child, the big sister who loves and is loved by everyone, not to mention being a true-born daughter and the heir to the title and estates. But Rhys and Gwyn might wish they hadn't taken me in."

"Never! They would be startled, maybe even a bit shocked, but they'd never regret making you part of the family." She drew a deep breath. "If I'm the big sister, you're the big brother who can always be trusted to protect and help the rest of us with our problems. You are as loved and essential to the family as I am."

Expression troubled, he said, "I'm always happy to help as needed. But if we can't return to behaving as brother and sister, I'll have to withdraw from the family."

"If you left us, that would certainly cause damage!" she exclaimed, horrified.

"It wouldn't be an obvious break. I'd just start spending almost all of my time on Home Office work and not be around the family for much of anything else."

She thought of the casual meals and riding and walking in the country, the regular activities that were the foundation of their family. Not just her and Cade, but every possible combination of Tremayne siblings. If Cade was never there . . .

She hated the thought. "You would be missed desperately if you stepped away from the rest of us."

"I'd be missed some," he agreed. "But that disturbance would be minor compared to the shock and revulsion if we were to marry, and if we want to be together, it must be marriage. Trying to have a secret affair would be even worse because we could never keep such a secret from gifted family members."

She frowned. "You and I and Bran have always been so close. Don't you think Bran would be able to accept us as a married couple?"

"My guess is that the odds are about even as to whether he'd accept or challenge me to a duel for taking advantage of you," Cade said wryly.

Tamsyn shuddered. "Surely not!"

"A duel is unlikely, but if you and I are together, I fear it would change things with Bran drastically. I would ... have trouble bearing that," Cade said. "This is one of the many reasons why we must step back before anything irrevocable happens."

Would the marvelous closeness between them be reduced to a brief passion? Or could it be love everlasting such as that between Gwyn and Rhys? She'd never thought of marriage before Cade made his declaration, but she was thinking about it now, and recognizing the potential for both joy and dire consequences. If Bran condemned them, the rupture in their friendships would be excruciating.

Their family was a complex network of individual relationships, like a delicate three-dimensional weaving of lace that connected each member of the Tribe with every other Tremayne. She had a horrible vision of those threads of love and trust being irrevocably sundered. Surely some of her brothers and sisters would be able to accept a marriage between her and Cade, but it was far too likely that some could not. They would see such a marriage as incest, as she had for so many years.

With sudden horror, she recognized that Cade was the one who would be blamed for seducing his sister even though that wasn't what had happened. Any fault was mutual, but as he'd said, she'd be seen as the innocent sister and he'd be condemned for taking advantage of her. Dear God, what would that do to him? He'd been thrown away by his appalling father. Being forced out of his family of the heart would be not only wrong, but devastating.

She shuddered as she thought of the reactions. "I don't want to believe that you're right," she whispered, "but I fear you may be."

Cade sighed, his expression deeply sad. "I can't imagine a happy outcome if we put our own desires ahead of the well-being of our family."

She'd always seen Cade as strong, utterly in control, and utterly reliable. Those same traits could cause him to walk away from the Tremaynes to avoid hurting others. The thought struck ice into her heart. She couldn't bear the thought of never seeing him again. It didn't matter whether her love for him was romantic passion or a deep, deep friendship. Either way, he was vital to her.

The night before, she'd felt as if Cade had opened a door in her spirit that had revealed a bright, rich future on the other side. Now he was closing that door. But if he was willing to withdraw from the family he loved, to spare everyone pain, she must show equal strength to make sure he wouldn't have to do that.

Summoning calm, she said, "You're right that we must step back for now—this is all too new. But I'm not sure that damage is inevitable. We must move ahead in a very carefully considered way until the situation becomes clearer. But please don't leave without telling me! *Please.*"

He hesitated before saying, "I promise I won't just disappear without letting you know, but I lack your optimism. I think the most likely result will be that I continue working for the Home Office but move farther away from Tremayne House and largely disappear from general family activities. And perhaps now that you've awakened the part of yourself you'd suppressed, you will find a man you can love who isn't your brother."

She made a face. Cade was rarely foolish, but he was certainly a fool to suggest that she could just turn around and find another man worth marrying.

More tactfully she said, "Foretelling ability is very rare even among the gifted, Cade. But I believe that the future holds many possibilities, not all of them dire."

He smiled wistfully. "I've always liked your optimism, Tam. I wish I shared it."

Chapter 27

The rest of the day was quiet as Cade and Tamsyn removed all traces of their stay from the cottage. He kept a wary eye on her, but she had stepped back into treating him as a brother, showing no signs of anger or frustration. She just looked thoughtful, which could mean anything. He tried to get a sense of her emotions, but she was very good at withdrawing into herself so that he couldn't read her.

After they finished up their food supplies with a last lunch, Tam said, "Because we're going to slip away in the night, should we muddy up Zeus's fine white coat so he won't be as easy to see?"

Cade considered. "Maybe some splotches so his outline won't be as clear. I'll take care of that."

"I'm sorry we must leave Zeus behind, but I'm sure Madame LeBlanc will see that he's well cared for." Tamsyn was folding the bedding, but she paused. "Will we get back to England safely? There is a war going on and I have a feeling our return won't go smoothly. What do you think? You've always been good at sensing danger."

Apart from a general sense that they'd make it to England, he hadn't thought much about their escape because most of his mind was engaged in thinking about Tamsyn. Damned careless of him not to be paying more attention when they were in enemy territory!

He stilled his mind, then reached out with all his senses. "There will be danger on our escape," he said slowly. "Something wholly unexpected, and perhaps disturbing, but I do feel we'll make it across the channel. Very frustrating not to sense it more clearly!"

Tam shrugged. "The limits of our gifts are maddening. But whatever happens, presumably we'll be able to deal with it or we wouldn't make it home."

She was right, but still he worried. He didn't like the unexpected.

The hours passed slowly, and fog settled in as dusk approached. That would help them to travel unseen.

They both had their carry bags slung across their bodies and were dressed for riding. In her boy's clothing and with her hair braided and pinned up, Tam looked like a well-bred schoolboy. They spoke little as they waited, but Cade wanted to memorize every detail of the cottage where, for a few brief hours, he'd been happier than he had ever thought possible.

It was almost dark when a light knock on the door was followed by the entry of two people. The single lamp that lit the cottage was sufficient to reveal the upright figure of Madame LeBlanc. A step behind her was a slim young man. He was dark haired, of medium height, and had a small-boned build similar to that of his grandmother.

Tamsyn rose from her chair to greet them. "I assume that all the arrangements are in place, Madame." She turned to the young man and offered her hand. "It's good to meet you, Andre Jameson."

He made a courtly bow over her hand, and when he spoke, his

English had a slight Scottish accent. "The pleasure is mine, Lady Tamsyn. Grandmère assured me that you'll get me safely to England and guide me when I reach there. I am most grateful."

Andre's eyes were dark and intelligent, and he had an aura of quiet power. Wondering what the young man's gifts were, Cade stepped forward and offered his own hand. "We'll certainly do our best. Both Tam and I think we'll make it safely across the channel, though not without some trouble."

Madame LeBlanc sighed. "Isn't there always trouble? But I have faith in your abilities. It's time we left. We have some distance to cover to our destination and your smugglers need to catch the tide."

Cade waited until the others had left the cottage before turning out the lamp. Then he stepped outside to where three horses were waiting. A moment later, Tam joined the group, leading Zeus. Cade's carefully applied muddy smears made the gelding less eye-catching.

After they were all mounted, Madame LeBlanc led their small group down to the sandy beach and turned left, heading south away from Calais. Cade took the rear position, all his senses alert for possible danger. The fog distorted sound. Visibility was limited, but the light-colored sand made it easy to follow the edge of the beach. Though the ride was easy, Cade's sense that they were approaching damage became stronger.

After they'd ridden for an hour or so, Madame LeBlanc halted her horse and waited for the others to join her. "We're almost there," she said in a low voice. "Captain Jones, the owner of the boat, is English and he's a good, reliable man. I've already paid him for the journey, but he won't mind if you give him a bonus when you're safely on the other side."

"Understood," Tamsyn said with a smile in her voice.

Something pinged in Cade's mind. He caught his breath and opened his senses as far as he could. "Men are waiting between here and the boat," he said softly. "An ambush."

He could feel his companions tense. "Can we go around?" Tam asked, her voice a mere breath.

Cade glanced at the sea cliff to their left. They'd have to backtrack to reach a place where the horses could go to higher ground, which would risk their boat missing the tide. "Not in the time available. We need to proceed on foot."

As they dismounted, he studied his three companions. They might not look like a military squad, but he knew that all were gifted and determined. "Is everyone here ready and able to fight?"

Madame LeBlanc reached up into her horse's saddlebag and pulled out two pistols and two ammunition pouches. She handed one of each to Cade and kept the other pistol and pouch. "Andre is already armed. Lady Tamsyn?"

"I'm not fond of firearms, but I have an experienced knife I can use if necessary," Tam replied as she flipped back her coat to show a sheathed dagger.

They tethered their horses by a pair of straggly wind-shaped trees. Then those who carried firearms checked that their weapons were primed and ready. But in a situation like this, using their gifts would be even more important.

Cade offered his hand to Tam. "Help me focus."

Her small, strong hand clasped his and his sensing ability expanded sharply. His feelings for her also flared, and she caught her breath until he could get them under control. Their gazes met in the dim light and he felt the impact of their mutual desire, all the more powerful for being suppressed.

Not now, alas, not now. He felt her wry agreement.

What lay ahead? He sensed pulses of energy. "Four men. Three of them are bored and not very alert. One has a fierce, rather jangled mind. I think he's the leader and the most dangerous."

He double-checked his impressions. Yes, what he was seeing was accurate. "I have some stealth ability that should make it possible for us to close in on them without being noticed. With luck, no one will have to die."

"I sincerely hope not!" Tamsyn murmured.

Cade dug into his carry bag and pulled out lengths of rope suitable for binding men's wrists. As he passed them out, he said, "I hope you're all good at tying knots. Now join hands so I can share the stealth energy."

Madame LeBlanc's clasp was firm and he was startled by the combined power of the four of them when Tam and Andre completed the circle. Andre was clever and brave and had faced danger in the past, and it was clear that Madame LeBlanc hadn't spent her life doing embroidery and accounts. Tamsyn, as always, was utterly reliable. Yes, his troops were ready and capable.

He sent energy into the circle, touching each of the others and incorporating their special strengths into the whole. Once the stealth energy was as powerful as they could make it, he said, "We're not invisible, but now we're less likely to be noticed as long as we move carefully. There are four of us and four of them, and we should all be able to get close enough to hold weapons to the heads of the ambushers to persuade them to surrender quietly. Tam, once they're subdued and their wrists are tied, can you do something to calm them down or send them to sleep so they don't cause trouble?"

"Yes," she said with no elaboration.

"That felt . . . very interesting," Andre said with surprise as they released their hands. "Can you teach me how to do it?"

"Perhaps. That depends on your own natural gifts. Once we're in England we can experiment." Cade described the locations of the ambushers and how they would need to move to reach their individual targets. The night was dark and the fog had persisted, but with the aid of the stealth energy, they should be safe. "Watch your footing so you don't fall or crash into anything."

Quietly they moved forward. The murmuring of the waves

covered any slight sounds they made. As they approached their targets, he smelled a whiff of tobacco smoke. Fools.

Since he knew Tam's abilities, he'd assigned her and himself to the longest route that circled around their targets.

As they moved inland from the sea, he kept mental track of the enemy and his own troops. Cade gestured for Tam to stay behind the first man they reached. The fellow was smoking a clay pipe. Cade continued on to the final man, the alert and surely dangerous leader.

His senses were working exceptionally well tonight, and he was able to determine when his friends were in place. He drew a deep breath, then stepped forward and jammed his pistol against the skull of the leader while he bellowed, "Halt and drop your weapons! You're surrounded. We'd prefer not to kill anyone, but we will if we have to!"

After a stunned moment, a spate of filthy French curses burst out. There were sounds of scuffling from Andre's man, which ended when Andre brought him down. There were thuds as other weapons dropped to the ground.

But not the leader's. He jerked away from Cade and spun around, his own weapon raised and ready.

It was Claude Bastien, and he was aiming his pistol straight at Cade's heart.

Cade's gifts included the swift reflexes of a predator, and as he dodged to one side, he grabbed the other man's wrist and twisted viciously hard until the pistol fell to the ground.

As Cade kicked the weapon out of Bastien's reach, he said in a hard voice, "If you wanted me dead, you should have killed me when you had the chance."

"I wish I had!" Bastien agreed, his hands still but his fierce eyes confused. "Are you going to shoot me?"

"Probably not." A swift glance showed that his friends had disarmed their opponents and were now tying up wrists. "Though I'm tempted."

He felt a twinge from Madame LeBlanc, who didn't want to

see her nephew killed even if he wasn't exactly her nephew. She would get her wish as long as Cade didn't have to kill Bastien to protect his friends.

Bastien frowned, his craggy face perplexed. "You really do look like me," he said in a puzzled tone. "I find that very annoying."

"I'm not fond of the resemblance either," Cade said dryly, keeping his pistol aimed at the other man.

"What was our father like?" Bastien asked abruptly.

This was a very strange conversation. "Jago Evans was a violent, selfish bully. He threw me out to die when I was five years old. I've done my best to be completely different from him. You should try to do the same." Cade frowned at his half brother, sensing something off balance in the other man. "Why did you ambush us? To kill? To capture? To torture?"

"I'm . . . not sure why I'm here." Bastien looked baffled, and Cade was beginning to wonder if he was quite right in the head. No wonder he hadn't sensed the Scorpion's distinctive energy this time.

Bastien turned to look at Madame LeBlanc. "I wanted to see my aunt Agnes, who has been avoiding me for some time."

"Because I don't like your behavior, Claude," Madame LeBlanc said tartly. "You have become far too fond of hurting people."

Bastien nodded as if that made perfect sense and turned his gaze to Andre. "I also wanted to see my young cousin. Why are you fleeing to Britain, Andre? I had hoped you would enlist your talents for France."

"Really?" Andre said coolly. "I thought you wanted to see me arrested and interned with the rest of the British men unlucky enough to be caught in France when war broke out again."

"I wanted that once, but it would be a waste of your talents." Bastien still seemed disoriented. He swiveled around and glared at Tamsyn, who had just finished putting the other three men to sleep. "Most of all I want to know what your little witch did to me!"

"I'm not a witch but a healer," Tamsyn replied in a calm voice. "I tried to remove the anger that makes you so dangerous and unpleasant, but I didn't have time to be thorough. I'm sorry I didn't do a better job. Do you want me to correct any imbalance I caused?"

"Can you do that?" he asked doubtfully.

"I believe so, but there might not be time. We have a boat to catch and the tide waits for no one."

"Please," Bastien said, his voice between an order and a plea. "*Try!*"

Cade swore silently, knowing that Tam would not leave until she had repaired the damage she'd done. "Madame LeBlanc, how much time do we have?"

The older woman said in a worried voice, "Perhaps half an hour. Is that long enough, Lady Tamsyn?" Cade guessed that she wanted Claude healed, but even more she wanted her grandson safe.

"It should be," Tam said, but she didn't sound sure.

"If we combine energies to support you, might that speed up the process?" Cade asked.

"I'm sure it would!" Tam replied.

"Please do it," Bastien said, a crack in his voice. "It's . . . hard to live with my mind in a storm."

"Very well then, Monsieur Bastien," she said. "Take a seat on that rock and let us begin."

Chapter 28

Ignoring the pistol Cade still had trained on him, Bastien obeyed Tamsyn and settled on the chair-height rock she had indicated. She was profoundly grateful to be able to correct the errors she'd made earlier when she had been mostly concerned with getting Cade out of the fortress. Touching another person's mind was a grave responsibility and she had betrayed her gift by forcing a change on him, and worse, not doing it well.

He asked uncertainly, "What will you do?"

"I'm not going to turn you into a different person," she explained in a reassuring voice. "You will still be yourself, but with pain and broken edges soothed and healed. It will be disorienting but not physically painful. Is that acceptable to you?"

"I won't recognize who I am without pain," he said starkly. "But yes. Do it!"

She placed her palm on his forehead and began a preliminary assessment. When she'd worked on him at the fortress, his mind had been like a thicket of thorns, filled with anger toward the world. She hadn't had time to discover why then, but now she sorted through his feelings and found fury at his official father, who tolerated Claude because he needed an heir, but who had despised his bastard son for his low-born smuggler father.

With his mother dead in childbirth, Claude had been raised mostly by men. His tutors had often been brutal. Though he'd received a decent education, he'd had very little kindness or understanding.

His anger had served him well when he started to work for the French government because he was excellent at seeking out and destroying traitorous Frenchmen and dangerous English spies. His work was legitimate, but as his aunt had said, he took far too much pleasure in inflicting pain, as he'd done on Cade. Remembering Cade's agony caused Tamsyn to freeze for a moment, but she reminded herself that she was here to heal, not to execute vengeance.

Her hasty earlier work had reduced much of his anger but had left his mind and emotions unbalanced. No wonder he was confused.

Cade's hand came to rest on her right shoulder, and a moment later Madame LeBlanc took gentle hold of her other shoulder. The rush of energy she received from them clarified what she needed to do, and she began to smooth away the confused edges of his emotions. Bastien needed balance. Peace. More awareness of the needs of others.

Her healing moved with amazing swiftness and she recognized that it was because of the added energy from Cade and Madame LeBlanc. At some point she felt Andre join them and she realized that he'd gone to collect their horses so they could ride on as soon as she was finished. She spared a moment of gratitude at how well all their gifts blended. Then she returned to her work.

When she'd done as much as she could, she asked quietly, "How do you feel, Monsieur Bastien?"

His eyes had been closed but they opened now, and his gaze was focused in a way it hadn't been before. After a long, fraught moment, he said unevenly, "My mind feels very different, but yet . . . I am myself."

She removed her palm from his forehead and stepped away. "It will take time for your mind to settle down, but you should soon be comfortable within yourself. Your men will wake soon, none the worse for their rest."

He stood up and shook his head, then stretched his long limbs. The resemblance to Cade was stronger now. "Thank you, Lady Tamsyn. Tante Agnes, I think you will find me less interested in hurting people. I hope we will see more of each other?"

"I hope so also. Please call on me tomorrow if you can, Claude. We have much to talk about." His aunt smiled and patted his cheek. "But now we must be off."

As she collected her horse, Bastien's gaze moved to Cade. "Take good care of my cousin and your little witch." His expression hardened. "It will be best if you don't return to these parts, Tremayne."

Cade's expression was like granite and Tamsyn sensed that he was thinking of the excruciating pain the other man had inflicted on him. The two of them would never be friends, but they were no longer sworn enemies. "I will gladly leave this side of the channel to you, Bastien."

Madame LeBlanc looked at the sky, then mounted, muttering several words that well-bred French ladies weren't supposed to know. Raising her voice, she said, "If we ride hard, we might be able to make our rendezvous. Follow me!" She set off down the beach at a speed that was surely faster than was safe.

Tamsyn was exhausted from all the work she'd done on Bastien. Not surprisingly, Cade noticed and caught her around the waist, then lifted her up onto Zeus's saddle. She looked down at him and said softly, "That was very presumptuous of you, Caden, yet for some reason I never mind when you touch me."

They shared a glance of intense intimacy. He smiled up at

her. "You look tired, Tam, and it's easy to lift you because you're just a little bit of a thing."

"*That* I mind!" She chuckled as she gathered her reins and took off down the beach after Madame LeBlanc. A few moments later she heard the hooves of two more horses as Cade and Andre mounted and followed.

A strengthening wind had blown the fog away and there was enough patchy moonlight to show the way. Reminding herself that Madame LeBlanc knew this coast well, Tam followed the older woman's lead as to changes of speed and avoiding obstacles.

She felt a rush of exhilaration as she flew through the night on the way to freedom and home. It was accompanied by a matching fear that they wouldn't be in time and the smuggler would have left without them, but Cade was right behind her so surely all would be well.

Several times the horses splashed ankle-deep in water and twice they swung briefly away from the sea when blocked by a tumble of rocks. Once in a shadowed area she almost missed seeing a large tree trunk that had been washed up onto the sand in front of her. She had just enough time to signal Zeus to jump and they soared safely over the obstacle.

After perhaps a quarter of an hour of riding, Madame LeBlanc crested a small hill and called over her shoulder, "Almost there!"

Tam caught up with her and saw a small cove below. Her breath spasmed when she saw the dinghy containing three men that was moving away from the shore, already halfway across the cove. *Too late!*

"*Halt, Captain Jones!*" Madame LeBlanc shouted with a note of command in her voice unlike anything Tamsyn had ever heard before. Command must be one of the older woman's gifts that hadn't been needed until now.

Her order echoed across the water and the dinghy paused.

Then it pivoted in a splashing of oars and headed back to the shore.

By the time the bow reached the shallows, all four of the riders had arrived and were dismounting. Jones barked in English, "You cut it pretty damned close, milady!"

"We ran into trouble," she explained as she swung from her horse in a spray of sand. "Here are my three passengers."

"Step lively, you lot!" Jones ordered.

Tamsyn scrambled into the dinghy with Cade's help. Andre turned to hug his grandmother, saying, "Thank you for all you've done for me, Grandmère!"

Her voice unsteady, she said, "Take good care, my dear boy. We may not meet again in this lifetime, but you will always be in my prayers."

"We will meet again." He kissed her cheek. "I promise it!'

None of the three travelers had much luggage, so it took only moments to transfer their bags to the dinghy. When the three passengers were aboard, Jones and his men pushed the small boat out against the waves. As soon as they were afloat, the sailors started rowing hard, the blades of their oars slashing through the water.

Cade settled by Tamsyn on a middle bench, his warm arm around her. No one spoke and the only sound was the crashing of the sea.

The dinghy plowed through increasingly rough waves to reach the sleek waiting cutter in the mouth of the cove. The ship was built for speed so she could escape the revenue agents who usually sailed in similar cutters. As the dinghy passed the bow, Tam saw the name *Sea Swan* painted on the bow, and the bowsprit was carved into the image of a swan lady. An elegant name for an elegant if illegal ship.

They took turns scrambling up a short rope ladder to reach the deck. As soon as they were all on board, half a dozen sailors began to swiftly raise the sails, Tamsyn caught hold of the railing as she watched the coast falling away behind them. Would she ever set foot in France again? For now, she was glad to see the last of it.

Jones approached his passengers, his gaze moving over them. "You're obviously the lady's grandson," he said to Andre, "but who are you two?"

"I'm Cade and this is Tam," Cade said. "We're both from London. We were caught in France when the war resumed."

Shivering in the sharp breeze, Tam asked, "Is there a space belowdecks where we can get out of the wind?"

Jones blinked. "So you're a lass. You should be safe at home doing your embroidery!"

She laughed. "I was always better at getting into trouble than doing fine needlework!"

The captain chuckled. "The weather is getting choppy so you need to keep out of our way." He beckoned to a young sailor. "Jem, take our guests down to the fore cabin, where they can get some rest. Give 'em some brandy to warm them up."

Jem led them to a hatch that opened to reveal a steep ladder. "Watch your step, miss."

The ship was rolling so Tam held on tight as she descended, hearing the snap of sails overhead. To the left she caught a glimpse of the dark hold, which was well filled with contraband.

The cabin was a cramped room lit by a dim lantern and containing a set of bunk beds, carefully secured storage, and a very small desk. She guessed it was the captain's office. With four people in the cabin it was crowded, and the ceiling was barely high enough for Cade to stand straight.

Jem opened a cupboard and pulled out a bottle. "Some of France's finest," he said with a grin, "but you'd best use the water in this jug to thin it down. It's going to be a rough passage. If any of you get seasick, please use that bucket as I'm the one who will have to clean up after you!"

"Thank you, Jem," Tam said warmly as she pulled off her wet hat, revealing her blond hair. "We're all experienced sailors so I hope we'll be all right."

Though he knew she was female, his eyes widened at the sight of her face. He swallowed hard before saying, "There's blankets in that chest, miss. Help yourself. The bunks have railings that flip up so you won't fall out." He demonstrated how the lower bunk railing worked. "There's food and ale in that basket if you're hungry. Now I need to get back on deck."

After Jem left, Andre sagged onto the lower bunk and buried his head in his hands. "So we're on our way!" he said in an unsteady voice. "I never thought I'd make it this far."

Tam sat beside him and rested a sympathetic hand on his shoulder. "You've had a long, long journey. It takes courage to go to a strange land. I hope you find the life you're seeking in Britain."

"I want to be free to learn and study to be an engineer like my father." He raised his head, his expression uncertain. "I also hope to meet a friend. Elizabeth Caton. Beth and I grew up together in India. Her father and mine were both engineers. They worked together for the Sultan of Mysore, but the Catons returned to Britain three years ago."

It was easy to read his feelings. "Elizabeth is very special to you?"

"She was." He shrugged. "Impossible to know how she feels now, but I very much want to find her once I'm in England."

Cade had been leaning against the wall opposite the bunks as he sipped his brandy. "Do you know where she's living now?"

"Her father works in the Royal Arsenal at Woolwich. That's part of London, isn't it?"

Tam gave Cade a swift glance, guessing they both felt a flicker of energy when the Royal Arsenal was mentioned. He gave her a slight nod. "Yes, it's in the southeast area of the city and there are a number of military and naval institutions there.

If her father is working at the Arsenal, he should be easy to find."

"I surely hope so." Andre swallowed the last of his watered brandy, then covered a yawn. "Would either of you mind if I take the top bunk? I've barely slept in days."

"Go ahead," Tam said. "We'll manage."

Andre took off his boots and coat, then climbed the ladder at the end of the bunk. As he rolled himself in a blanket, Tam said, "Sleep well. Tomorrow we'll be in England."

He gave her a slight, sweet smile, then murmured good night. He slid almost immediately into the regular breathing of sleep.

"Sleep sounds good," Cade said quietly. "If we lie on our sides, we'll both fit on the bottom bunk. Unless you'd rather sleep alone? I can take the floor."

"Don't talk nonsense," she murmured as she stripped off her boots and coat. She flipped the railing of the lower bunk into place and estimated that they'd both fit, barely.

Smiling, Cade also stripped off his outer clothing, then crawled into the bunk, his back against the wall. Tam climbed in beside him, her back to his front.

As she pulled the rough blanket over both of them, she gave a sigh of pleasure and relaxation. Cade's arm went around her waist. He was so wonderfully warm after a chilly night of riding. She loved the physicality of his body surrounding hers, and they fit together perfectly.

"Sleep well, my love," he whispered as he brushed a kiss against her hair.

She loved hearing the endearment. Once she and Cade reached England, they would have to figure out how to have a future together. Surely there would be a way.

She thought of all the members the Tribe of Tremayne. She loved each and every one of them; the bond she felt with each was special and unique.

But as she thought back, she realized that her bond with Cade had always been especially special, if one could say such a thing. She'd loved him since they'd first met as children. For all the years since he'd been considered a brother, but he'd always been in a category of his own. He'd been her best friend, the one she turned to first, and she loved and trusted him.

She'd met Bran at the same time, and she also loved and trusted him entirely. But if she was defining relationships, she'd say that Bran was truly her brother while Cade was . . . something different. *More.*

Cade was a loyal and loving brother to all the Tremayne sisters, but apparently he'd also put Tamsyn in a different category all her own. He'd recognized that difference early but kept it hidden until he'd spoken those words of love when his mind was in chaos. Once spoken, the words couldn't be unheard, and they were changing how she thought of him.

Bran was a wonderful brother. Cade was her one and only beloved. It was so obvious now. How could she and Cade explain that to the rest of the family without causing grave damage? Particularly when all the Tremaynes had at least some ability to sense emotions.

That was a problem for another day, but she believed it could be solved. She *had* to believe that because the closer she and Cade became, the less she could imagine being separated from him.

She wriggled comfortably against Cade, feeling his breath and warmth and strength. The ship was rolling gently, like the rocking of a cradle.

She drifted into sleep with a smile on her face, and dreamed of what it would be like for them if—*when*—they fully became lovers.

Chapter 29

Cade didn't want to sleep and miss any of the delight of having Tamsyn in his arms, but fatigue won. As Captain Jones had warned, the channel seas were rough, but the cutter was steady on her path north.

He was jolted to full wakefulness by a deep boom that echoed over the waves like a cannon shot. Damnation, surely it *was* a cannon shot!

Tamsyn also woke, asking sleepily, "What the devil was that?"

"I suspect it's a revenue cutter," he said grimly as he swung over her to get to his feet. As he yanked on his boots and coat, he said, "Stay here. I'll go up on deck to see what's happening."

She muttered an oath and flipped the railing down, then sat up on the edge of the bunk. "I hope you're wrong, but I don't think you are."

Andre rolled restlessly on the upper bunk but didn't wake. Cade left the cabin at top speed, saying, "I'll let you know what I learn."

As soon as he emerged from the hatch onto the deck, he was

hit by a fierce wind. A burly sailor stood at the wheel, fighting to keep the cutter on course. Jones stood beside him, facing the stern as he scanned the sea with a spyglass and a grim expression.

"Revenue cutter?" Cade asked.

"Not sure yet," the captain said tersely. He lowered the spyglass, muttering, "They say it's bad luck to sail with a woman on board."

"Don't blame Tamsyn for this," Cade said in a hard-edged voice as he looked in the same direction as Jones. It was dawn and the sky was beginning to lighten, though a heavy overcast made visibility poor. "Surely revenue cutters are one of the dangers of the smuggling trade."

"Yes, but not the only danger." Jones raised the spyglass again, then swore. "I think it's a French patrol ship."

Cade frowned. "Is that better or worse?"

"Worse. Either side would prefer to capture us and our cargo rather than blow us to bits, but if it's the Revenue, we'll be taken to England. Maybe end up in jail, though you'd probably be safe since you're a trapped Briton coming home."

"And if the French capture us, every man on the ship will be arrested and interned," Cade said flatly. God only knew what would happen to Tam as the only female on board.

Another cannon shot boomed, and Cade flinched as he saw a splash where the ball hit the water not far to port. A second shot tore through one of the head sails and barely missed the single mast. The cutter lurched and lost speed.

Cade squinted and managed to see the French ship in the distance. It was larger than the cutter with two masts, and it carried more sail. It was just a matter of time until the ship caught up.

Tamsyn's voice sounded behind Cade. "I presume we can't outrun the French. Does this ship carry any guns?"

"Nothing to match the French artillery." Jones was grim-faced.

Cade swore under his breath. He should have known Tam

wouldn't stay below. He glanced over and saw that she had a secure grip on the ship's railing. Behind her was Andre, his face pale and his grip on the railing white knuckled as he saw his dreams of England slipping away. Trying to keep his voice steady, he said, "Grandmère told me the *Sea Swan* is a lucky ship. But maybe it isn't today?"

"The French haven't caught us yet," Jones said gruffly. "But it wouldn't hurt to pray for divine aid."

Tam peered at their attacker. "It looks like a squall is coming this way. Could that conceal us from the enemy?"

"We might be able to do something with that," Cade said, thinking it was time to see if he could change the weather even a little bit. He concentrated on the squall, willing it to draw closer and grow stronger.

They all stared as the squall indeed strengthened and moved between the *Swan* and the French. Tam said, "Cade, do you think we might be able to invoke stealth so that we seem to disappear in the squall?"

Cade inhaled sharply. "It's worth a try." He turned to the captain. "Did the French lady tell you that we three passengers are all gifted?"

Jones lowered the spyglass, frowning. "No, she didn't, likely because she knows how some folk feel about them. I'm fine with gifted people if they do their jobs. Think you can do something to help us escape the French?"

"We invoked stealth when we were riding to meet you, and it allowed us to encircle the men who were waiting in ambush for us," Tamsyn said.

"A ship might be harder to conceal," Andre said, but his tone was thoughtful rather than defeated.

"What other choice do we have?" Cade said. "Captain Jones, are any of your crew gifted? For something like this we work by joining our abilities. The more power we have, the better our chances of escape."

"My boy Jem is gifted," the captain said. "So is my helmsman here and one of my other sailors, Matt." He issued an order to Jem, who immediately went off to summon his crewmate.

Jones waved his helmsman away and took over the wheel himself. "See what you can do with them, Gibbs."

Scowling, Gibbs muttered, "I ain't got any of them weird talents."

"You might not want to admit it, but you always know where the *Swan* is and where the best breezes are," Jones said. "Those are powerful gifts for those of us who live on the sea."

"Every bit of power helps, Mr. Gibbs." When Tamsyn smiled at the helmsman and took his hand, his expression became more cooperative.

"How do we do this?" Jem asked as he returned with Matt, another young sailor.

"We join hands. Tam and I will each put a hand on the ship's railing so that we connect with the *Sea Swan*. Then just relax and let your energy flow. I'll direct it toward the ship," Cade said. "This may take a while. If it's too much for you, speak up so I can adjust as you leave."

Tamsyn added, "You should be able to feel each person's energy, and it's a good feeling. Ready?"

Nods and curiosity all around. Cade closed his eyes and reached out to the others to join them into a cohesive group. The energies flowed together easily and he realized that the six of them together were generating great power. He also recognized how much of the smoothness of the joining was because of Tam, who clearly had a gift for blending energies. He and Tam and Andre were the most powerful of the group, but the three sailors made significant contributions that were tuned to the sea.

When he felt that he had full command of the energy, he

started with a light touch on the squall. It strengthened immediately, and wasn't that interesting? He needed to explore weather working later.

He shifted his focus to making the *Sea Swan* hard to detect. He envisioned the ship's shape and its sails blending into the gray waves, impossible for their French pursuer to detect.

He heard an awed curse from Jones and sensed that the captain was changing the vessel's course so they wouldn't be where the French ship was looking. More westerly. That felt like a wise decision.

He wasn't sure how long the group held hands and created stealth, but it was a long time. Then a moment came when it felt all right to release the energy. "I think we're safe now, so we can let go," he said, realizing he was shaking with fatigue.

"Well, that was interesting!" Jem exclaimed. He was on Cade's right side and he released their hands, opening and closing his fingers to loosen them.

"If this is what it means to be a member of the Tribe of Tremayne, I want to join!" Andre exclaimed. "Do you do this sort of thing often?"

Cade shook his head. "It was a new technique for a dangerous new situation." He surveyed the others who had joined the gifted circle. Gibbs, the helmsman, was impressed at what they'd done and seemed more willing to accept the gifted side of his nature.

Jem and Matt were very pleased with themselves and wanted to learn more. And Tam—when her warm gaze met his, he felt as if they had almost read each other's minds while they were working so closely together.

"If we're safe now, Captain Jones, I plan to return to my bunk and sleep," Tam said as she leaned wearily against the railing. "We did good work, but I'm exhausted. I think we all are."

The captain looked them over. "You look like a bunch of half-dead flowers. We can manage on this course for the next few hours." He glanced at the sea ahead. "We'll be landing farther west than I originally planned, but I know a good safe place. Get some food and rest now."

Food. What an excellent idea. As was rest. Feeling ready to sleep the clock around, Cade followed Jem and Tamsyn and Andre below to the cabin they'd spent the night in.

When they reached the cabin, Jem said with amazement, "That was something, it was! I feel like I learned a lot about being gifted." He hesitated. "And maybe my gift is stronger now?"

"It might well be," Tam said. "This is new for us, too!'

Inside the cabin, Jem picked up the food basket and lifted the lid. "Bread and cheese and hard-cooked eggs. There are a couple of jugs of ale here, too."

"What about you, Jem?" Tam asked. "Surely you need food and rest as well."

"There's an aft crew cabin like this but larger," he explained. "Gibbs and my friend Matt will already be there. Andre, would you like to join us? There's more space there and we can ask you about being gifted while we eat. There are more bunks there as well for resting up."

"I'd like that," Andre glanced at Cade and Tamsyn. "That will leave more space for you two."

What a very thoughtful young man Andre was. As soon as he and Jem left the cabin, Cade drew Tamsyn into his arms. As she leaned into him, he held her tight, needing to feel her warmth and softness and healing strength. They breathed together for long moments and he felt her restoring his strength and sanity. Then, because they were alone, he kissed her while backing against the door so no one could interrupt them.

Tam kissed him back with sweet enthusiasm, her mouth and body equally soft. When she pulled back a little, she whispered, "I can feel myself getting stronger. Or am I imagining that?"

"I feel it, too," he agreed. "Sharing energy to accomplish a particular task has interesting effects."

Tam bit her lip thoughtfully. "We'll have to talk to Gwyn and Rhys about this."

"And Bran since he's the expert in analysis." He smiled down into Tamsyn's eyes. "For now, let's eat and then renew our acquaintance with the bunk bed."

"The sooner the better!" Tam gave Cade a shy glance. "Even though we now have two bunks, I'd like to share one with you again."

"So would I!" Cade crawled into the lower bunk as he had the night before.. Tam joined him and latched the railing to hold them in place. She felt so utterly right in his arms. He wondered if they'd ever be able to fully consummate their love.

He hoped so, but for now, this was enough.

Chapter 30

It was dusk when the *Sea Swan* deposited her passengers at the pier in a tiny fishing hamlet. As the cutter temporarily moored at the pier, Captain Jones said, "I'd meant to leave you near Brighton, but as you know, we needed to sail farther west." He gestured at one of the hills that bracketed the small harbor. "This is at the western edge of Littlehampton. There's a nice inn up the High Street, the King's Arms. A good place to get dinner and spend the night. The owners can set you up with horses or a carriage tomorrow."

"Thank you for getting us here, Captain," Tam said as she gave him a bonus payment.

He glanced at the bills. "I should be paying you for keeping me and my ship from being captured by the French!"

"But you did get us here safely." Cade smiled. "Perhaps we'll meet again if we should need a talented smuggler in the future."

Jones gave a booming laugh. "I'll welcome that if it happens! But for now, I have customers in Cornwall waiting for my cargo."

As the *Swan* set off to sea, Cade took Tamsyn's carry bag and added it to his own. As the three of them walked along the pier to the shore, Tam said feelingly, "I'll be glad to sleep in a proper bed tonight! A bunk bed is just not the same!" The mischievous slanting glance she gave Cade made him smile.

The narrow street that ran up the hill was lined with small, neatly kept stone cottages. There were no people in sight, but a snoozing hound in the street raised his head to study them, then went back to sleep.

The King's Arms had a weathered sign board hanging out into the lane. As Cade and Tam and Andre approached, a well-dressed man emerged from the door and turned to look down toward the pier.

The man stopped dead in his tracks and the last rays of the setting sun illuminated his dark hair and familiar beloved face. *Bran!*

Chapter 31

Bran gave a whoop and surged forward to Cade with a rib-crushing hug. "Damn, I'm glad to see you! I wasn't sure if I'd ever lay eyes on either of you again!"

They weren't usually so affectionate, but Cade hugged his brother back with all his strength. He felt the pain and anxiety that Bran had endured, and now this rush of relief. The embrace reminded him of when they were small children escaping certain death at the baby farm. Cade had known how to fight, but Bran was the one who created hope. They had become true brothers then and forever.

"It's a great relief to see both of you." Bran released Cade and pulled Tamsyn into his arms. "Tam, you're a miracle worker!"

Not afraid of tears, she hugged him back and said in a choked voice, "How did you find us?"

He grinned. "I was taking a quick trip to Portsmouth, and it was time to stop for the night. I had a feeling that there was some place I should be. And it was here."

"That's how intuition works," Tam said with amused understanding.

Moving out of Bran's embrace, she caught Andre's arm and pulled him forward. "Bran, meet Andre Jameson, a gifted young gentleman whose remarkable grandmother was instrumental in freeing Cade and getting us safely back to England. Andre, this is my brother Bran Tremayne."

Bran turned and caught Andre's hand. "Welcome! Are you a new addition to the Tribe of Tremayne?"

Andre smiled as they shook hands. "Perhaps not a full Tremayne but maybe a cousin? Meeting your brother and sister has been remarkably interesting."

For an instant Cade saw something quick and unexpected as Bran's gaze flicked from Cade to Tamsyn, but when he spoke, it was to Andre. "All Tremaynes are interesting. It's a requirement. Along with being gifted."

"Andre definitely qualifies," Tam said. "Since he grew up in India, I want to hear about elephants!"

"Then your timing is excellent," Bran said. "Mrs. Williams, who owns the King's Arms with her husband, is preparing dinner now and there are rooms available as well. We can discuss our adventures, including elephants, over dinner."

Tam took his arm. "Lead on, Bran! A clean room and good dinner will be most welcome. I can even put on a dress again! But where's Merryn? Aren't you still on your honeymoon?"

"We should be, but needs must," he said regretfully. "Rhys really wanted me to make this visit to Portsmouth. Merryn and I reached London three days ago. We're staying at Tremayne House so she can become better acquainted with the younger Tremaynes. I considered bringing her along to Portsmouth, but Gwyn persuaded us that she and the younger sisters needed to introduce Merryn to the delights of the metropolis."

Tamsyn chuckled. "You're wise to stay away."

"Very likely you're right, but I miss her!"

As they reached the entrance to the inn, Cade said, "You've become the Home Office's official expert on possible dangers in royal dockyards?"

"Apparently. Portsmouth is even larger than the Devenport Royal Dockyard," Bran said. "I'll tell you more about that later."

As he opened the door to the inn, he said more seriously, "I've been rather worried. For a while earlier you both seemed to . . . to disappear from my mind. Usually, I have a sense of both of you, so losing that sense was . . . disturbing."

Cade thought a moment. "Perhaps that was when the three of us and three gifted sailors on the smuggler's cutter worked to wrap the ship in stealth, for lack of a better description. We were being pursued by a French naval vessel that we couldn't outrun. The stealth worked on the French, but it didn't occur to me that the effect would be so broad."

Bran's eyes widened. "I definitely want to hear more about that!" He glanced around the entry hall. "I'll go find the Williamses. I believe there are two vacant rooms, one each for Tam and Andre. There are two beds in my room so Cade can stay with me and we can talk all night."

"Just like old times," Cade said with a smile, though he hated the idea that he and Tam wouldn't be together. How quickly he'd become used to sharing a bed, or a bunk, with her. To being able to touch her and feel her warm spirit.

After Bran left in search of the proprietors, Andre asked, "Does he always have that much energy?"

Tam laughed. "Bran likes organizing things." She sank into one of the wood chairs in the hall. "I'm more than happy to leave matters in his hands."

Her faith wasn't misplaced. It was only a few minutes before Bran returned with the proprietors. "Mr. and Mrs. Williams," Bran said, "Let me introduce you to my brother and sister, Tamsyn and Cade Tremayne, and our cousin Andre Jameson."

"Welcome to the King's Arms!" the landlady said warmly. "You've just enough time to take your belongings to your rooms and wash up before dinner is served. Come along with me, lass."

As she escorted Tamsyn upstairs, Mr. Williams took charge of the men. Andre was given a small but spanking clean room of his own, and Bran took Cade to their larger shared room.

When they entered, Cade pulled his battered carry bag from where it was slung across his chest. "I presume you took the bed by the window, as is your custom?"

"Of course," his brother said.

Cade dropped his bag on the nearer bed and turned to the washstand. "It's so good to be back in England, where all we have to worry about is spies and saboteurs instead of imprisonment and torture."

"I can only imagine just how good that feels," Bran said seriously as he sat on the edge of his bed. "I presume you never want to set foot in France again."

"Too right!" Cade went to the washbasin to scrub, then dry his face. "But I definitely want to discuss the interesting results we've been getting by energy sharing."

He combed his hair and made a half-hearted attempt to straighten his travel-worn clothing. Then the two of them headed down the stairs, closely followed by Tamsyn and Andre. Tam had donned a simple blue gown and looked modest and maidenly, though rather wrinkled. Completely and irresistibly adorable.

They were directed to a small dining room, which they had to themselves, and were soon indulging in a thoroughly British meal of cheddar cheese soup and a large and very tasty shepherd's pie, accompanied by bread and cheese and pickled onions.

Cade had enjoyed the wine that was always available in France, but a fine English ale tasted very good tonight. Andre approached the meal a little warily. But being young, hungry, and adventurous, he ate his share with gusto after the first tastes.

When the first rush of eating slowed, Cade asked Bran, "Is

there a particular danger threatening the Portsmouth Naval Yard?"

"Not that I know of," Bran said as he buttered a piece of bread. "But now that war has resumed, all military installations are at risk of damage from French agents. The Commissioner of the Portsmouth Yard is interested in whether someone like me can train gifted members of his forces to better detect potential danger."

"An interesting question," Tam said thoughtfully. "Do you think you can provide effective training?"

"I have no idea," he said. "But it will be interesting to find out. Now I want to hear how you used shared energy so effectively that the enemy lost sight of your smuggler's ship."

"It might be easiest to demonstrate," Cade said. Tamsyn sat on his left and Andre on his right, so he joined hands with both of them. "Bran, close your eyes while we try invoking stealth. You can tell us what you sense and then what you see."

Bran obediently closed his eyes. Cade glanced at Tam and Andre as he shared energy with them and then summoned stealth. It was easy compared to the hard work they'd done to protect the *Sea Swan*.

After a couple of minutes passed, Bran gave a soft whistle. "Interesting. Even with my eyes closed, I could sense all three of you. And then you slipped out of my mind. Andre first, probably because I've only just met him. Then Tam, then you last of all, Cade."

"Presumably because you've known me the longest," Cade said. "What happens when you open your eyes?"

Bran's eyes opened. Looking bemused, he said, "I can see all three of you, but if we weren't all sitting at the same table only a few feet apart, I think my gaze would slide away from you. Very interesting."

"The next best thing to invisibility," Tam observed. "I wonder if any of us can do this alone, or if Cade has to be part of the link?"

They experimented further. Cade definitely had the strong-est gift for this particular action, but all of them had some abil-ity now that they knew how to tap into it.

The dinner ended when Mrs. Williams provided a large pot of tea and a plate of small currant cakes. Another round of eat-ing and drinking followed. When they were about to break up, Andre said, "Dining with the Tribe of Tremayne is amazingly educational and entertaining! Are all of your meals like this?"

Bran laughed. "Not usually, but we've had much to discuss." He considered. "Do any of you three want to join me on my visit to the Portsmouth Royal Navy Yard? It would be inter-esting to see if this energy-sharing technique might be useful in detecting potential threats to the facility."

"Thank you for the suggestion, but I want to go home! We should be getting back to London," Tam said firmly.

"You can send a message to Rhys and Gwyn that you're both safely back in England and that you've found a new cousin," Bran said persuasively. "You'll only be delayed a cou-ple of days."

Tam stood and covered a yawn. "I'll sleep on it. For now, Mr. Williams has promised me hot water for washing up, after which I'll collapse on that very fine bed in a place where Cade and Andre and I can all feel *safe!*"

"Can't argue with that!" Bran said with a smile. "We can dis-cuss the possibility of Portsmouth in the morning."

Cade trailed the others up the stairs to their rooms. He'd hope for an unobtrusive private moment with Tam, but that didn't turn out to be possible. They exchanged glances when she turned at her door to say good night, and her smile made it almost like a kiss. Alas, not close enough.

He followed Bran into their shared room and immediately pulled off his coat and boots. Bran did the same, saying, "I know you've had a very difficult time. I want to hear as much as you want to talk about, which probably isn't everything."

Cade thought back through the eventful weeks since Bran

and Merryn's wedding. He'd known excruciating pain and bone-deep fear . . . and so much more. "You've always been an excellent listener. But much of what happened you already know, and some things really shouldn't be talked about."

Quietly Bran said, "Does that include you and Tamsyn?"

Cade froze. "Is it so obvious?"

"It is to me. We each have things we don't care to talk about, but we've never really kept secrets from each other."

Cade straightened up and studied his brother's expression. "Are you horrified?"

Bran's brows drew together. "My first reaction was shock and surprise. My second was *not* to be surprised. When Gwyn and Rhys brought us to Tremayne House, frozen and half starved, Tam welcomed us to the family with open arms. She was wonderful and I knew I would love her as my sister forever. You had your own relationship with her that was equally strong, but different. Unique to the two of you. Looking back, I realize that you've always loved her, but not as a sister."

Cade sank down on the chair beside his bed. "You notice too damned much!"

"One of the downsides of being gifted," Bran said dryly. "I'm guessing that you never spoke about your feelings to Tam or anyone else."

Voice hard, Cade said, "Of course not. But Claude Bastien, my unwanted half brother, thought we were married and said as much to me. In my addled state, I believed him. After Tam rescued me, I kissed her as if she was my wife."

Bran's brows arched. "That surely set the cat among the pigeons!"

"Much mutual confusion followed," Cade agreed, thinking back to the satisfaction and shock of that kiss. "I apologized for the kiss, but . . . we found that what I'd said changed . . . everything. Yet I can't see a future for us because of the damage our relationship would cause to the rest of the family."

Bran nodded gravely. "What does Tam think?"

"She's more optimistic than I am." Cade smiled involuntarily. "She always has been. One of the many reasons I love her."

"She's very lovable," Bran said. "But as you both know, the situation will be . . . challenging."

"I'm all too aware of that." Cade drew a deep breath before asking the hardest question. "What do you think will happen in the family if Tam and I say we're in love and want to marry? Will Rhys and Gwyn forbid me to ever enter Tremayne House again?"

"Nothing so drastic," Bran said reassuringly. "I think they'll be surprised, or at least Rhys will. Gwyn is less likely to be because she has a better sense of the emotions of all her children."

"Whereas Rhys is a protective father to all of us and might disown me for taking advantage of his beloved eldest daughter," Cade said flatly.

"Anyone who believes that Tam can be taken advantage of doesn't know her very well," Bran said dryly. "I expect that after the first shock, Rhys will see reason. If there's going to be trouble, it will be among the younger members of the family, particularly the girls. They all adore Tam and have her firmly on a pedestal. Some might have trouble seeing her as a woman in her own right rather than as an icon."

Cade frowned as he thought of the younger Tremayne brothers and sisters. "I think you may be right. They'll surely blame me for behaving badly where Tam is concerned."

Bran nodded. "Some will think it's romantic, others will be appalled."

"What about Cameron? I've always suspected that he might be half in love with Tam himself. That makes me the villain again."

"Perhaps, but he rather idolizes you. He might think that you're a worthy mate for the Tremayne golden girl."

Taken aback, Cade said, "Why would he idolize me? That's ridiculous!"

"You underestimate the effect you have on others." Bran's

expression became troubled. "I think there's a reasonably good chance the family will eventually accept a marriage between you and Tam, but I have no idea how any given family member will react, nor how long acceptance would take."

Cade wished Bran's analysis was more optimistic, but it sounded realistic. Bran was always honest with him. He asked quietly, "How do *you* feel, Bran? Your opinion matters more to me than anyone else's."

"I want you to be as happy as Merryn and I are," Bran said, his gaze direct. "If you and Tamsyn are right for each other, I hope and pray that you can find a way to be together that everyone can accept."

"Thank you," Cade said awkwardly. "It would be very hard if you disapproved."

"This brings up an important question," Bran said slowly. "Is she as committed to you as you are to her?"

Cade's first reaction was to retort that of course she was, but then he forced himself to be objective because that question was critically important. Leave it to Bran to ask it. "I think so, but I'm . . . not quite sure. I've been in love with Tam for years, but this is new for her."

Though the mutual attraction was strong, he wondered uneasily if Tamsyn might be confusing the discovery of passion with deep, lasting love. He hated that thought, but in fairness to her, the issue must be considered. "With everyone in the family gifted, I suspect that she and I can't even talk to each other without other Tremaynes noticing now that we're back in England."

Bran's expression became thoughtful. "There may be a way around that. Your gift for stealth. If you want to go to her room tonight to talk or anything else, you should be able to do so unnoticed."

Startled, Cade said, "I hadn't thought of using stealth in such a personal way."

"Why not? It could be a useful way to give you and Tam the chance to work out your future without having an audience watching and judging."

"An excellent idea." Cade smiled a little. "Ideas have always been your specialty."

"Here's another one. Don't call on Tam until she's had time to wash up." Bran laughed. "She's surely cherishing having hot water and won't want to be interrupted. And get that expression off your face!"

Cade groaned. It was hard not to imagine Tam blissfully enjoying the hot water as she washed her bare curves. Her blond hair would be pinned on top of her head and a few silken tendrils would curl around her neck. "You're right. And now that you mention it, I could use a good washup, too. I'd love fresh clothes as well, but I don't have much with me."

"I brought along a change of clothing for you," Bran said.

Cade stared at him. "You were that confident you'd find me?"

"Not exactly confident, but hopeful." Bran reached under his bed and pulled out his traveler bag. "If you want to go down to order some hot water, I'll unpack the outfit I brought."

"You are the best of brothers!" Cade exclaimed.

Bran laughed. "Indeed I am!"

Chapter 32

Tamsyn usually enjoyed the freedom of wearing boy's clothing, but after doing that continuously for so long, it was a pleasure to dress as a female again. She hung up the blue morning gown she'd worn to dinner in the hope that some of the wrinkles would fall out, and after her delightful hot-water washup, she donned a soft shift to sleep in. Mrs. Williams had lent her a cozy shawl for the evening, and she felt thoroughly pampered.

As she combed the tangles from her freshly washed hair, she wondered if Cade and Bran really would talk all night. Quite possibly, and much of their discussion would surely be about her and Cade.

She was starting to braid her hair in preparation for going to bed when there was a soft knock on her door. As she crossed the room to open it, she wondered who would be calling at this late hour, but she couldn't sense who was on the other side of the door. Which was interesting because she almost always knew.

She opened the door and blinked in surprise to see Cade. He was wearing only a shirt and trousers, both fresh, probably supplied by Bran. Cade looked equally tense and yearning.

"Come in." She stood back so he could enter. "I didn't feel you there."

"Bran suggested using stealth so I could visit with you in private," he explained as he closed the door.

"What a very fine idea!" She stepped up to him and rose on her toes to slip her arms around his neck so she could draw his face down for a kiss.

Passion flared as his mouth opened against hers and his beautiful strong hands stroked down her back, kneading and caressing and bringing every fiber of her being to life. The kiss lasted for a gloriously long time. As heat and a golden glow rose between them, she thought dizzily that she didn't need Mrs. Williams's shawl anymore.

Then Cade broke the kiss and stepped back, luckily keeping his hands on her shoulders or she might have lost her balance. "This isn't why I came here," he said unevenly.

She tilted her head. "No?"

He swallowed hard, his face tight in the lamplight. "At least, not the main reason."

He was serious, she realized. She stepped away, glad she hadn't dropped the shawl since she was cold again. "Have a seat."

She gestured at the room's one wooden chair, then perched on the edge of the bed, pulling the shawl tight. "Did Bran sense what's between us?"

Cade sighed. "Of course he did."

"Not surprising considering how well he knows us both." She bit her lip. "What was his reaction?"

"He wants us both to be happy and if it's with each other, we have his blessing," Cade said tersely. "But..." His voice trailed off.

"Of course there's a 'but,'" she said a little tartly. "Does he think a romance between us will shatter the Tribe of Tremayne?"

"Not necessarily." Cade paused as if searching for words.

198 Mary Jo Putney

"But he's concerned that we're moving too quickly. I've always known that I love you, but for you it's a new idea. Desire can be a kind of madness and it might masquerade as love when in fact, it's only madness."

She drew her knees to her chest and wrapped her arms around them as she considered his words. "That's a fair point, but Bran may be worrying unnecessarily. Don't desire and love often go hand in hand? They seemed to when Bran and Merryn met."

"Yes," Cade agreed, "but our situation is more complicated. *Much* more complicated."

She studied his strong, concerned face. Cade and Bran were the oldest Tremayne sons and they'd modeled themselves after Rhys, who was the most responsible, compassionate, and protective father imaginable. As the bastard son of a smuggler, Cade in particular was always willing to put his own needs last if he thought doing so would help another family member. The dear, foolish man.

"Cade, your desire to protect me from my own possible errors is admirable but unnecessary. I have the right to make my own mistakes."

He frowned. "I didn't think you ever made mistakes."

"They're rare," she agreed, "but I'm quite sure I'm not making one now. Though your declaration of love was a shocking surprise, it released a part of myself that I'd been suppressing. Because of that, I'm sure of what I'm doing." She uncoiled from her position on the high bed and slid to the floor. "And it's not a mistake."

She moved forward and embraced him again, leaning into him both physically and emotionally. "I know you don't ever want to hurt me in any way."

"I would die first," he said unsteadily.

She smiled up at him. "Isn't that rather melodramatic? I don't want you to die. I want you to trust me enough to make my own choices and my own mistakes." She laughed a little. "Which we have both admitted are extremely rare!"

His expression eased. "I can't think of any mistakes you've ever made."

"I could give you a list, but what I want you to accept is that I have the right to choose my own path, and what I choose is *you*."

She raised her face for another kiss, and when their lips met with intoxicating desire, she rolled her hips against him. His response was instant and unmistakable.

"I can't resist you," he said a little helplessly.

"You aren't supposed to resist!" she said as she caught his hand and tugged him toward the bed. "We are here together now, wanting each other equally. I trust you to take care of me when I need it, and you need to trust me to care for you equally. Can you do that, my darling man?"

He began to laugh. "I've never been able to win an argument against you!"

"Why would you want to when I'm right?"

He laughed again. "I bow to your matchless wisdom, my darling lady!"

She backed into the bed. It was high so Cade swooped her up and laid her tenderly in the center of the mattress. He stretched out beside her and skimmed his hand along her body from the curve of her cheek, over her breasts and belly, down to her thighs, pausing there to let the heat of his palm warm her. Everywhere he touched came alive with golden yearning, a desire for *more*.

"You are so lovely. Perfect and exquisite in all ways."

She chuckled. "I'm grateful for the sweet words, and for the fact that the light is rather dim here!"

He shook his head, smiling down at her. "You are beautiful in all light and all situations."

"Even when I'm rumpled and wearing clothing that has been saturated in seawater so I must taste like a lightly salted fish?"

"Especially then because you shine with beauty and grace

even when you look as if you've been washed and salted." He bent forward and kissed her throat. "Not salty at all. In fact you smell like lavender."

"Mrs. Williams was generous with her handmade soap."

Needing to touch him back, she brushed his cheek with her fingertips. He'd shaved and she felt only the faintest prickle of whiskers, erotic and masculine. A golden sensation curled through her, increasing her desire. She knew that Bran saw silver when something important was at stake. Was this golden glow she felt with Cade similar? She didn't really need to discuss it with Bran. She already knew that this golden glow was a gift beyond price.

She slipped her hand around his neck and pulled his head down for another kiss. His mouth was a miracle, deliciously Cade, amazingly stimulating. She'd been kissed by aspiring suitors and had never found their caresses very interesting. But Cade? "You have the most wonderful mouth," she murmured.

He gave a mock growl. "The better to eat you with, my delectable little morsel!" He nibbled down her neck, and didn't that feel wonderful? The air sparkled with golden light.

Her shift had buttons almost to her waist, and he undid them one by one as his lips moved sensuously over her bare skin until they reached her breast. She gasped as a sensation shot directly from her nipple to her loins.

She was even more shocked when she realized that he'd drawn her shift up around her waist and his fingertips had drifted to the incredibly sensitive area between her thighs. His delicate stroking created a wholly improbable amount of heat and desire. Panting, she buried her fingers in his dark hair to bring him even closer.

Then his lips followed his fingertips to that frighteningly sensitive place. "Cade!" she gasped as his magically gifted tongue triggered a cascade of sensations that exploded into searing need even more intense than what she'd felt that amazing night of discovery they'd spent together at the cottage.

Her body thrashed out of control yet felt safely held by his strength and protective body as she reached a peak unlike anything she'd ever experienced. "*Cade!*"

The fierce sensations flowed away, leaving her limp with astonishment and satisfaction. Cade rested his cheek against her belly as he whispered, "My darling, darling princess."

When her mind had returned to rationality, she said huskily, "Act One was a stunning success. Now it's time for Act Two."

She wriggled so that she was lying on her side beside him, her hand free to roam his body. She sensed his emotions, his profound pleasure with how he'd satisfied her, but his body was tense and controlled until she unbuttoned his fall and slid her hand under to clasp that pulsing length of fascinating male flesh.

He gave a strangled gasp. "With a very small amount of effort on your part, you can end this right now and get that sleep you wanted!"

"Sleep can wait. I want to complete what we have begun." She tugged at his hip to roll him over onto her, but he caught her hand.

"We can't go that far," he said seriously. "Yes, you get to make your own choices, but one risk I refuse to take is the chance of getting you with child. That would be unforgivably irresponsible on my part, and certainly far too soon when we're still discovering each other!"

"I agree that this is not the right time for a child," she agreed, "but I will now tell you one of the secrets of Tremayne females."

He frowned. "There are secret female mysteries? I think I'd rather not know!"

"This one is simple, and I learned it from Gwyn. A gifted Tremayne woman won't become with child unless she wants it to happen."

"How can that be?" he said, startled. "There are methods that can reduce the chances of conceiving, from sheaths to withdrawal to vinegar-soaked sponges, but none are entirely reliable, and except for withdrawal, none are available at the moment."

"I see you've made a study of the matter," Tamsyn said admiringly.

"If Gwyn has secrets for females, Rhys had lectures for his sons so there would be no accidents," Cade said dryly. "His goal was to make sure that no female would ever be harmed in any way at the hands of a Tremayne male."

"Is that one of the reasons you feel that you might be wronging me?" she asked quietly. "Because you're not."

"It's difficult not to feel that I'm breaking one of the cardinal rules of being a Tremayne," he said haltingly. "No matter how much you point out that we're not blood kin, my feelings for you still seem . . . *wrong.*"

She caught his hand and drew it to her heart. "Then I must be glad that Bastien scrambled your mind enough for you to speak up! But to return to the previous subject, what Gwyn said is very simple. A strongly gifted woman will not conceive unless she wills it."

"I'm having trouble believing this," he admitted.

"Think of Gwyn. She bore three children, with two years between each of us, but remember how she almost died when Caitlin was born?"

He shuddered. "None of us ever forgot that! You saved her life."

"With the help of every gifted person in the household, if you recall." Her brows drew together. "Now that I think of it, that healing was a very powerful example of what can be possible when gifted people share their abilities to reach a common goal. Like the stealth you wield, it's a powerful technique and we should explore it further. But the point I wanted to make was that after she almost died, she was never with child again because she feared for her health, so she told her body not to conceive."

"It's still difficult to believe."

"If we can't believe Gwyn, whom can we believe?" Tam said reasonably. "And if you don't quite believe her, trust me when I say that there will be no unwanted consequences from whatever we do tonight!"

"You're very convincing," he admitted.

"I want to have this time with you now because when we reach London, we'll have to tell Gwyn and Rhys about us," she said, knowing it was impossible to predict what would happen after that.

"So we shouldn't waste this opportunity." He released his breath in a long sigh. "I surrender, my dearest love."

"Then it's time we removed the rest of our clothing because I really want to be skin to skin with you," she said mischievously.

"An excellent goal." He sat up and pulled off his shirt, revealing his broad, powerful chest with its artistic dusting of dark hair. By the time he'd shed the rest of his garments, Tamsyn had untangled her shift from around her waist and tossed it away. Now she lay on her side waiting for him, her eyes warm with welcome.

Cade stretched out beside her and leaned forward into a kiss. She drank him in, amazed how a simple kiss could make every cell in her body thrum with desire. He began stroking along her side, bringing warmth wherever he touched.

A little shyly, she stroked him in return, her hand drifting down until she could clasp him and feel the fierce pulse of his desire. He sucked in his breath at her touch. "You're like a spark to tinder, Tam!"

"Then let us enjoy the fire together," she breathed. It took very little mutual caressing to return both of them to eager readiness.

When the time felt right, Cade rolled up and positioned himself above her, saying apologetically, "This first time will certainly be uncomfortable and quite possibly painful. Let me know if you want me to stop."

"Virginity is something I want over, so I swear I won't want to stop," Tam said, smiling as she opened her arms to him. "Come to me, my beautiful man!"

Exercising all his control, he slid into her gradually. She felt herself expanding, at first startled by the sensation of fullness and then welcoming it. His soft words and commanding movements were rousing the madness again. When they were fully joined, they were both very still for long moments, the only sound their mutual rough breathing.

She cautiously moved her hips against him once, then again when he caught his breath. Enjoying the sense of power, she rocked into him with delight.

His control shattered and he surged into her with all his love and gifts of power, sweeping them both into spiraling madness. It was beyond anything she'd ever imagined, a joining of mind and body that ravished all her senses as the whole world turned golden.

Her culmination triggered his release and together they shared joy unbounded. After, as she lay warm and protected in Cade's arms, she looked forward to a future where they would continue to explore and discover new depths of loving as long as they both should live. There would be challenges ahead, but by God, together they would meet and overcome them!

Aloud she said, "I'm glad that we've had this time together before we reach London and reveal our love to the rest of the family."

He sighed. "Yes, we must tell them. Who knows what will happen next. Trouble, I think."

"I feel that things will work out for us," she said slowly, "but that may just be my native optimism. Or should that be naïve optimism?"

Cade chuckled. "We're both supposed to be powerfully gifted, but we're just as confused about the future as anyone else!"

"Think how dull life would be if we always knew what would happen!" She snuggled closer to him. "You have become the most glorious surprise ever, my darling Cade. Sleep well. . . ."

Chapter 33

Cade slept very well with Tamsyn in his arms, and it was near dawn when he woke. After a few moments of savoring the pure bliss of being with her, he reluctantly swung from the bed before bending to kiss her temple, saying softly, "Thank you, my darling girl."

She made an agreeable humming sound but didn't quite wake up. Smiling, he pulled on his clothes and silently left the room. He tried not to wonder when, if ever, they would have another such night of privacy and passion.

The inn was quiet and he hoped he could return to his bed without waking his brother, but as he entered the room, Bran shifted in his bed by the window and muttered, "Your stealth energy works very well."

"Good." Cade divested himself of his clothing again and slid into his bed. With luck he could get a couple hours more sleep before rising for breakfast.

Knowing that Bran deserved at least a summary, Cade said, "As you suggested, I asked Tamsyn if things were moving too quickly for her. She was quite firm in asserting that was not the case."

Bran chuckled. "If she's decided that, the subject is now closed. But I'm glad you discussed it."

After a long silence, Cade said, "We're going to reveal our relationship to Rhys and Gwyn when we get back to London."

"I think that's a wise decision and gives you the best chance of a successful outcome," Bran said. "Together you can figure out the best way to proceed."

Even though Cade had used stealth, Bran had probably guessed what Cade and Tam had been doing besides talking, but the subject was private. Instead he said, "I'm getting an increasingly strong feeling that all four of us—you, me, Tamsyn, and Andre—should go to the Portsmouth Royal Dockyard. Just for a couple of days."

Cade wouldn't mind having more time before confessing to Rhys and Gwyn. "Do you know why there was a request for your presence?"

"The Commissioner of the Dockyard is Sir Charles Saxton. He had a long and honorable history as an officer in the Royal Navy before he was appointed Dockyard Commissioner at Portsmouth. His reputation is impeccable, but Rhys said that he's rather traditional, which makes it somewhat surprising that he'd request aid from the Home Office's gifted department."

"Is he concerned about anything in particular?"

"I'm not sure." Bran's voice turned amused. "Plenty of people who have no use for those of us who are gifted are willing to believe in intuition."

"Which of course has nothing to do with being gifted," Cade said with a chuckle. "It's a much safer word."

"A sea captain as capable as he was must have good intuition," Bram said. "Perhaps Saxton senses something is wrong, or perhaps one of the men under him is worried. Rhys told me that the Yard is enormous and contains a number of major industrial facilities. With the resumption of war, they're also expanding the Dockyard, so there must be many opportunities for French agents to cause trouble."

"And since the sea and the Royal Navy are all that stand between us and Napoleon, the safety of the dockyards is very important. Do you have more specific information about the one in Portsmouth?"

Bran covered his mouth with a yawn. "Yes, but I'll save it for the morning. I'm hoping to persuade all three of you to go with me."

"I will," Cade said, yawning himself. "As you spoke, I got the feeling that I should be with you."

Bran made an approving sound, then fell asleep again, probably to dream of Merryn. As Cade burrowed into his bed, he hoped he'd dream of Tamsyn.

At breakfast that morning, Bran told the others about the Portsmouth Yard. "All the naval yards are being expanded now that we're at war again, and Portsmouth was already the largest British yard. It's also the largest manufacturing site in Britain and quite possibly the world."

"Which means there are many, many targets for determined French agents," Tamsyn said thoughtfully. "I'll go with you."

Bran turned to Andre. "Are you interested? It would be a short visit."

Andre hesitated. "I'm anxious to get to Woolwich to find Elizabeth."

"Quite understandable," Tam said. "If you're uncertain what to do, try closing your eyes and letting your mind become still, then see if one of the possibilities begins to seem like the right one."

Andre did as she suggested, his face relaxing. After a minute or so while the others continued eating, he opened his eyes again. "How interesting! I realized that I should go with you to Portsmouth. That's a useful technique, Tamsyn." He smiled.

"I'm interested in all matters of engineering, but I also hope to learn more about using my gifts by following the three of you around."

Bran laughed. "You're welcome to do so. We all have thoughts on being gifted—and we don't always agree by any means!"

"I have had very little training," Andre said hesitantly. "When Grandmère told me about your family, I hoped you would be able to teach me more."

"We're happy to," Cade said. "We've all benefited by being members of the Tribe of Tremayne."

"And new cousins are welcome." Tamsyn studied Andre through narrowed eyes. "I feel that you are going to be very helpful."

"But many of the Tremayne family are working against France," Cade said seriously. "Half of your heritage is French. Are you comfortable allying yourself with France's most determined enemy?"

Andre nodded. "I've thought of this, but half of me is also British. Though there is much I love about France, I do not support Napoleon, who yearns to conquer all of Europe and beyond and doesn't care how many people die in his quest."

Bran gave a nod of approval, then finished off the last of his tea and stood. "I'll go arrange for a carriage so we can be off soon. Luckily, none of us have much baggage."

Andre also stood. "I look forward to spending hours in a carriage with you where you won't be able to avoid my questions!"

They all went upstairs to their rooms. Cade came up last and went to Tamsyn's room as no one else was there to see. He tapped quietly, then entered.

Tam was efficiently packing her few garments into her carry bag. She looked up with a smile. "You're ready to go?"

"Not yet. I wanted to give you a hug before we set off."

"What a fine idea." Tamsyn walked into his arms and they held each other. She smelled delicious. As she settled against him, she said softly, "The more I think about Portsmouth, the more I feel we're going to find something important there."

Cade frowned. "Dangerous?"

Tam hesitated. "Somewhat. And I think it will lead to something more dangerous. It's good that we're going together."

With a sharp flash of intuition, Cade realized that this visit would, indeed, lead to something critical and dangerous. His arms tightened around Tamsyn. "We'll all be alert," he said out loud. And his silent message was *I'll keep you safe, my love. I promise.*

Chapter 34

It was late afternoon when they arrived at the Portsmouth Royal Dockyard. As Bran had said. the Yard was even larger than the one in Devenport. Even the porter's lodge that guarded the main entrance was a substantial building in its own right with several guards stationed at the gate.

Bran said, "I'm supposed to meet with Chief Howard, who is the head of security for the whole Dockyard. His office is here in the porter's lodge." Looking cool and confident, Bran led the way in and presented his Home Office credentials to the officer on reception duty, explaining that his companions were part of his team.

The officer studied the credentials, then gave a nod. "Chief Howard is expecting you. Smith, escort Mr. Tremayne and his colleagues to the chief's office."

Smith, one of the younger guards, bobbed his head and led them across the large, bustling entry hall to an office in the corner of the building. After announcing the visitors, he departed.

The office was cluttered with books and papers, and a large map of the dockyard was pinned to the wall on the left. Chief Howard rose from his desk to greet them. He was a dark-haired man in early middle age with alert eyes. Tam suspected that he was also at least a little gifted.

Howard scanned them. "Which of you is Bran Tremayne?"

"I am," Bran said. "When I considered the size of the Portsmouth Royal Dockyard, I thought that a larger team might be useful. This is my sister, Miss Tremayne. My brother, Cade Tremayne, and our cousin, Mr. Andre Jameson."

Howard arched his brows when he looked at Tamsyn. "I believe your sister is more correctly styled Lady Tamsyn Tremayne?"

Tam smiled at him. "I didn't think our reputations would have preceded us!"

Howard's serious gaze held hers. "My brother is the sailing master of the *Royal William*, which was almost blown up in Devenport. He says he and his friends would have died if not for you Tremaynes."

Tam caught her breath when she remembered how narrowly disaster had been averted. "Did he suggest that you contact Lord Tremayne at the Home Office if you had concerns about the Portsmouth Dockyard?"

"Yes," Howard said. "He mentioned Bran Tremayne, Cade Tremayne, and Lady Tamsyn Tremayne." His gaze went to Andre. "I don't know if you were present, Mr. Jameson. If you were, I didn't hear your name."

"I've just arrived in England," Andre said. "An engineer in training. I believe there is much for an engineer to learn here in Portsmouth."

"Indeed there is. There are almost seven hundred ships in the Royal Navy, and it's the Navy that keeps Britain safe. Portsmouth is not only the largest Royal Dockyard, it's also the largest industrial complex in Great Britain.." He frowned, looking tired. "There are so many important things being done here that could be vulnerable to attack by French agents."

"If we can help, we will," Bran said. "Have you been sensing a particular threat, or is your concern more general?"

Howard thought. "I have many general concerns, but lately

I've been feeling as if something specific is being threatened. I have no idea what that might be. There are so many possibilities!"

"Can you use that map to give us an idea how the Yard is laid out?" Cade asked.

"Excellent idea." The chief stepped up to the map and his visitors gathered around him. His pointing finger circled the sprawl of the dockyard. "You can see how many basins and wet and dry docks we have. New ships are being built and older ships are being repaired. Here's the smithery, which is huge and as noisy as the hammers of hell. That's where the anchors are made. Next to it is a copper-smelting furnace and a refinery used for recycling the copper sheathing that's used on ships' hulls. The copper needs to be replaced every five years so that's a substantial operation."

"I've heard about your revolutionary block mill," Cade said. "Where is that?"

Howard tapped an area near the middle of the Yard. "Here. We now have two steam engines that drive the block mills and the sawmill and the woodworking shops." He glanced at Tamsyn. "Blocks are pulleys that control the rigging and lines on a ship. A ship of the line might have as many as a thousand blocks of different sizes, but in the past, procuring them has always been a problem. Our new mills make blocks much more quickly and the quality is consistent."

"This place truly is extraordinary!" Andre breathed with engineering lust in his eyes.

"What area of the Yard do you consider most vulnerable?" Bran asked.

Howard frowned. "There are many places doing vital work and none is invulnerable. "

They all gazed at the map. "It's hard to know where to begin looking," Andre said.

"I have a thought," Tam said. "Bran, you love experimenting with new techniques. What if the four of us turn our backs to the map? Chief Howard can ask us one at a time to point out the area we feel is most endangered. If we feel strongly, we can select a second or even a third spot. When we've all done that, Chief Howard can tell us which areas we singled out and we can discuss what was chosen and then perhaps visit those sites."

"I like that idea," Bran said. "Shall we see if this works, Chief Howard?"

The chief looked surprised, but said, "It's worth a try. Now all of you turn away. Who will go first?"

"I will," Cade said. "I had an idea when the chief was outlining the different facilities."

All but Cade turned to face the opposite wall. Tam felt him gathering his intuition. Then he tapped the map briskly. Howard gave a thoughtful "Hmmm," then asked, "Who's next?"

"I'll try," Bran said.

Cade moved to stand by Tam, his back to the map. Bran took longer before tapping. "There and perhaps also there, but that feels less urgent."

Andre said, "I'd like to try now." He turned to face the map and there was a longish pause.

Tam said, "Don't think too much. Let your intuition guide you."

Andre drew a slow breath, then tapped. "Thank you for the advice, Tamsyn. It helped."

Chief Howard said, "Will you take a turn, Lady Tamsyn?"

"Of course." She turned to face the map and studied it with unfocused eyes. A sudden image of fire snapped into her mind. "Here!" she said, tapping hard. "Fire and soon!"

Her three companions turned around. "What were the results?" Cade asked.

Howard was staring at the map in amazement. "You all picked the block mill for your first choice."

"That has to mean something," Andre said.

"I think it means we have to get over there right now!" Cade said.

Howard headed to the door. "Lady Tamsyn, will you wait here?"

"I'm going with you," she said briskly. "If I can't keep up, leave me behind and I'll catch up with you soon."

As the five of them swept out of Howard's office, the chief signaled to two of the armed guards. "Come along!"

The group set off at a swift pace, heading to the interior of the Yard. Tam was a swift walker but she said to Cade under her breath, "If I'd known we'd be running around the Yard, I'd have worn trousers!"

He took her hand to help steady her. "Since you're just a little bit of a thing, I can carry you if necessary."

"Ha!" she snapped, but didn't say more because she didn't have breath to spare.

They were moving between seemingly endless storehouses and workshops. There was a clamor of tools and machinery and beyond the building, ships' masts were visible. A heavy bell rang and workers began pouring out of the buildings to head for home, moving in the opposite direction from their party.

Finally they reached an incredibly long building. Howard waved a hand at it. "This is the Double Ropehouse, where very long lengths of rope are made in one piece because they're stronger than spliced ropes. Over the years there have been several fires here because of all the fiber used. The last time that happened, it was caused by arson. Now water for firefighting is piped around the Yard so it's less likely there will be another serious fire."

Tam studied the length of the building, but the fire she'd seen hadn't been here. They turned a corner and Howard gestured at a massive three-story building in front of them. "That's the block mill building just ahead."

Bran said, "Tamsyn saw fire. You said that the block mill included wood shops?"

"Wood shops and sawmills, among other things." The chief scanned the area with narrowed eyes. "I don't see anything out of order at the moment."

They started to circle the building and turned into the alley that ran between the block mill building and a large storehouse.

Tamsyn's intuition was on high alert. Something odd flickered in the alley ahead of them. There was something there she couldn't quite see. . . .

She stretched her intuition to the limits, then caught her breath. "Ahead of us are two men using stealth to conceal their movements!"

Cade looked where she pointed and swore under his breath. "Bran, take my hand so we can combine our energies!"

Tam was already holding Cade's hand and Bran and then Andre joined the connection. She felt a rush of power and realized that Cade was trying to overcome the stealth being used by the men ahead.

There was a shimmer and suddenly two men wearing workmen's smocks became visible. They were running away from the block mill as fast as they could.

Howard gasped as they became visible, then bellowed. *"Halt!"*

Instead, the men sprinted harder, heading for the end of the block building, where they could turn out of sight and perhaps get lost in the maze of buildings and crowds of exiting workers.

The chief shouted again, *"Halt or we'll shoot!"*

One of the men pivoted around to face them and yanked a pistol from under his smock. He cocked it and fired, but his shot didn't hit any of his pursuers.

Howard ordered his guards, "Fire!"

The guards were armed with rifles, more accurate than pistols, and their two shots were almost simultaneous. The weapons were deafening in the confined space between the two brick buildings, and the air filled with the acrid smoke of black powder.

Both of the fleeing men jerked and went down. When the pursuers reached the fallen men, Howard bent over the one on the left, whose head and neck were covered with blood. "Good shooting, Morris! He's dead but I hope the other one is alive because I want to hear what he has to say."

Tamsyn saw a faint glow of light about the man on the right, but it was flickering, and she guessed that he was mortally wounded. She crossed to him, with Cade in tow. This was the man who had fired his pistol, and because he was turned toward his pursuers, the bullet had struck his chest and he'd been knocked onto his back.

Tam knelt beside him and Cade placed a hand on her shoulder to help her study the man's energy. He was young and ablaze with fury and defiance as he gloried in the knowledge that he was dying for France and Napoleon. He was also taking fierce satisfaction in the knowledge of the damage he'd arranged.

She rested a hand on his arm and said quietly in French, "You're gravely injured, citizen. Do you have any last messages or prayers you'd like to make?"

He tried to spit but he didn't have the breath to do it well. He did manage to snarl a few filthy French curses at her. Later she'd have to ask Cade what some of the words meant, though she could make a good guess.

She laid a hand on his cold forehead and continued speaking in French. "As an agent of France, you've done a brave and dangerous deed. But will your action today kill men you worked with who may have become friends?"

For a flickering moment she felt regret as her words struck home. She also sensed images of what he'd done and gave thanks that there should be time to undo his work. Again softly, she asked, "Were you working alone or are you part of a larger group?"

This time there was a jumble of words, place names, gone in an instant. She repeated them to herself so she wouldn't forget.

His defiance dissolved into fear and he grabbed at her hand as he whispered a desperate "*Mama?*"

"You are not alone," she said quietly.

He exhaled raggedly, then breathed no more.

Chapter 35

As Tamsyn felt the young man die under her hand, she gasped and began shaking, near fainting. Cade's arm came around her, warm and protective. "It's all right," he said softly. "You're safe now."

She saw that he had knelt beside her on the dusty street. She half turned and burrowed into his arms, wanting to disappear into him.

More distantly, she heard Bran say quietly to Chief Howard, "Tamsyn's strongest gift is for mental health and healing, and I've seen her do extraordinary things. But using her gifts is exhausting."

Bran was right—this particular incident had taken a great deal out of her—but she must speak of what she'd learned as soon as possible. She knew that the young man she'd shadowed into death had been named Jacques and he'd desperately wanted to aid his country and his hero, but in his final moments he'd been terrified by approaching death. She hoped he was at peace now. But that information wasn't important compared to what else she'd learned.

Cade was stroking his hand down her back, bringing her back to herself. Raising her head, she said, "This man, Jacques, and his companion over there were French. They came to England pretending to be Belgians fleeing the French conquest of their country. When they applied to work here in the Yard, they quite convincingly claimed they wanted to work against Napoleon."

"Are there others like them working here?" Cade asked calmly.

She needed to explain further, but first she must stop the potential damage. "They're the only ones here in the Portsmouth Yard. Since they were both assigned to work in the wood shops, they decided that setting fires there would produce the maximum damage."

"Did you see anything more specific?" Bran asked. He'd settled down on her other side and was resting a supportive hand on her back. Tamsyn was developing a much greater appreciation for the way physical touch enhanced mental gifts.

She visualized what she'd seen so that she could describe it properly. "They developed little time-delayed fire starters. Black powder and a slow-burning beeswax candle set in a little wooden box. Jacques had stealth magic so they were able to obscure the locations. The boxes were set in places where there was wood to catch fire easily. They lit the candles before they left so they were late leaving their jobs."

"Do you know how many of their nasty little bombs have been set?" Bran asked.

"A dozen?" Tam shook her head. "Thirteen. Make sure your men find them all, Chief Howard." She frowned. "I think they might have done something to cause one of the steam engines to explode, but that was less clear. Get your engineers to make a thorough inspection."

"Anything else?" Cade asked.

"When I asked if they were working with others, I heard

place names." She closed her eyes as she remembered. "Plymouth. Portsmouth. Chatham. Sheerness. Deptford." She hesitated, then added, "Gibraltar?"

Howard swore under his breath. "Those are the most important Royal Navy Dockyards in Britain, plus Gibraltar, which is vital for our ships in the Mediterranean. Since Britain lives or dies by our navy, the French must be trying to undermine us in as many ways as possible."

"We can discuss this more later, but for now we have to find those firetraps and see if anything has been done to the steam engines," Bran said as he rose to his feet. "Tam, are you all right?"

She managed a smile for him. "Fine. Just . . . tired."

"Glad to hear that," Howard said gravely before he began giving orders to one of his guards about bringing more people to aid in the search. To Bran, he said, "Can you help us search?"

"Of course." Bran glanced at Andre. "Will you join us? I think your talents will be particularly useful in this."

"I am eager to help," Andre said firmly.

"Tam needs time to recover," Cade said. "I'll look after her. Chief Howard, can you recommend a good nearby inn where I can get us rooms for the night?"

"The Admiral's Inn is nearby and said to be very comfortable," Howard said.

"I'll take Tam there and send the carriage back to wait until Bran and Andre are done."

Bran nodded. "Book rooms for all four of us and we can talk over dinner. Shall we begin, Chief Howard?"

As Howard and the others organized their search, Cade asked Tamsyn, "Can you stand?"

She drew a deep breath. "I'm . . . not sure."

Cade helped her to her feet, but she swayed and nearly fell. He immediately caught her up in his arms and started walking back toward the porter's lodge.

It was a relief to close her eyes and relax against him, but she muttered threateningly, "If you say that I'm just a little bit of a thing, I will *bite* you!"

"I wouldn't dare say that!" he said with a chuckle; then his voice turned serious. "What you did was extraordinary, Tam. You've saved lives and prevented massive destruction. Reading the French agent's mind as he lay dying? I've never heard of anyone else who could do that. Your gifts of the mind keep growing in amazing ways."

"It wasn't exactly mind reading, but . . . yes, it was different from anything I've done before," she murmured. "Gifts seem to respond to what is needed."

"That fits with Bran's theory that a person who is powerfully gifted can develop new abilities if the need is compelling." Cade was silent for the length of a warehouse. "I tried to affect the weather when we crossed from France and the revenue cutter came after us. It seemed to work."

Becoming more alert, Tamsyn said, "Very interesting. Research is needed."

"We can set Rhys on it."

She wondered if Cade was beginning to find her heavy, but he seemed to be able to manage her weight over the longish walk without any problem. She sighed and let her head rest on his shoulder. She suspected that being held by him was helping to restore her depleted energy.

A gruff voice asked from nearby, "Is the young lady ill?"

"No, my wife is merely tired from so much walking around the Yard," Cade replied.

Tam waited until they left the other man behind. "Wife?"

He smiled down at her a little wistfully. "A man can dream."

So could a woman. She let herself relax into a doze so she could dream of them being together and accepted by their world. Surely that was possible. . . .

Chapter 36

The Admiral's Inn was close and rather grand, as Chief Howard had promised. It was also spacious, and Cade was able to get a pair of connecting rooms for himself and Tam, plus separate rooms for Bran and Andre. Despite Tam's claims that she was fine, she didn't protest when he carried her up the stairs to their rooms.

Tamsyn's room had a comfortable-looking four-poster bed, wide enough for an admiral and his wife. Cade set Tam on her feet while he pulled back the counterpane. "Shall I help you out of your gown and stays so you can relax better?"

"Please." She turned so he could undo the ties of her gown and then unfasten her stays, leaving her in her shift.

As he peeled off her outer garments, she said, "You'd better invoke some stealth now. If anyone in our family should sense our activity, this would be considered a highly compromising position!"

"We've well and truly compromised each other, but yes, locked doors and stealth are desirable." He lifted her and laid her gently down on the wide mattress, then removed her half boots before crossing the room to lock the main door to the corridor outside. Returning to the bed, he asked, "Is there anything else you need?"

"A glass of water?" she asked in a thin voice.

On the desk was a pitcher and a pair of drinking glasses, so he poured water for both of them. It had been a long day and the spring weather was getting warm.

He emptied his glass in one long swallow, then helped Tam sit up so she could drink also. As she swallowed, he admired the elegance of her slim neck and tried, without success, not to stare at the soft curves visible under the light fabric of her shift. "Now you need to get some sleep."

She handed her empty glass to him and lay back on the bed with a tired sigh. "Will you lie down and hold me until I fall asleep? I . . . I need you close."

"Your wish is my command, my lady." He stripped off his coat and boots, then lay down on the bed behind her and drew her into his arms.

She gave a soft sigh of relaxation and settled back against him, drawing his upper arm over her waist. She was so delicate, yet so strong. She also had a deliciously shaped backside. Once again he told his lower self to behave.

Aloud he said, "I'm glad we have this private time together. I have no idea how we'll manage in London. I have trouble imagining setting up a love nest where we can be together in secret. It seems . . . so undignified. You deserve better."

"So do you. We must take it one day at a time, and we'll start by telling Gwyn and Rhys. They might have some magical solution," she said, her voice stronger than it had been. "But now that you mention it, since private time might be difficult to come by soon, we shouldn't waste it now."

He laughed a little. "Are you suggesting what I think you are?"

"No," she said demurely as she rolled onto her back. "I'm suggesting what I hope you'll suggest."

There was a mischievous twinkle in her eyes, but he hesitated briefly. "Are you sure? You burned an immense amount of energy earlier."

"Yes, but I've become stronger while you're holding me." She looked mischievous again. "It would be an interesting experiment to see if closer holding would restore my energy entirely."

He couldn't stop himself from laughing. "If you're willing to participate in this experiment to increase our knowledge of how energy can be rebuilt, it will be my pleasure to assist you."

"I'm sure we'll find this very educational," she said before she pulled his head down into a slow, delicious kiss. Energy sparked between them.

In deference to her fatigue, he started gently, but as they kissed and caressed each other, desire increased to a bonfire. Her shift was easily moved and her clever hands deftly unbuttoned his fall.

As she clasped him, she said, "Surely you don't need to disrobe entirely when you'll just have to get dressed again later. It would be a waste of time."

He gasped as she squeezed him. "We wouldn't . . . want to waste time," he managed to get out.

She was ready, more than ready, and they came together with smooth fire. He dizzily sensed that no matter how many times they might make love in the future, each occasion would feel as rare and special as this joining did.

They culminated swiftly and held each other as the intoxicating waves of passion subsided. She said with a catch of laughter, "Our experiment suggests that this is a swift and delightful way to recharge one's energy."

He chuckled and drew her against him. "I rather think that now you have all the energy and I'm a mere shadow of my former self."

"Further experiments will be needed," she said with mock seriousness.

He drew her closer so that all her soft curves melded against him. "I can't imagine giving this up forever. Maybe we should emigrate to the American colonies. They say that Boston is a pleasant place."

"An appealing thought," she said with a sigh. "But with the war resumed, we're needed in England and will be for years to come."

"Speaking of which, Bran and Andre should be returning soon. I'll go down to the kitchen and see about getting a dinner served up here in my room. There's a good-sized table and several chairs in there."

"I'm sure that admirals like to hold elegant private dinner parties here," she said. "Or do you think they prefer wild orgies?"

After a moment's thought, he replied, "I'd rather not speculate on what admirals do for entertainment." He skimmed his hand from her shoulder to her knee, loving the silky texture of her pale skin. "You, my experimenting lady, look very fetching now, but you need to get dressed again."

She covered a yawn, then sat up in the bed. "I have the feeling that Bran and Chief Howard were successful in their search, and I haven't heard any explosions, but I want to hear more of the details."

"As do I." Cade swung from the bed and straightened his clothing, then donned his coat and boots again. "We'll have a council of war over dinner."

The Admiral's Inn had a very obliging kitchen. A quarter hour after Bran and Andre returned, a fine meal of roast beef, boiled new potatoes, and sweet young peas was served in Cade's room. Tam was already there, looking misleadingly demure.

"You look much recovered, Tam," Bran said.

She gave him a quick hug. "Cade took good care of me. But now I want to know what happened after we left. Andre, you seem to be vibrating with excitement."

"I am!" he said. "It was the first time I've been part of such a serious mission. I found it most interesting and rewarding."

"He did very well," Bran said. "Especially with the steam engine. He used his intuition to find what the French agents had done that might have led to an explosion."

"You must have a strong gift for mechanical things," Cade said. "What about the firetraps? Did you find them all?"

"Yes, and the last one was close to going off," Bran said. "Unlucky thirteen indeed. But we got to it in time."

Tam said, "I've been thinking about the fact that there seems to be a network of French agents working to cause trouble at the Royal Navy dockyards. Could Dubois, that unpleasant fellow we met at the Devenport Naval Yard, have been part of this network?"

"I think it likely," Bran said slowly, "though we have no proof." He frowned. "It isn't generally known yet, but Napoleon wants to invade England and is massing soldiers and ships in the Boulogne area. I don't know how long it will take for him to assemble his invasion force because it's a huge undertaking, but there is no question that he wants to cross the channel and conquer Britain."

Not liking the sound of that, Cade set his wineglass aside. "So the more he can weaken the Royal Navy, the better his chances of success."

"Exactly," Bran said. "I think in the coming years, many of the efforts of our branch of the Home Office will be bent on protecting our naval installations."

His words produced a long silence, which he ended by taking a sip of his red wine. "Very good wine."

"An inn that wants to lure admirals needs a good wine cellar," Tamsyn said. "This tastes French."

"Probably smuggled to England," Cade said. "Possibly in the same ship that brought us over."

"That's an interesting thought." Andre contemplated his glass of wine before taking a sip. "We have reason to be grateful to smugglers."

"The smugglers are probably bringing over French agents as well," Bran said dryly. "I'm going to stay here for several days and discuss further security measures with Chief Howard. Andre, will you stay and join the discussion? You have good instincts in this area."

Andre hesitated, torn. "I'd like to be part of this, but . . . I want to get to Woolwich to find my friend Elizabeth."

"Of course you do," Tam said warmly. "It's a southeastern area of London, and we can easily go that way on our return to Tremayne House."

Andre smiled, looking a little bashful. "You probably think I'm foolish. Elizabeth and I might not even recognize each other after all this time."

"We Tremaynes take affairs of the heart very seriously." Bran's gaze touched lightly on Tam and Cade. "You can join the dockyard security discussion when I return to London. Rhys, the father of the Tribe of Tremayne, is also head of our Home Office department of gifted agents, and he'll have very good ideas about what changes will need to be made."

"I look forward to meeting him," Andre said. "Do you think he might consider me as a possible agent even though I am young and not well trained?"

"I think it very likely," Bran said. "He looks for talent and commitment. Which is why we have female agents like our Tamsyn."

Andre blinked at Tam. "You're an official agent for the Home Office?"

She batted her blue eyes at him, looking totally frivolous. "Yes, and a good one. Most men don't take me seriously."

Cade laughed. "You've seen what she can do, Andre! Talent and commitment. Rhys would be a fool not to have her as an agent, and he is not a fool. You might want to be a part-time agent while you pursue your engineering studies."

"I would like that if it's possible." Andre inclined his head respectfully at Tam. "I am honored to have seen your abilities, Lady Tamsyn!"

Thinking it was time to return to business, Cade said, "If we leave early in the morning, we should be able to make it to Woolwich by late afternoon. The roads are good from here to London."

"London!" Tam said dramatically. "Life will return to normal and I'll have more than one gown to wear!"

Her gaze met Cade's and turned bleak, and he knew they were thinking the same thing. They would have tonight to be together. After that, when would such closeness be possible again?

Chapter 37

The carriage ride to London was indeed smooth and swift. Tamsyn dozed for the last part with her head on Cade's lap. She thought it was as close as she could get to him without being scandalous.

She awoke when Cade patted her on the shoulder in a very non-scandalous way. "Time to wake up, Tamkin. We've entered Woolwich."

She sat up and covered a yawn. "That was a very easy journey, Cade. Have you been playing with the weather again?"

"Yes, and it seems to be possible." He brushed a lock of her hair from her cheek in a way that was a bit more than brotherly.

Andre had been staring eagerly out the window, but he swiveled around and stared. "You can really do that, Cade?"

"More experimenting is required, but I think it's possible to have some effect," Cade replied. "I'll never be a wizard standing on a cliff calling down lightning to smite my enemies, but it seems I can encourage weather that might already be happening."

"That is extremely interesting!" Tamsyn looked out the window thoughtfully. "There are some heavy clouds ahead, north of the Thames, which could bring rain to the Royal Arsenal soon. Shall we see if we can push those clouds away?"

She caught first Cade's hand, then Andre's. Once more she felt the surge of power that came from connecting with other gifted people. They all gazed out the window at the heavy clouds and concentrated.

Slowly the clouds began breaking up. Tamsyn gave a whoop of excitement and squeezed her companions' hands. "This is definitely a gift worth further exploration!"

Andre continued gazing out the window. "There seems to be no end to the possibilities."

"So it seems," Cade said. He gave Tam's hand a private squeeze before releasing it. "Of course we three are unusually gifted to begin with."

"You know Woolwich a bit, don't you, Cade?" Tamsyn asked. "What can you tell us about it?"

"Well, the name Woolwich probably means that long ago this was a place where large amounts of wool were shipped because wool was England's most important product for several centuries." Cade grinned. "Also, the Arsenal is called the Warren because an early owner had a vast rabbit warren there. The earth was full of tunnels that were home to rabbits that could be hunted for food."

Tam blinked. "Really? Are there still rabbits there?"

"I imagine they've moved out in search of quieter lodgings. Having artillery tested overhead can't be very restful."

Andre pulled out a worn and frequently folded slip of paper with writing on it. "This is where the Caton family lives. Do you know where that address is?"

Cade studied the paper. "Yes, and it's a very pleasant area and conveniently close to the Arsenal."

He signaled the carriage to stop and had a brief conversation with the driver about their destination. As they started again, Tam asked, "Is your Elizabeth gifted?"

Andre gave a twisted smile. "She's not my Elizabeth, and I don't know if she's gifted or not. We didn't talk about such things."

Tam gave an understanding nod. "We Tremaynes talk about gifts a great deal among ourselves, but for many people, the subject is still one to be avoided. I hope when you see her again, you'll be able to talk about being gifted since it's an important part of you."

Looking daunted, Andre said, "I never thought of the possibility that she might despise me for what I am!"

"She might not," Cade said, "but it's always something to consider when you meet others who don't know what you can do."

Andre sat tensely as the carriage drove the last distance to the Caton residence. They pulled up in front of a handsome house, not a mansion but freestanding and large enough to have an attractive garden.

As soon as the wheels stopped rolling, Andre swung out of the door, then stood still as he gazed uncertainly at the house.

Before he could start walking to the entrance, the front door flew open and a slim young woman with cinnamon-colored hair bolted outside. "*Andrew!* I thought I felt you coming!"

His face shining, Andre raced toward her. "*Beth!*" They met in an embrace of laughter and tears.

Tam and Cade exited from the carriage but didn't move toward the house, giving the younger couple time for their reunion. "I'm guessing that his Beth is also at least somewhat gifted," she remarked.

Cade smiled. "Indeed she is. They both must have grown a great deal in the time that has passed, but they're off to a good start."

Beth said to Andre — Andrew? — "It's been so long since I've received a letter from you. I had a feeling that you were traveling, but it's such a long way from India, I didn't know when or even if you'd make it to England! You seemed to have many problems."

"I did." Keeping an arm around Beth, Andre turned her to make introductions. "Lady Tamsyn Tremayne and Mr. Cade Tremayne, I'm pleased to introduce you to Miss Elizabeth Caton." He added, "Beth, they made it possible for me to travel the last stretch from France."

Beth was a pretty girl with bright hazel eyes, and the smile she gave her visitors was dazzling. "Thank you! With France and England at war again, the journey must have been almost impossible."

"Andre's grandmother was of great aid to us, so we all helped each other, Miss Caton," Tam said.

"Please call me Beth, for I think we will be friends."

Her warmth was irresistible. Tam shifted her gaze to Andre. "Do you prefer Andre or Andrew?"

He smiled. "I was christened Andrew and my Scottish father always called me that, but my French mother called me Andre and it seemed wise to use that name when we returned to France. Either name will do." Turning to Beth, he asked, "Is your father home? I look forward to seeing him again."

"He's at work at the Arsenal and won't be home for a while. Would you like to come in to refresh yourselves and perhaps have tea?" Her gaze went back to Andre as if she hated looking away from him. "If Papa isn't back by the time we finish our tea, I can take you to him at the Arsenal. It's not far. Mr. and Mrs. Tremayne, if you would like to see the Arsenal, you could join us."

"I'd like that very much," Cade said, not bothering to correct her assumption that they were married.

There was a note in his voice that made Tam think he believed they should visit the Arsenal. She also had a sense of uneasiness. But she'd be glad for tea and refreshments. It had been a long time since breakfast.

Cade had washed up and was heading to the drawing room for tea when his path crossed with Tam, who was going in the same direction. Since no one else was around, he drew her into a hug. He would never tire of holding her.

She hugged him back, but said, "I'm sensing trouble coming soon, rather like I did before we visited the Portsmouth Yard. Can you feel it?"

"Yes, but I'm not sure if it's potential trouble at the Arsenal, or at the Woolwich Royal Naval Dockyard which is nearby. You sensed the name 'Woolwich' from the French agent and that could refer to either place."

"Or both. We'll be seeing Rhys later this evening so we can tell him that the royal dockyards are being targeted," Tamsyn said. "Perhaps that will distract him from his shock when we confess our sins."

Cade flinched inside at the thought of what lay ahead, but they had no choice. He doubted either of them could conceal their feelings from their parents. "We need to talk to Rhys and Gwyn together. She's always more understanding."

"While Rhys may become a very protective father." Tam sighed. "I think they'll both be shocked, but just now I prefer to think of tea and cakes." She took his arm until they entered the drawing room. The housekeeper and cook had produced a splendid array of cakes and sandwiches, and conversation was lively as Andre and Beth caught up with each other's doings during the time they'd been apart.

When the handsome brass clock struck the hour, Beth glanced up at the time. "Papa will be leaving work soon. Shall we go meet him?"

"I'd like that," Andre said, his gaze going to Tamsyn and Cade. "If they're interested, can my friends come also?"

"I don't see why not." Beth stood and turned to her visitors. "Would you like to see what the Warren is like? It's very interesting."

"I would indeed," Cade said as he also stood. "What does Mr. Caton do?"

"He works in the Royal Laboratory and is in charge of the group that is developing battlefield rockets," she explained. "He and Andrew's father learned a great deal about such things in India."

"I've read about how effective and frightening those rockets were when they were used in India," Cade said. "Improved rockets will be a valuable addition to Britain's arsenal in the years ahead." Which meant that this facility would be a prime target for French agents.

The four of them left the house and walked toward the Arsenal. The guards at the gate greeted Beth cheerfully and allowed her guests to enter when she vouched for them.

The Arsenal was large and bustling with activity. With so many explosive materials around, Cade wasn't surprised to see axes and other firefighting equipment fastened to the outside walls of most of the buildings. As they walked past a broad alley filled with stacks of cast iron artillery pieces, Tamsyn said to Cade, "I think I'm becoming jaded about vast military installations!"

"They do have similarities," he agreed. "The Woolwich Royal Navy will seem even more familiar if we visit there."

"With luck I won't have to," Tam said, her voice tense. She glanced at the sky. "Those heavy clouds are coming back again. I wonder if we could make them rain if something catches fire?"

"I hope you're not foretelling disaster," Cade said, feeling distinctly uneasy. He and Tam had fallen behind the other couple so they could talk more freely. She took his hand during the rest of the walk to the Royal Laboratory.

As they approached the impressive building, a well-dressed

older man who looked much like Beth was coming down the steps from the laboratory. He waved cheerfully to Beth, then stopped in his tracks. "Andrew Jameson! Is that really you?"

"Mr. Caton, I'm so happy to see you!" Andre rushed forward and caught the older man's hands. "I just arrived in England and of course I immediately wanted to see you and Beth."

"Especially Beth!" Caton said, beaming. "Hasn't she turned into a beauty?"

"She has always been beautiful," Andre said earnestly.

It was enjoyable to watch young love blooming, but Cade's sense of foreboding was increasing exponentially. His worried gaze traveled to the long storehouse opposite the laboratory a moment before a series of powerful explosions sounded inside the structure.

As the ear-numbing sounds ricocheted among the buildings, fires blazed up in several spots along the length of the storehouse. "Firetraps like those set in Portsmouth!" Tam gasped.

Cade swore and caught Tam's hand hard. "Shall we see if we can summon rain?"

As shouts rose furiously from all sides, Cade and Tamsyn raised their gazes to the clouds and visualized rain. Masses of heavy rain coming *now!*

The sky darkened and a cold wind blasted from the river. An initial spattering of raindrops was rapidly followed by a soaking deluge, but the fires had already caught hold in the storehouse.

Mr. Caton gave a cry of dismay. "That storehouse is full powder and ammunition! Come back into the laboratory—the brick building will provide some protection if there's an explosion!" He grabbed his daughter's hand and pulled her up the steps with him.

Cade swore again when he saw the flames flashing higher inside the building. He shouted at Caton, "Are there people inside?"

Caton hesitated, then pointed at a small wooden addition to

the brick storehouse. "Probably only in that office on the end. It might be empty at this hour."

His guess was proved wrong when three men staggered out into the rain, coughing as the wooden office addition crumbled behind them. The gabled roof fell almost intact to the ground. Cade barked, "No! There are men trapped inside!"

He jerked free of Tamsyn's hand and raced toward the burning structure, grabbing a fire ax from an outside wall as he ran. Andre gasped in horror, then grabbed a second ax and followed.

Tamsyn summoned every ounce of power she had and aimed it at the storm clouds. *Harder, harder, pour down right there.* The rain helped prevent the fire from spreading, but it wasn't enough to douse the flames inside the storehouse.

Cade and Andre were hacking at the wooden frame of a broken window set in the end of the collapsed addition, fragments of wood flying in all directions. After widening the opening, Cade stopped chopping for a moment and leaned inside to grab the flailing arm of a man and yank him out to safety.

Coughing and covered with soot, the man said hoarsely, "My son! My boy is right behind me!"

Face grim, Cade studied the fallen gabled roof, took a deep breath, then bent over the bottom sill of the window and plunged swiftly into the remnants of the building amidst broken glass, smoke, and flames. Instants later, the remnants of the roof fell inward, collapsing into the space below.

Tamysn felt the suffocation and blazing heat as intensely as if she was inside with Cade. Felt his fierce determination as he grabbed onto the boy, the struggle for breath, and then... darkness. Horrified, she breathed, *"No! Nooooo!"*

She saw that workmen were racing toward the collapsed building, most carrying axes and crowbars and other tools. "There are two people in there!" Tam called in her most commanding voice.

"We'll do our best!" one of the men said grimly. Working furiously, the newcomers chopped into the roof, yanking chunks away with leather gloved hands to open the area inside.

Barely able to breathe, Tam drew as close to the workmen as she could without getting in the way. She sensed that Cade's life force was flickering. "Please!" she begged. "My husband is in there and I think he's still alive!"

"Better pray you're right!" the leader of the workers growled as he and another man expanded the open area of the collapsed structure.

It seemed hours had passed while they worked to get to the trapped victims, though Tamsyn knew it was only minutes. She dimly noticed that the rain began diminishing as soon as she stopped paying attention to the clouds.

After massive pieces of roof and rafters were carefully lifted away, the lead workman called, "I see them!"

Two burly men stepped warily into the hole and hauled out an unconscious Cade. A young boy of about twelve was clasped in his protective arms.

"Jemmy!" The man Cade had rescued earlier needed help to wrench the boy from Cade's grip. Jemmy was crying and gulping for air, but alive. Surely Cade must be also. . . .

Cade had been laid out on the roadway, and the workmen didn't seem to know quite what to do yet. "Looks like a goner," one of the men muttered.

Frantically Tam pushed her way through the group of men and knelt by Cade. She rested one hand on his heart and the other on his forehead. He was still alive, but barely, his beloved face losing the golden light that made him who he was. "Caden Tremayne," she barked at him, "don't you *dare* leave me!"

She rested both hands on his chest and poured all her power into him, but it wasn't enough. She could feel that he was still slipping away.

A strong hand clamped on her shoulder. Andre. "Use my power!" he ordered.

She took him at his word and felt an increase in her energy, then a smaller one as Beth took Andre's hand.

Not enough, *not enough*. She remembered how they'd knitted the energy of several family members together to bring their power to Cade when they were in France. She could do that again. She *would* do it again!

She reached fiercely for her most powerful family members. Bran, as close to Cade as two brothers could be, Merryn, who also loved Cade and would do anything to spare her husband the devastation of losing his brother. Rhys, the powerful and protective father who had always given everything he had to give. Gwyn with the power of her healing gifts and her compassion. Cameron, the next brother, who had always looked up to Cade and Bran.

One by one she grasped the power of every member of the Tribe of Tremayne, all the way down to six-year-old Emily. She felt their shock at this invasion of their minds, but as soon as they understood what she was doing, they freely poured their power through her into Cade. *Heal, heal, heal . . . !*

Slowly Cade's life force brightened and she felt his heartbeat growing stronger. As he grew stronger, she grew weaker, but she couldn't stop, not until she was sure that he was safe.

The river of power flowing through her began to diminish when the others had given all they could. Just a little more to be sure. . . .

She felt the wet earth on her face as she fainted, then felt no more.

Chapter 38

Tamsyn emerged from the depths of darkness to a soft light and her own familiar bed. Disoriented, she opened her eyes and whispered, "Mama?"

The mattress dipped as Gwyn moved to sit next to her. She was beautiful and blond and Tamsyn would look very much like her in future years. Except that Gwyn was taller. Everyone was taller than Tam.

Her mother rested a warm hand on Tam's forehead. "You're all right now, aren't you, my dearest girl? How do you feel?"

"Beyond . . . exhausted." With sudden horror, she tried to sit up but sagged weakly back onto the bed. "*Cade!* Is he all right?" She thought she could sense him, but that might have been hope rather than truth.

"He's in the room next to this one, somewhat battered but less drained than you, I think." Gwyn brushed back Tam's damp hair. "When Cade was well enough to be moved, that nice young Mr. Jameson organized transportation to bring you home. He rode with you the whole way."

Tamsyn exhaled with relief. "Andre is wonderful. We've decided that he's a Tremayne cousin. Can we keep him?"

Gwyn laughed. "He's already created a place for himself!"

Thinking back to that dizzying river of power she'd created to save Cade, Tam asked, "Did I drain everyone in the family? It was extremely rude to pull all that power without asking first, but I couldn't think of anything else that might work,"

"The power was freely given, and there's no one as exhausted as you." Gwyn's hand came down to hold Tamsyn's. "You've explored new territory, my love. Rhys and I have never seen such a blending of energies. It was amazing." Her voice caught. "Cade would have died if not for you. I would have lost my oldest son."

Tam closed her eyes, shaking at the memory of how close it had been. "I wouldn't have been able to bear that," she said in a raw whisper, knowing it was time for the confession. "Cade and I had decided that as soon as we reached Tremayne House, we would tell you that we're in love and want to be together always. We've hoped you won't exile us from the family, but we realize that there is much potential for grave damage. We're prepared to move away so we won't cause more trouble."

"It was quite a shock to recognize how you felt about each other," Gwyn said wryly. "I was perhaps . . . not as shocked as everyone else. I knew that you and Cade had a special bond, but I didn't realize that you would fall in love like this."

Tam opened her eyes. "We're not blood kin, but we *were* raised as brother and sister and we feared that we'd be exiled. Have we horrified some of the younger Tremaynes? Neither of us want to hurt anyone."

"We would never have exiled you!" Her mother squeezed her hand. "But I agree that if you two had just showed up and announced that you were in love, it would have been much more difficult. You and Cade are so important to everyone in the family that it would have been a devastating shock for some of the younger children to learn that your relationship had changed so drastically. Most have come from difficult backgrounds, and they need to feel that they are safe. That their new world is firm beneath their feet."

"That's just what we feared," Tam said hesitantly. "But from the way you're talking, it sounds as if that hasn't happened?"

"No, because your call for help was propelled by the intensity of your great love for each other," Gwyn said softly. "Every Tremayne felt that love right down to their marrow. They loved you already as individuals and now they love the two of you together. You changed everyone's mind about what is acceptable."

"Really?" Tam breathed. "It seems . . . too good to be true."

"Really." Gwyn smiled. "It was a drastic way to announce that you two want to marry, but very effective."

Tam closed her eyes against tears. "It was agonizing to think I might have to choose between the family and Cade," she whispered. "I would have chosen Cade, but it would have hurt forever if we'd lost everyone else." She thought of young Emily, who had arrived at Tremayne House terrified and weeping. She hadn't slept until she fell asleep in Tamsyn's arms.

"Luckily, you won't have to lose anyone," Gwyn said. "Cade's near-death experience turned out to be a blessing in disguise."

The door to Tam's bedroom opened and Cade limped in with his arm slung over Rhys's shoulders. Tam was surprised to notice that Cade was a little taller. His left arm was bandaged and he looked thoroughly bruised and abraded, but he was definitely alive.

"As soon as he could struggle out of his bed, he insisted on coming in here to see Tamsyn," Rhys said with amusement. "The lad has become much heavier over the years. When he first arrived at Tremayne House, he didn't weigh much more than a plucked goose."

"A shortcoming I overcame quickly by eating half my weight daily," Cade said affectionately.

He broke free of Rhys's support and lurched over to the bed on the other side from where Gwyn was sitting. There he more or less collapsed on the mattress beside Tam, wrapping his good arm around her to pull her close. "Tamkin . . ." he murmured, his deep blue eyes intense. "You almost killed yourself to save me. Don't you dare ever do that again!"

"Only if you promise to stop playing hero!" She gave a small laugh. "Though I don't suppose you can. You were born to protect. To be a hero."

Gwyn rose from her perch on the bed and said indulgently, "Rhys, I think it's time we let the children get some rest."

Rhys laughed as he opened the door for his wife. "I'm sure they'll have much to discuss first, starting with their marriage. They need to set a good example for the younger members of the family."

As the door closed, Cade said, "I think we should get married as soon as possible."

Thinking scandalous thoughts about his powerful body and rugged good looks, she said, "The sooner the better! But let's wait until we're both strong enough to walk down the aisle on our own."

"You are so beautifully sensible," he murmured before kissing her temple. "And so impossibly beautiful. I most certainly want to marry you before you can change your mind, Lady Tamsyn."

"You know I won't, love." She caught his gaze, her eyes serious. "No one else would ever do for either of us, Cade. I was sure that I was destined to be the helpful maiden aunt because no man had ever caught my interest, while you kept your love a secret because you thought it was impossible." She brushed a kiss on his mouth. "I'm so very glad we were wrong!"

"So am I," he laughed. "Shall we see just how tired we really are? I'm feeling remarkably recovered."

"What an interesting coincidence." She pulled his head down for a serious kiss. "So am I!"

And the world turned golden. . . .

Author's Note for
Golden Lord

England and France have a very long history of fighting each other. After the French Revolution, the Revolutionary Wars continued from 1792 until 1802. The Peace of Amiens lasted for fifteen months between 1802 and 1803, with both sides busily rearming and ignoring the treaties they'd just signed—1803 saw a return to battle for the Napoleonic Wars, which lasted until the bloody conclusion on the fields of Waterloo in 1815.

The Peace of Amiens ended when Britain declared war first, but the French retaliated immediately, including Napoleon's unprecedented order to arrest all British males between the ages of eighteen and sixty. In those days, people didn't carry around birth certificates or drivers' licenses to prove their ages, which meant that a well-grown fourteen-year-old boy could be caught up in the net, and the same for senior citizens who were particularly well preserved.

Michael Lewis's excellent book, *Napoleon and his British Captives,* tells the story of the chaos that ensued. Other European nations were horrified by Napoleon's outrageous action against civilians, but Napoleon rather enjoyed outraging people.

Most of the interned British men ended up in the provincial city of Verdun, where a whole Britons-in-exile community grew up. Many men had family members with them, and there were barbers and tailors and musicians, and even a racetrack. As internment camps go, this one wasn't bad. But the prisoners didn't get home until 1814, after Napoleon's abdication.

Great Britain's safety was dependent on its island status and the strength of the Royal Navy, the most powerful navy in Europe then, and quite possibly in the world. The Royal Navy Dockyards were some of the most industrialized facilities anywhere and they created cutting-edge war ships and weaponry.

The Royal Arsenal, known at the time of this story as the Warren, created and stored vast amounts of weapons and ammunition. Not surprisingly, destructive fires were not uncommon, so I felt free to create one of my own.

I have a favorite quote that sums up how Great Britain was protected by the English Channel and the other seas around it during this period. Admiral Lord John Jervis, the 1st Earl of St. Vincent, said in a letter to Parliament:

"I do not say, my lords, that the French will not come. I say only that they will not come by sea."

Please read on for an excerpt from SILVER LADY
by Mary Jo Putney, available now!

SILVER LADY

Mary Jo Putney

Together they faced the past . . .

A sense of duty sends Bran Tremayne to Cornwall to con-
front his heritage of British nobility. Abandoned at birth, Bran
wants nothing to do with the embittered remains of his family.
But as a special agent for the Home Office, he senses trouble
brewing along the coast. And he can't turn away from the vulnerable woman he encounters in the Cornish countryside.
Merryn's amnesia makes her past a mystery to them both, but
with her life in danger, the only thing Bran knows for sure is
that the beautiful stranger needs his protection . . .

But would they share a future?

Leaning into Bran is difficult enough, but can Merryn trust
the strong bond—and the powerful passion—she feels for her
rugged rescuer? She has no choice once Bran uncovers that she
is at the center of a plot between French agents and Cornish
smugglers. From misty woodlands to stormy shores, the two
join forces with a band of loyal Cornishmen to bring down a
common enemy. Yet will their growing love survive the coming peril?

Chapter 1

❦

London, 1780

The play had been good, but an icy wind bit to the bone as Rhys and Gwyn Tremayne emerged from the Theatre Royal. "Our carriage should be down to the left," Rhys said. "And the sooner we get into it and head for home, the better! Shall we end the evening by sipping brandy in front of a roaring fire?"

"That sounds most appealing," Gwyn said as she took his arm. Then she halted, feeling a powerful intuition. "But not yet. Let's take a bit of a walk first."

"You sense something that needs to be found, Lady Tremayne?" Rhys asked mildly. Since his wife was one of the best finders in Britain, he knew better than to argue. He merely raised an arm and gestured for their coach to follow them.

"Something, or someone." Gwyn drew her cloak more closely around her as she purposefully started threading her way through the mass of waiting carriages and playgoers who were happily discussing the show they'd just seen.

Two turns took them from Covent Garden into a narrow

lane. Halfway down, Gwyn paused, then turned left into a dark alley barely lit by capricious moonlight. It dead-ended at a wall, where a pile of rubble had accumulated against the dingy brick. Heedless of her expensive cloak, she knelt on the frozen ground and said softly, "You can come out now, my lad. You're safe."

There was a rustling sound, but no one appeared. "How does warm food and a fire and a bath sound?" she said in her most persuasive voice.

A child's voice snarled, "Don't want no bath!"

"Then we'll start with the food and the fire," she said peaceably. "Will you show yourself? We won't hurt you."

Rhys stood silently behind her, knowing a frightened child would fear a rather large grown man more than a soft-voiced woman. The rubble shifted and a small, filthy face became visible. A boy child, perhaps five or six years old.

Gwyn brushed back a lock of fair hair, then peeled the kidskin glove from her right hand and offered it to the little boy. He hesitantly took it. As she clasped his freezing fingers with her warm hand, his eyes widened and he sighed with relief.

"You can tell I'm safe, can't you?" Gwyn said.

The boy frowned up at Rhys. "You may be, but not sure about *him*!"

"I'm safe, too," Rhys said in his most reassuring voice. "I'm very good at protecting others."

Unconvinced, the boy narrowed his eyes warily. As Rhys stood very still, Gwyn said soothingly, "I'm Gwyn Tremayne. What's your name?"

The boy hesitated, as if his name was too precious to share. After a long moment he said, "Caden."

"Caden. That's a good Cornish or Welsh name. My husband and I come from Cornish families." Knowing there was more to find, she moved her gaze back to the rubble pile. "Your friend can come out, too."

Caden gasped and jerked away from her. For a moment she feared he'd try to bolt, but a thin, childish voice emerged from the rubble. "It's all right, Cade. These are the people we came to find."

An even smaller boy emerged from the rubble, his ragged garments almost indistinguishable from the trash around him. His gaze on Gwyn, he said, "I'm Bran."

"For Branok?" Again Gwyn offered her hand and Bran took it without hesitation. His small fingers felt as if they were carved from ice. In the darkness it was hard to see the boys clearly. Though both were dark-haired, there was little other resemblance. Bran's eyes were light, Caden's were dark, but the color wasn't visible in the shadows. "Are you brothers?"

The boys exchanged a glance. "We are now!" Caden said fiercely, challenging anyone who might deny that.

They both had soft West Country accents, and she wondered what their story was. How had they made their way to London? Bran seemed to have the ability to read people's nature and to decide what must be done. Caden surely was gifted as well, perhaps in other ways.

Learning more about them could wait. What mattered now was getting the boys out of this vicious cold. "Come with us now and we'll take you to our home, where you'll be warm and well fed."

Bran stood shakily and almost fell over from weakness and cold. Her heart hurting at the sight, Gwyn said, "I'll start warming you now." She leaned forward and scooped Bran into her arms, then rose to her feet. The child weighed almost nothing, and his torn shirt revealed something on his right shoulder blade. If she had to guess, Gwyn would have said it looked like a tattoo of a dragon.

It was a question for another day. She pulled him inside her cloak, covering everything but his head. His thin body was cold against her. "Is that better?"

He peered out of the folds of her cloak with a smile of great sweetness. "Much better, ma'am."

"No! You won't take him away!" Caden exclaimed as he lurched to his feet.

"Don't worry, Caden, we won't separate you," Rhys said as he lifted the larger boy in his arms and tucked his own cloak around him as Gwyn had done with Bran. Caden struggled some, but the warmth seemed to soften him.

They carried the children back to the wider street, where the carriage waited. Their driver, Jones, gave them an expressive glance, but didn't speak. This was not the first time he'd seen them rescue children.

Rhys opened the carriage door. Knowing Caden wasn't comfortable with being carried, he set the boy in the vehicle. "There are carriage robes on the seats to warm you." The child scrambled inside and there was a rustle of fabric as he pulled a robe around himself.

Rhys then helped Gwyn into the carriage. She continued holding Bran as she settled on the forward-facing seat. Before climbing in and closing the door, Rhys called up to the driver, "Home now, Jones."

As the carriage rattled westward over the cobblestones, Gwyn asked, "How did you boys come to be here in London?"

The silence stretched so long that she wondered if either of them would answer. Then Caden said warily, "What's it mean to be 'gifted'? My da called me that before he threw me out of the house."

Gwyn's heart constricted at the thought of such a young boy being treated in such a beastly manner, but his question confirmed what she already knew. "Gifted people are just better at some things than most others are. Better at sensing emotions, perhaps. Better at persuasion, or maybe better at finding lost objects. Perhaps good at telling if someone is lying or telling the truth. Small gifts, but often useful."

Bran asked, his small voice hard, "Why do people hate us?"

As Gwyn wondered how to explain bigotry, Rhys said in his deep, calming voice, "Sometimes it's from fear. Sometimes from envy. Some people just need to hate anyone who is different."

It was a good explanation. Gwyn said softly as she cuddled Bran against her, "Some people hate, but there are also those who love you exactly as you are."